P9-DDH-271

KISSING THE RANCHER

"How's your tattoo?" Josie asked.

Evan raised an eyebrow. "Wanna see it?"

"Yes, please."

He grabbed hold of the hem of his Henley, yanked it over his head, and turned to one side. "I think it looks great."

"Hmm . . ." Josie breathed.

"You're not looking at it."

"I'm just taking all of it in," she said as she admired his flat stomach, lightly haired chest, and tight biceps. "The tattoo is merely the icing on the cake."

"Yeah?" He stood up, came around to the other side of the table, and held out his hand. "May I kiss the winner?"

Josie hastily wiped her mouth on her napkin and jumped to her feet. "Sure!"

He drew her into his arms, and she raised her head to meet his steadfast gaze.

"Thanks for making me do this."

"Right back at you."

She slid her fingers into his damp hair and locked her mouth against his, her other hand on his bare shoulder. He groaned her name and kissed her back with a direct fierceness that surprised and intrigued her. She forgot everything except the taste and scent of him as she explored his body and leaned right into all that hard, warm flesh . . .

Books by Kate Pearce

Published by Kensington Publishing Corp.

Romancing the
RANCHER

The Millers of Morgan Valley

KATE PEARCE

ZEBRA BOOKS
KENSINGTON PUBLISHING CORP.
www.kensingtonbooks.com

ZEBRA BOOKS are published by

Kensington Publishing Corp.
119 West 40th Street
New York, NY 10018

Copyright © 2022 by Kate Pearce

This book is a work of fiction. Names, characters, businesses, organizations, places, events, and incidents either are the product of the author's imagination or are used fictitiously. Any resemblance to actual persons, living or dead, events, or locales is entirely coincidental.

All rights reserved. No part of this book may be reproduced in any form or by any means without the prior written consent of the Publisher, excepting brief quotes used in reviews.

To the extent that the image or images on the cover of this book depict a person or persons, such person or persons are merely models, and are not intended to portray any character or characters featured in the book.

If you purchased this book without a cover you should be aware that this book is stolen property. It was reported as "unsold and destroyed" to the Publisher and neither the Author nor the Publisher has received any payment for this "stripped book."

All Kensington titles, imprints, and distributed lines are available at special quantity discounts for bulk purchases for sales promotion, premiums, fund-raising, educational, or institutional use.

Special book excerpts or customized printings can also be created to fit specific needs. For details, write or phone the office of the Kensington Sales Manager: Attn.: Sales Department. Kensington Publishing Corp., 119 West 40th Street, New York, NY 10018. Phone: 1-800-221-2647.

Zebra and the Z logo Reg. U.S. Pat. & TM Off.

First Printing: January 2022
ISBN-13: 978-1-4201-5259-3
ISBN-13: 978-1-4201-5260-9 (eBook)

10 9 8 7 6 5 4 3 2 1

Printed in the United States of America

ACKNOWLEDGMENTS

*Thanks to Sian Kaley and Jerri Drennan
for their always contrasting and interesting critiques.
Thanks also to the lovely ladies who offered me advice
about getting a tattoo, speaking Brazilian Portuguese
and how to cook traditional Brazilian dishes.
I apologize for the lack of names
but I'm in the middle of moving
and left most of my paperwork back in Hawaii.
This is the last of the Miller books.
I hope you have all enjoyed reading them as much as
I've enjoyed writing them.*

Chapter One

Miller Ranch
Morgan Valley, California

Evan Miller kicked off his boots in the mudroom, washed up, and walked through into the large family kitchen where the smell of coffee and fried bacon still hung in the air. He scowled at his oldest brother, Adam, who was seated at the kitchen table chatting with their father.

"Where were you? I had to muck out all the stalls by myself."

"It's a nice change to see you working hard," his father, Jeff, said and held up his phone. "We had some good news."

"What would that be?" Evan helped himself to coffee, which at least warmed his hands. Even in summer it could still be cool in the mornings in the shadow of the Sierra Nevada mountain range. His brother Kaiden emerged from the pantry with a fresh loaf of bread and grinned at him as they both sat down at the table.

"Danny went and did it."

Seeing as Danny wasn't talking to him right now, Evan had no idea what was going on, and he sure as hell wasn't going to beg for info.

"So what?" Evan sipped his coffee.

Kaiden sat back. "Jeez, I suppose you already knew, seeing as you and Danny are so close. Kudos for not blabbing, which isn't like you."

"I suppose this has to do with Faith?" Evan hazarded a guess.

"Yeah." It was Jeff's turn to chip in. "Somehow they ended up in Vegas yesterday and got hitched!"

Evan sucked in his gut like someone had punched him, and covered up his shock with a nonchalant shrug. "Not exactly a surprise."

"I'm guessing either Silver or Mom helped them with the planning." Kaiden shook his head and whistled. "I never thought Danny had it in him to move so fast."

"He saw a good thing and he went for it," their father said.

"And you're okay with this, Dad?" Kaiden raised an eyebrow. "I thought you'd be pissed."

"Why? I told him not to let her get away."

"Faith's not a wayward steer," Adam said. "She's perfect for Danny. We could all see he was still in love with her."

All three of them nodded. Evan shot to his feet again.

"What's up?" Adam asked.

"I left my phone in the tack room." Evan was already halfway out the door. "I'll be back in a minute."

He stepped into his muddy boots, grabbed his heavy jacket, and set off for the barn, his phone already securely in his pocket. He bypassed his supposed destination and went to stare out over the pastureland and foothills that comprised the majority of the Miller property. His breath condensed in the fresh, morning air as he propped his arms on the top of the gate, his brain barely registering the amazing view.

Danny hadn't told him.

His closest brother in age, his best friend, and the person who always set him straight, hadn't bothered to share that he was getting married. The worst thing was that Evan knew exactly why. The last time they'd been together Danny had gotten mad at him for revealing some personal information about him and Faith over the family dinner table. He'd only been trying to protect his favorite brother, but Danny hadn't seen it that way and had gone off on him.

"Hey."

Evan didn't turn his head as Adam came to join him at the fence. At least he didn't have to deal with wise-cracking Kaiden. It took a while for Adam to actually say anything, which was just like him. He wasn't a man who wasted words.

"I guess Danny didn't tell you?"

"Why would he when he was barely talking to me before he left." Evan sighed. "You know what happened, I screwed up. I apologized to him and to Faith, but apparently he's still mad at me."

"Or he simply had to make a quick decision and only had time to ask for help from someone who had the means to get him there and get things done fast."

"Like someone with money or power, you mean." Evan snorted. "Neither of which I have or will ever have."

"Danny probably wanted to keep it quiet as well."

Evan finally glanced over at Adam's calm face. "Thanks."

"You aren't known for your ability to keep a secret, Bro."

"So, two strikes already against me," Evan said bitterly. "I can't keep a secret, I don't have any money, and let's not forget that Danny currently hates my guts."

"I bet he's not even thinking about you right now," Adam suggested mildly. "And you know what? That's okay. Maybe he needed to put himself and Faith first for once."

"I get that." Evan grimaced. "I also get that I screwed up, and that despite everything that went down, he *wanted* to fall in love with her again and didn't need me getting involved."

"Sometimes love doesn't give you a choice." Adam smiled. "Look at me and Lizzie."

"Yeah, when are you two going to get married anyway?" Evan asked, eager to change the subject.

"As soon as Lizzie's okay with it and we've worked out how to balance our lives together."

"That could take a while."

"Yeah, but that's okay." Adam glanced over at Evan again, his expression serious. "Maybe it's time for you to start thinking about what you're going to do with your own life, rather than worrying about everyone else's."

Evan turned to face his big brother. "Like, *seriously?* You're going to lay that on me right now?"

"Why not?" Adam shrugged. "Danny was right. You're not a kid anymore. You can't just drift along, never committing to anything or anybody."

"I do my work." Evan pushed away from the fence to confront his much-taller brother.

"Now you do."

Evan winced. "Wow, did Dad send you out to get at me, or is this all on you? I suppose technically you are my boss now since Dad's supposed to have stepped back. Are you firing me?"

Adam shook his head. "See? This is just like you, turning a genuine attempt to help you into some kind of dramatic ultimatum. You've got a job here until you die, Evan. You know that. But is that what you really want?"

"I'm done talking." Evan turned around and headed to the barn. "I've got fences to mend."

"Okay, fine," Adam called after him. "If you're determined to leave, do me a favor and check in with Ines at Rio's place? I was going to go myself, but it looks like I'm stuck here for a while doing Danny's chores."

Evan briefly raised a hand to acknowledge his brother's words and kept going. When Adam didn't attempt to call him back or apologize, Evan's indignation continued to rise, fueling his escape. He saddled his horse, Joker, grabbed his fencing supplies, and rode out toward the far boundary of the ranch.

He was sick of his family telling him what to do. When Kaiden had taken on the Garcia Ranch project, Evan had stepped up and done more than his fair share of his brother's chores without a single word of thanks from anyone. So, what if he was content to remain a ranch hand for the rest of his life? He would've thought that a man like Adam, who was always complaining about the scarcity of available labor, would be *begging* him to stick around.

Evan rammed his Stetson down on his head and picked up the pace. If there was any way he could give them all the finger and ride off into the sunset right now, he'd absolutely, one hundred percent, do it. He gathered Joker and set him toward the boundary fence. If he took a couple of shortcuts across the other ranches, he'd be at the Martinez Ranch in no time at all.

What was wrong with loving the place he'd grown up in anyway? Why did he have to think beyond that? Evan slowed Joker to a walk as Adam's words continued to repeat in his brain.

A job here until you die . . .

He stared down at the Martinez spread—the old ranch house with the new outbuildings Rio had added since taking over from Adam's old in-laws and saving the place from housing developers. Evan wasn't sure if Rio was home. Between his interests in his father's billion-dollar company, Howatch International, and his gig as a commentator for the Professional Bull Riders TV show, he was a busy man.

The ranch had originally been intended for Adam and his now-deceased wife, Louisa. But after his father-in-law's recent death, Adam had given up that claim and secured Ines's financial future at the ranch where she lived with Rio and his fiancée, Yvonne, who ran the café and bakery in Morgantown. Ines loved having the company and that Rio could speak Portuguese with her now that Carlos had gone.

Despite his father's hatred of all things rodeo, Evan had taken to sneaking off to the Martinez place where Rio not only trained aspiring bull riders but had also set up a bull breeding program for the PBR. For the first time in his life, he was glad he hadn't been built like his two linebacker brothers and was the shortest and lightest male in the family. It made riding any horse or bull competitively so much easier.

He clicked to Joker, leaned slightly back in the saddle to compensate for the slope, and made his way down the hill toward the new barn, his gaze scanning the fenced pastures for a sight of the new bulls and any activity. The place was disappointingly quiet. He reminded himself he wasn't here to mess around but to check in on Ines.

He dismounted in front of the barn and led Joker toward the shade to tie him up. A shrill whistle drew his attention to the enclosed paddock at the other end of the building. After making sure Joker was double-tied, because he had a tendency to get free, Evan walked through the shadowed barn and back out into the glaring brightness of a typical blue-sky California day.

Someone was practicing on one of the smaller bulls. Evan leaned up against the high railing and watched as the diminutive rider struggled to stay on board the relentlessly kicking bull. He slowly counted down the eight precious seconds it took for a ride to be scored and was impressed when the rider managed to hang on long enough.

He stuck his fingers in his mouth and whistled his appreciation as the rider rolled clear and came up on his knees, his hat falling to the ground.

"Nice job."

One of the hands persuaded the bull back into its pen

and the rider came toward Evan, dusting off the Stetson on his chaps.

"Who are you?"

Evan recoiled. "You're a girl."

"So what?" Her eyebrows rose over her dark brown eyes. "Girls can ride bulls."

"Not that I've noticed."

She pointed back into the paddock. "What was that? A mirage?"

"Maybe." Evan considered her. She had a slight accent, which gave her voice a huskiness he found ridiculously attractive. "Does Rio know you're riding his bulls?"

"No, I just sneak in here when he's not around. Next question?"

"I kind of admire that." Evan nodded. "Won't he be mad if you get hurt, though?"

For the first time, she smiled. "Probably. Doesn't mean I'm going to stop."

"It's a dangerous sport."

"Duh. I know that."

For a moment they just stared at each other and then Evan grinned and offered her his hand.

"I'm Evan."

"Josie." She shook his hand, her grip firm.

"I came to see Ines."

"Oh! She's expecting you—just go on through the mudroom to the kitchen. I'll join you after I've washed up."

"You live here?"

Josie came through the railings and looped the chain back over the post. "I do at the moment."

"You're one of the hands?" Evan started toward the house.

"Not quite, but I help out when I can." She pointed at the rear door. "Go through there. It's not locked."

Evan resisted the impulse to tell her he knew the way. The fact that she seemed to have no idea who he was in a place where everyone knew his entire family history for four generations was refreshing. He guessed Adam had let Ines know he'd be coming at some point, which was kind of annoying. He didn't need his big brother checking up on him.

Josie stopped and turned back, her long, black braid swinging over her shoulder. "Don't you need your tools?"

He studied her carefully. "I need to see what's up first."

"Makes sense." She nodded. "See you in a bit."

"Looking forward to it already," Evan called out as she headed toward the tack room.

He went into the mudroom, took off his boots, and padded through into the kitchen where he found Ines, hands on hips with her back to him, staring at the open dishwasher and shaking her head.

"*Bom dia,* Ines," Evan said.

She spun around. She was a small woman who always wore her silver-streaked hair in a braided bun on the top of her head. "Evan, how lovely to see you." She came over to kiss him on both cheeks. "I thought you were the repairman."

"What's up with it?" Evan joined her in staring at the dishwasher.

"It's not draining properly. I told Rio I didn't need one

of these things and that I was quite happy washing up my own dishes, but he wouldn't hear of it."

Evan crouched down and looked inside the dishwasher where two inches of dirty water still lingered at the bottom. "That's not good."

"I was thinking about running it again, but Josie said I might end up flooding the kitchen, and that the best thing to do was call the repairman."

Evan stood and leaned over to check the air gap sticking out of the countertop. "Have you looked at this?"

"I don't even know what it is," Ines confessed.

Evan tried to unscrew the cap, but it was stuck. He reached into the back pocket of his jeans and pulled out one of his gloves to get a good grip.

"That's better." Even as he released the cap, he saw the problem. He eased the chunk of what looked like half-chewed gristle out of the pipe, which then gave a satisfying gurgle and spewed out a mixture of bubbles and water. "That should clear it."

Ines peered over his shoulder. "There was something stuck in there?"

"Yup, blocking the airflow." He dropped the mangled piece of meat in the trash. "It should be fine now, but I'll just check the pipes under the sink for any further blockage. Has the water been running through the faucet okay?"

"It hasn't been great," Ines admitted.

Evan rolled up his sleeves. "Then let's take a look."

After cleaning up in the barn, Josie walked into the kitchen to find the plumber laid full out on the floor, his head and shoulders under the sink, which gave her an opportunity to check out his flat stomach and long legs. The fact that he still looked like a cowboy but was actually a tradesman made her want to smile. But she already knew that Morgan Valley was a small town where everyone took on multiple roles.

There was a knock on the open back door and a cheery hello as another guy, complete with a toolbox came into the kitchen and stopped dead.

"Morning, Ines. Why's there a Miller under your sink?"

Evan was a Miller? Josie winced as the sound of a thud came from the cabinet quickly followed by a curse as Evan slid into view, rubbing his skull. His short hair had more than a hint of red in it.

"Hey, Bart. Just trying to help out." He pointed at the pipes. "Looks corroded to me, but you're the expert."

Bart set his toolbox on the tiled floor. "I thought this was a dishwasher issue."

"I fixed that part." Evan got to his feet and grinned at the older man. He really was ridiculously attractive. "The pipes are your problem."

"Thanks for nothing," Bart said, but as he was smiling back at Evan, Josie didn't think he was really offended. "Don't expect a cut of my bill."

"Wouldn't dream of it," Evan said, his gaze finally settling on Josie. "Hey."

"Hey."

Ines touched her shoulder. "Why don't you and Evan go and get acquainted while I finish up with Bart? I just made a fresh pot of coffee and some banana muffins. You can take them through to the family room."

"That would be great." Josie turned to Evan, who was

regarding her with great interest. "Do you want to grab a couple of plates and I'll get the coffee?"

"Sure." He was already on the move and obviously familiar with the layout of the recently renovated kitchen as he found the plates first go. "Shout if you need any more help, Bart, okay?"

Bart muttered something uncomplimentary. Josie fought a smile as she poured out two mugs of coffee and set them on the tray with the muffins, cream, and sugar. She walked through to the sunny family room where she found Evan standing by the large woodburning fireplace.

"You're Rio's sister."

Josie set the tray down. "Wow, when did you finally work that out?"

He pointed at the mantelpiece above the fireplace. "You're in the photos with Rio and his mom."

"You should be a detective. Isabelle is my mom, too. Rio and I have different fathers. I gather you're a Miller."

"Yeah, the youngest apart from Daisy."

"Your brother Adam was married to Ines's daughter." Josie sat down and added cream to her coffee.

"Correct." Evan sat in the chair opposite and took his coffee black. "He's very fond of her and this place."

"It really is lovely. So peaceful and tranquil."

Evan made a face. "If you like that kind of thing."

"You don't?"

He set his mug back down. "I don't know anything else. I've never been anywhere."

"Like ever?"

Josie couldn't keep the surprise out of her voice. She'd traveled between Brazil and the USA since she was a small child and had gone even farther afield with her job at Howatch International.

"Nope." He eyed her consideringly. "Never felt the need until recently."

"I suppose it's good you're happy here and know that you belong," Josie said cautiously. "I've never felt like that about anywhere I've lived."

"The thing is—" Evan said, and then stopped, his brow furrowed.

"Go on," Josie said encouragingly. "You can say anything you want. I'm not going to tell anyone."

He grinned. "You have no idea how appealing that is to someone who lives in a small town where every damn thing you do gets reported back to your family." Evan paused again. "I want to change some stuff and I don't know where to start."

"Like what?" Josie leaned toward him. If she wanted to avoid facing her own problems, solving someone else's was a great opportunity to procrastinate. It was central to her nature to want to fix things.

"Stupid shit, stuff I've never been able to do because—" He half smiled. "You're going to think I'm nuts."

"Does it matter if I do?" Josie asked. "Let me put it this way. I'm here for at least a month on vacation, I've got a lot of time on my hands, and helping you achieve your goals seems like a great idea."

"You're going to help me?" Evan looked taken aback.

"Isn't that what you want?"

He studied her for a long, unnerving minute. "I don't even know you."

"You know I'm Rio's sister and that I'm willing to help."

He frowned. "Hold up a minute. Number one, you don't know what I want to do, and number two, your brother would kill me if I got you into trouble."

"My brother's not here right now, and if you're worried, why don't you draw up a to-do list, and I'll decide whether I want to help you or not?" Josie offered.

Evan sipped his coffee. "Maybe I'm not the only one who's nuts around here. What's up with you?"

She met his hazel-eyed gaze and tried to be honest. "I . . . need to focus on something that isn't related to my work or myself."

"What do you do workwise?"

"I'm a VP of Finance at Howatch International."

"That's Rio's dad's company, right?" Evan helped himself to a banana muffin and devoured it in two bites.

"Yes. Rio insisted I had to take a load of unused vacation days off before I lost them." It was a lot more complicated than that, but Evan didn't need to know everything. "I decided to come here and help out on the ranch."

"Doesn't your mom have a ranch in Brazil?"

"I . . . didn't want her fussing over me." Josie tried for a smile. "She already thinks I work too hard and I didn't want to admit she might have a point."

Evan nodded. He'd obviously met Isabelle and knew about her flair for the dramatic. "So, I'd be like your pet project or something?"

"Not exactly. I mean, I'm just offering to help if you need someone." Josie blew out a breath. "Okay, it was a stupid idea. Why don't we forget I suggested it and have some more coffee?"

"Hell, no. How about this?" Evan held her gaze. "We *both* write out lists and help each other out. I bet you have some stupid stuff you'd love to do on your vacation." He rose to his feet. "Let me get more coffee while you start thinking."

Chapter Two

After agreeing to meet Josie at the Red Dragon Bar in town that evening, Evan left the Martinez place and fixed fencing for three hours, his mind abuzz with ideas. When he got back home, he spent some time rubbing Joker down and making sure he had plenty of water before heading into the house. For some reason, he was reluctant to see everyone, and was relieved there was no one around when he entered the kitchen.

Being stuck close to home after heart surgery meant his dad had an unnerving habit of appearing from nowhere, asking questions about Evan's work, and why was he back home when there was still plenty to do. Although Evan had some sympathy with his dad's plight of being confined, the endless questioning was already starting to grate on him. As the youngest son, he'd always had plenty of cover to do his own thing, but with Ben and Kaiden no longer working full-time on the ranch, he was way more visible than he liked.

He stopped and stared out of the window that faced the rolling foothills and the long dancing lines of the white paddock fencing. Was this it? Would he be staring at this view when he was ninety while Adam's kids ran the place and laughed behind their backs at their old uncle Evan who'd never been anywhere or done anything in his life?

His cell buzzed and he took it out of his pocket.

"Yeah?"

"Hey, it's Danny."

Evan straightened up. "Hey."

There was a long pause before Danny sighed. "I guess you're still mad at me."

"Why would you think that?" Evan shut off the faucet and took the filled jug over to the coffee maker. "You don't owe me a thing."

"I had to move fast, and Silver offered to help, and—"

Evan cut him off. "Hey, I'm in the middle of something right now. Can you call Dad if this is urgent?"

"Evan, it's lunchtime. I know you." There was a hint of amusement in Danny's voice. "You're either in the kitchen getting something to eat, or out on the ranch having a chicken salad sandwich. That's why I called, because I knew exactly where you'd be."

"Maybe I'm not," Evan insisted.

"Bro . . ."

"Gotta go." Evan cut off the call and returned his cell phone to the back pocket of his jeans.

Sure, Danny would probably be complaining to Faith about how juvenile he was being, but he didn't care. He wasn't ready to talk to his brother yet and that was the end of it.

The smell of coffee wafted over from the machine and Evan opened the refrigerator to find the fixings for his favorite sandwich. He stared at the mayo, chicken, tomato, and lettuce he'd automatically selected. Was he really that predictable? And, even if he was—so what? Just because all his siblings were marrying movie stars, hotshot lawyers, or making out big-time in the IT stock market didn't mean he had to.

There was nothing wrong with being like Adam, finding a local girl to settle down with, and running the family ranch. Evan went into the pantry to fetch the bread. Except Adam would own the ranch and Evan wouldn't.

"Jeez . . ." Evan spoke into the quiet stillness. "Maybe you'd better take Josie Martinez up on her offer and finish writing that list, loser."

Josie sat opposite Ines at the kitchen table and listened to her chat about her neighbors, the valley, and all kinds of delicious gossip to bring Josie up to speed with what was going down in her brother's new home. It seemed a world away from San Francisco and Boston where she spent the majority of her days, scurrying between appointments in the narrow-shadowed streets between skyscrapers.

Burnout—that's what her doctors had called it—which was a kind way of saying she wasn't up to the job. Not that anyone had made her feel bad for taking time off. In fact, they'd insisted on it. Had she been messing up so badly by that point that they'd all been relieved to see the back of her?

"Josie?"

She blinked and looked across at Ines's concerned face. "I'm sorry, I missed that."

Ines reached over and took her hand. "It's my fault. Rio said you needed to rest, and here I am chatting away without a care in the world." Ines hesitated. "If there is anything you'd like to talk to me about, I'm more than willing to listen."

Josie automatically touched the small scar on her cheek, hearing the sounds of breaking glass and the pounding of her heart, as she attempted to make herself as small as possible imprinted on her brain like a photograph. The flashbacks came at the most inconvenient moments and she couldn't seem to stop them.

"I'm just glad to be here." She smiled at Ines. "Although, I guess it is going to take me a while to slow down to country time."

"I bet." Ines squeezed her fingers and then withdrew her hand. "Have you finished eating? At least we have a working dishwasher to put our dirty dishes in now."

"After two experts worked on it." Josie joked as she rose to take her plate over to the sink.

"Evan Miller is a very nice young man. He's always willing to help out and he never makes me feel bad about asking."

"I don't know much about him," Josie said casually. "He's the youngest, right?"

"Of the five boys. Daisy is a couple of years younger than him." Ines carefully rinsed the plates and Josie stacked them in the dishwasher.

"Daisy, the tech millionaire?"

"Yes, she's done very well for herself." Ines smiled. "Jeff Miller doesn't usually have a complimentary word to say about his children, but he's very proud of her."

"So, Evan's got a lot to live up to," Josie said thoughtfully.

"I don't think it bothers him. He's too busy living a carefree life at home."

Josie considered that as they finished clearing the table. Evan hadn't seemed very happy with his life when she'd talked to him earlier. She was already half regretting her offer to help him out. What if she just made things worse and he ended up alienated from his family?

She checked the time on the kitchen clock. She'd go for a long ride to get her head together. The idea of writing her own list of stupid things to do hovered tantalizingly in her mind. . . . Maybe it was time for her to get a little funky in her thinking. When she got back, she'd decide whether she was going to meet Evan at the bar in town or leave him well alone. The last thing she wanted to do was mess up someone else's life.

Evan checked his cell phone and realized he hadn't given Josie his number to contact him in case she decided not to come. There were several messages and texts from various members of his family, but he was definitely ignoring those. He settled himself onto the barstool and took another sip of his beer. She'd probably decided he wasn't worth her time and he couldn't blame her.

Midweek, the bar wasn't full, as most of the ranchers and cowboys were busy with the harvest or rounding up cattle, and only came in on the weekends. There were a few tourists scattered around and the occasional lucky person who lived in town and could walk to the bar.

Evan's mother had recently bought an apartment in the converted old movie theater across the way and had given them all a key.

The smell of fried onions and garlic wafted in from the dining end of the establishment where Bella Williams and her staff offered good old-fashioned diner food and plenty of it. Evan's stomach growled, and Nancy who was working behind the bar grinned at him.

"Hungry?"

"You could say that." Evan drank more beer. He'd ducked out of the house just before Adam had announced a family Zoom call to congratulate Danny and Faith.

"Why don't you go and eat, then?"

"I'm waiting for someone."

"Like a date?" Nancy perked up. Evan belatedly remembered that she was an even worse gossip than he was and knew everyone in the valley.

He gave her the eye. "Like I'd tell you if I was."

"Man, I thought you Millers had run out of women around here."

"I've never dated you," Evan pointed out.

Nancy smiled sweetly. "That's because I haven't asked you. I prefer my men older and less responsible than you'll ever be."

"So, you're saying I'm boring?"

Nancy considered him, her head on one side. "You're . . . 'okay.'"

"Wow, thanks for the vote of confidence." Evan checked his cell again. "I'll have another beer when you're ready."

"Make that two."

He swung around to see that Josie was standing right behind him. She'd left her hair loose and wore an embroidered white shirt, jeans, and flowery cowboy boots. Her lipstick was as red as the roses on her shirt and her boots. Even as he smiled at her, Evan couldn't help but wonder how much of his conversation with Nancy she'd overheard.

"You came." Evan pulled out the barstool next to his.

"I said I would." She hesitated as she climbed onto the seat. "I forgot to ask you for your cell number."

Nancy handed them both a beer and went to help another customer. Evan lowered his voice. "Does that mean you wouldn't have come if you'd had it?"

She sighed. "I don't know. I could've gotten it from Ines if I'd really wanted to. I guess I'm worried about sticking my nose into your business and screwing things up."

"I like your nose," Evan said encouragingly.

Her lips twitched. "You're incorrigible."

"I don't know what that means, but it sounds good." He gestured toward the diner. "Have you eaten yet?"

"Yes, but I could always go for some dessert."

"Great, because I'm starving." Evan got down and offered her his hand. "I left before dinner so my dad wouldn't give me the third degree."

"Ines said he's a hard man." Josie didn't let go of his hand as they walked through to the diner and Evan was totally okay with that.

"He's stubborn, opinionated, and a complete pain in the ass," Evan confirmed. "But sometimes even if his mouth is still going off at you, his heart is in the right place."

As the youngest of the Miller boys, Evan knew that

compared to his older brothers he'd gotten off lightly with their dad and none of them let him forget it.

Sonali Patel was just coming out of the kitchen and smiled when she saw Evan.

"Hey! Do you want a table?"

"Yes, please."

"Where's Danny this evening?" Sonali asked as she gave them menus and set tall glasses of ice water on the table.

"He's . . . in Vegas."

"Really?" Sonali's eyebrows rose. "I saw him the other day and he didn't mention he was going on a trip."

"I don't think he planned it that far ahead."

Evan tried desperately to be noncommittal, which wasn't his strong point. As far as he knew, no one in Morgan Valley was aware of the marriage, apart from the Millers and hopefully the McDonalds.

Luckily, someone else claimed Sonali's attention. Evan picked up his menu and used it as camouflage until Josie tapped on the front.

"You hiding in there?"

He lowered the menu. "Not from you."

"From Sonali? Is she sweet on your brother?"

"I damn well hope not, seeing as he just eloped to Vegas with Faith McDonald."

Josie's mouth formed a perfect O and Evan groaned.

"Don't tell anyone I said that, okay? It's still a secret."

"I have no one to tell except Ines." Josie moved her water to one side and unwrapped her silverware from the paper napkin. "Your secret is safe with me."

Evan shoved a hand through his hair. "My family are right. I blab out everything."

"Maybe that's better than being a professional liar. I've met way too many of those in my line of work." Josie's mouth twisted. "A dose of the truth is quite refreshing, actually."

"Danny told me I was getting too old to just throw stuff out there without a thought for the consequences." Evan grimaced, aware that he was doing it again but already confident that Josie wouldn't mind. "I mean, there should be some limits, right?"

"I guess." Josie didn't look convinced. "I'd still rather get the truth than the lie though."

"I hurt him," Evan said slowly. "I was trying to protect him, and I got a lot of things wrong and interfered when I should have kept my mouth shut."

Josie reached over and took his hand, her brown eyes full of sympathy. "But he's your brother, right? He'll forgive you."

"I hope so. I did apologize."

"Then everything will be okay."

Evan wished he had her confidence. Part of his current feeling of being off-balance came from his fight with Danny. They'd stuck together through their parents' acrimonious divorce and supported each other against their older siblings. Danny was Evan's best friend, and he wasn't sure how to go on without that certainty in his life. But did Danny even need him anymore when he had Faith?

Sonali appeared, her tablet in hand. "Now, what can I get you two to eat?"

"What do you recommend?" Josie asked.

"The beef, obviously—it's organic and locally sourced

as are our vegetables. But we've also got a great coconut shrimp special." Sonali looked expectantly at Josie.

"I'll try that," Josie said.

"It comes with either rice or fries or macaroni salad."

"I thought you were only having dessert?" Evan intervened in the discussion.

"I changed my mind." Josie grinned at him and then turned back to Sonali. "I'll have the rice, please."

"I'll have the same as Josie, but with fries," Evan said. "Thanks, Sonali."

"You're welcome." She turned back to the kitchen.

Evan held out his beer bottle. "Cheers."

She clinked hers against his. "*Felicidades.* Now, how about you tell me one of the things on your list?"

"You don't want to start?"

"Nah, it was your idea so you should definitely go first," Josie encouraged him.

Evan pulled out his phone, ignoring the all-caps text from his dad, and opened notes. "I haven't prioritized them yet."

"Okay, so maybe start with an achievable goal?" She looked at him expectantly.

He scrolled through his options. "I want to get a tattoo."

She blinked at him and he frowned. "What's wrong with that?"

"I thought everyone had tattoos," Josie said.

"Like where would I get one around here?" Evan asked. "I suppose I could've asked my dad to brand me on the ass while he was doing the rest of the herd, but somehow it didn't appeal."

"I suppose not." Josie was definitely trying not to laugh

as Sonali returned to set some condiments on the table. "I wonder where the nearest place to get a tattoo *is*."

Sonali cleared her throat. "I hope you don't mind me eavesdropping, but I have a friend who does really great tattoos."

"Yeah? Are they local?" Evan asked.

"She is at the moment. Kashvi normally lives in L.A., but she's waiting for her new studio to open and she's come to stay with me and Dev right across the street." Sonali smiled. "She has all her kit with her so I'm sure she'd be happy to work on you, Josie."

"It's not for me," Josie said.

"*You* want a tattoo?" Sonali stared at Evan.

"Yeah." Evan met her skeptical gaze. "To go with the other dozen hiding under my clothes."

"Okay." Sonali nodded. "I have your number. I'll check in with Kashvi and let you know if she's good to go."

"Great."

Evan sat back and noticed that Josie was still smiling at him. He didn't think he'd met anyone who appeared to be so in tune with him.

"Do you have a tattoo?" Evan asked.

"Yup."

"Where?"

"None of your business." Josie drank some beer.

"Does Rio?"

"Yes, he has a massive one all over his back and shoulder. It's some kind of poem or script."

"I think I should probably start small," Evan said thoughtfully.

"I would," Josie said. "If this Kashvi is any good, she'll

talk you through the options and the recovery period in some detail."

"If she says yes, will you come with me?"

"Of course! I wouldn't miss it for the world."

Two days later, Josie ascended the steps to the apartment Sonali shared with her brother, Dev. Evan was right behind her. It was late afternoon, and according to Evan he was supposed to be out on the ranch somewhere counting cattle. After picking Josie up they'd driven into town and he'd hidden his truck behind the gas station before walking along the back street to Sonali's place.

Josie knocked on the door and it opened to reveal a diminutive woman dressed all in black. Her arms were bare, and Josie was transfixed by the vibrant tattoos of birds, vines, and flowers that encircled her flesh.

"Hey, you must be Josie and Evan. I'm Kashvi. Thanks for offering to let me keep my hand in while I'm here."

She gestured toward the pristine kitchen where she'd set up a chair swathed in plastic. "I've done everything I can to keep the place sterile and my tools are always kept like that."

"Looks good," Josie said as Evan had suddenly gone very quiet. She nudged his elbow. "You okay, *mano?*"

He nodded, his solemn gaze fixed on the chair like he was visiting the dentist for an extraction. Where had her wisecracking cowboy gone?

As Kashvi went to scrub her hands, Josie lowered her voice. "You still want to do this? You don't have to."

"If I can't do this, how the hell am I going to move on

to anything significant on my list?" Evan whispered. "I have to cowboy up and get through it."

"You've got this." Josie went up on tiptoe and kissed both of his cheeks. Even as his hand reached to encircle her waist, Kashvi called out to him.

"Why don't you sit down, and we can talk about what you want to do? Sonali didn't seem to think you wanted anything too complicated."

Evan set his Stetson down on the table and moved off like a condemned man approaching the gallows. Josie fought a smile. When she'd decided to visit her brother's ranch, she hadn't envisaged holding a cowboy's hand while he got a tattoo. She hadn't expected to kiss him either, but that was another conversation entirely.

The instant attraction she felt for Evan had come out of nowhere. After growing up on a ranch, she usually avoided cowboys like the plague. Sure, they were amazing with horses, but they tended to lack some social skills and often preferred animals to people. They'd also treated her like their kid brother so the thought of having any romantic feelings for any of them had been zero.

"So, what are you thinking of having done, and where?"

Kashvi pulled up her stool and smiled at Evan who was gripping the arms of the chair so hard, Josie could see the white of his knuckles from across the room.

"Something to celebrate my heritage."

"Okay." Kashvi nodded. "Like what exactly?"

Evan looked appealingly at Josie who came to sit on his other side.

"It needs to be somewhere he can deal with the after-care himself and not too visible," Josie said. "Obviously, he has a very physical, outside job, so it needs to be somewhere it won't tear."

"Good to know." Kashvi looked at Evan. "How big?"

"That depends on how much you're going to charge me." Evan finally spoke up.

"Don't worry about that." Kashvi leaned forward and patted his hand. "You're doing me a favor. I'll be charging you the family rate."

After doing some research, Josie had also spoken with Kashvi on the phone and confirmed she'd help pay for the tattoo so Evan wouldn't get sticker shock.

"Are you left or right-handed?" Kashvi asked.

"Right."

"Then we'll do it on your left side," Kashvi said. "Easier for you to care for and you use that side less. If I were you, I'd go for your left bicep. Tattooing over muscle is a lot easier than being close to the bone."

"If he's anything like all the other cowboys I've known, he'll have great biceps," Josie added helpfully.

"Would you mind taking off your shirt, Evan?"

"Sure."

Evan undid the top three buttons of his denim shirt and pulled it over his head, ruffling his auburn hair in the process. Both Josie and Kashvi stared at his forearms and the muscular bulge of his biceps.

"Well . . ." Kashvi cleared her throat. "You're definitely in good shape." She winked at Josie. "Could you take your T-shirt off, too?"

Being on Evan's right side meant that at least Josie could drool quietly over his awesome physique without him noticing as his entire attention was fixed on Kashvi who was still talking.

"So, any idea what you actually want on that arm of yours?"

"Joker's head," Evan said.

"And Joker is . . . ?"

"My horse."

"Ah! That makes sense." Kashvi picked up her tablet and swiped through some kind of picture gallery. She handed the tablet to Evan. "Something like this?"

Josie craned closer to look. "You did all those?" she asked.

"Most of them." Kashvi pointed at the second picture. "That's one of my favorites. I love the clean, black lines."

It was Evan's turn to nod. "I like that one, too. It even looks a bit like him." He glanced over at the door as if already planning his escape. "How long do you think it'll take to get it done?"

Kashvi considered the picture. "As it's all one color, probably about an hour and a half, maybe two if you're a wriggler."

"I can just about stay that long," Evan confirmed.

"Where exactly does Jeff think you are?" Josie asked.

"I told him I was helping Ben count cattle at his place. Ben agreed to cover for me if Dad checked."

Josie tried to remember exactly which Miller brother Ben was and recalled Ines telling her that their parents had thoughtfully named their kids alphabetically.

"Ben's your second oldest brother, right?"

"Yup. He and Silver bought the Perez Ranch."

"Silver Meadows?" Kashvi was busy tracing something out on a piece of transparent paper. "I did a tattoo for her last week at her place. She's supernice."

"She is." Evan snorted. "I bet it was something romantic, like Ben's name in a heart."

Kashvi laughed. "You'll have to ask her about that." She presented Evan with the piece of paper. "Normally I'd print this out, but as I've done something similar before, I think you'll get the idea from this drawing." She leaned over and applied the paper to Evan's bicep. "How's the size and placement?"

Evan looked it over and then flexed his muscles, which made Josie want to purr. "I like it."

"Great! How about the design? Do you want to customize it further? What are some features of Joker you could add in there?"

Evan took the paper and studied it, his face a picture of concentration.

"Joker has this bit of mane that whatever you do it always falls down between his ears and onto his brow. It's kind of cute."

"Do you have a picture of him?"

"Yeah." Evan pulled his cell phone out of his jeans and flicked through the photos. "He's very photogenic."

He handed his phone to Kashvi who smiled. "He sure is. I think I can get some of his quirkiness into this image. Just give me a minute to redraw."

Evan waited quietly in the chair, his fingers tapping on the arms as Kashvi and Josie chatted about something in the design. He reminded himself that he wanted to do this—that no one was forcing him, and that he was a big, strong boy. Why he'd decided to start with the tattoo and not some of the other stupid things on his list was beyond him. But he hadn't expected Sonali to have a professional tattoo artist as a friend who just happened to be staying in town. . . .

Wasn't this his problem all along? The way he either sat back and did nothing, or rushed into things before he thought them through?

Kashvi sat back on the stool beside him, her expression serious. "Before we start, I want to remind you that tattoos are permanent, and that aftercare is a very important part of the procedure. Once I ink you, it's going to cost you ten times as much and take ten times as long to get rid of it—and your skin will never be the same again. Are you still sure you want to go through with this?"

Evan glanced at Josie who was regarding him expectantly.

"Yeah."

"Okay, then." Kashvi handed him the new draft of the tattoo. "What do you think of this?"

"It's *awesome*." Evan couldn't believe how she'd managed to get a sense of Joker right in there. "He's going to love it."

A small snort escaped Josie and he glanced over to find her grinning at him like a fool.

"Hey, he's my best friend," Evan protested. "I helped birth him and then brought him up."

"That's so sweet." Kashvi went to wash her hands again and then pulled on a pair of gloves. "Shall we get started?"

As soon as she laid one gloved finger on him, Evan tensed like a bull about to erupt from the bucking chute. He'd just remembered how much he hated needles.

"Evan," Josie said quietly. "Look at me."

He turned his head away from the whirring sound of the needle and focused all his attention on Josie's big, brown eyes, wide, generous mouth, and arching dark eyebrows. Seeing her now, this close up, he could see her likeness to her half brother, and yet she was still uniquely herself.

Even as the needle began to scratch into his skin, he considered the kiss she'd given him, and the way he'd wanted to pull her closer and make it into something even better. He'd always loved women, but he tended to keep them as friends because—he jumped as the needle tone changed.

"It's okay, Evan." Josie took his right hand in hers. "Just relax."

"I'm trying," he murmured. "It reminds me of when we had kittens in the house. I woke up one morning thinking someone was pricking my toes with a pin, and discovered a kitty attached to my big toe."

"That's a great description." Kashvi didn't look up as she outlined the shape. "If it gets too much for you at any point, just let me know, and you can take a break."

Seeing as his father would expect him back to do the evening chores, Evan wasn't planning on hanging around. He resolved to sit as still as a statue and not complain. He'd never been a big fan of needles, but at least he had something pretty to look at while Kashvi worked.

Eventually, just when he was beginning to think he couldn't bear another minute of the continual pricking, Kashvi stopped.

"I think that's it."

Evan turned his head to squint at the design on his upper left arm. "Cool."

"Okay." Kashi stripped off her gloves, rewashed her hands, and put on a new pair. "A healing tattoo is basically an open wound, so it's easily irritated. I'm going to apply a thin layer of sealant and slap a bandage over it. For the next few weeks, depending on how fast you heal, you're going to gently wash the tattoo with antibacterial, unfragranced soap and pat it dry. Do that twice a day and moisturize the hell out of it. You also need to keep it out of the sun, don't swim, and not scratch or pick at it when it scabs over. Got it?"

Evan nodded.

"I've got a sheet of written instructions for you and I'll put my cell number on there so you can call me if you have any problems." Kashvi gently covered the tattoo with a bandage. "You can take this off tomorrow and follow the instructions on the sheet."

"Thank you."

With a bit of help from Josie, Evan put his T-shirt back on and then added his other shirt. His arm felt kind of awkward after being stuck in the same position for two hours. Kashvi handed him the aftercare instructions and he folded them up and put them in his pocket.

"How much do I owe you?" Evan asked as he got out of the chair.

Kashvi, who was busy sorting her stuff out at the sink, didn't turn around when she answered, "My hourly rate's about one hundred and fifty dollars, so let's go for that."

"But it took almost two hours," Evan pointed out.

She swung around to smile at him. "And you get the family rate, which is fifty percent off, okay?"

"I wouldn't argue with her," Josie said. "She might want her tattoo back."

"If you can get me cash, that would be even better,"

Kashvi said hopefully. "Then I don't have to pay the credit card fees."

"I can get you cash." Evan put his card back in his pocket. "There's an ATM in the post office just down the street. I'll go right now."

"Thanks so much!" Kashvi came over to pat his right arm. "It was a pleasure working on you, Evan. I really hope Joker likes it."

"He will." Evan grinned as he headed for the door, Josie at his side. "I'll be right back with your money."

He went down the stairs at a gallop and the heat of the sun hit him square in the face. Being stuck inside wasn't his thing and two hours of inactivity made him want to run around like a wild horse.

"Hey, slow down." Josie spoke from behind him as he crossed the busy road and headed for the post office.

He swung around to look for her and all at once the whole world went upside down and he staggered back against the nearest building.

"Evan!"

He vaguely heard Josie calling him through the sparkling black-and-white stars now encroaching on his vision, and then his legs gave way. The next thing he knew, he was sitting on a bench with Josie crouched in front of him, her gaze anxious.

"Are you okay?"

"What happened?" Evan frowned. "Did I trip up the steps?"

She took his hand and cradled it between both of hers. "You almost passed out."

"Hell, no, I didn't!" Evan protested.

"It was probably a reaction to having the tattoo." Josie

wasn't having it. "You rushed off really fast and at some point, your brain caught up with your body, and you just had a moment."

Evan leaned his head back against the wall of the post office and briefly closed his eyes. No way had he almost passed out. Millers never fainted.

"It must have been the heat." Evan regrouped and fixed Josie with a challenging stare. "I'm probably dehydrated or something."

She rolled her eyes and eased her hand free of his. "Fine. Whatever, cowboy. Are you good to go or do you need to drink something before you get your money?"

Evan eased his weight over his booted feet and cautiously stood up.

"I'm good. How about we get the money, take it back to Kashvi, and then go get some coffee at Yvonne's place?"

Chapter Three

"So, how are things, *irmã?*" Rio asked.

For once, as she stared at the screen, Josie was glad her big brother was hundreds of miles away and not sitting right in front of her. He knew exactly why she'd abandoned her colleagues so abruptly, and she still wasn't ready to deal with either his sympathy or his possible disappointment.

"*Bacana!*" Josie smiled. "Yvonne's giving me free food at the café and keeping me company at home. Ines is mothering me and I'm enjoying working with your ranch hands and breeding team."

"Jaime told me you'd been hanging out with him. He says you're an asset. At least I think that was the word he used."

"Ha ha." Josie reminded herself that everyone on the ranch owed their loyalty to Rio and not her and wouldn't think twice about reporting back to her brother as to what she was up to.

"What else are you doing except riding my bulls?"

"He told you that?" Josie feigned shock. "Like I'd do that without your permission."

"He said it was a pity you weren't up for competing because the PBR could do with a few more women bull riders."

Josie sat back. "I'm humbled."

"He's got a good eye for what makes a successful bull rider." Rio grinned. "Maybe there's a new career for you?"

Josie's smile dimmed. "Does that mean you don't want me back at Howatch International?"

"Of course, I do. It means that I want you to feel free to do whatever makes you happy." Rio leaned toward the camera, his expression serious. "As someone who changed careers myself, I'm not going to call you out for making the same choices."

"Somehow, I don't think I'm going to make the leap from corporate finance to world-champion bull rider quite like you did, *mano,*" Josie said dryly.

"Why not? Jaime says you're good enough to compete."

"But I can't manage the massive bulls and you and the other breeders are focused on making the stock bigger and meaner every year."

Rio looked thoughtful. "Maybe that's something I should look into. We could specialize in a different kind of bull, one that allows women to compete equally."

"In your dreams," Josie said, making a face.

"Ines says you've been seeing a lot of Evan Miller."

"Wow, at the abrupt change of subject, Bro." Josie blinked at him. "Evan's a nice guy."

"I know." He frowned.

"And we're just friends."

"Awesome. I was going to say you could keep each

other out of trouble, but on reflection, I think you'll make each other worse."

"I'll do my best to stay out of jail. Evan's looking to change his life right now and I'm just going along for the ride."

"Evan is?" Rio's dark eyebrows rose. "Now I've heard everything." He hesitated. "Just have fun, little sister, okay? Take the time to heal and decide what you want to do next. There's no rush."

"Because Howatch International can easily go on without me?"

"It's a big company, Josie. We have the resources to cover most calamities. It doesn't mean you wouldn't be welcomed back with open arms. I just want you to think about what *you* want to do, and not what you think you ought to be doing—if that makes sense."

"Kind of." Josie nodded.

"I talked to Dr. Tio at the medical center the other day. He says they've now got a full-time therapist attached to the clinic."

"Thanks for the not-so-subtle hint," Josie said. "I'll contact him, I promise."

"Okay." Rio smiled. "Nice talking to you, kiddo."

"Same, old man."

"Love you."

He winked and ended the call, leaving Josie sitting at the table staring at a blank screen.

The ranch house was quiet around her. Ines had gone to help Yvonne at the café, leaving Josie all by herself for the first time. Not that she was ever totally alone. There were at least half a dozen ranch hands hanging out over at the bull breeding barn. . . .

Her cell buzzed and she picked it up to see a link to Dr. Tio's number sent by her brother. She reminded herself that Rio hadn't become a world champion for nothing. His relentless drive for success served him well in all the worlds he currently straddled.

Did she want to go back to work?

She pictured her office and smiled. Everyone in her department was awesome and she missed them a lot. But, if she resumed her job, she'd have to go back to living in the city. Even though she was alone, Josie slowly shook her head. She couldn't go back to her apartment. The thought of living there after her space had been invaded was too much to deal with right now.

She needed to talk to Rio about putting it on the market. There were plenty of places she could rent if she went back.

With a muttered curse, she clicked on the link Rio had sent her and was put through to Dr. Tio's clinic. She made an appointment with the therapist for the end of the following week. She had no idea if that person would work out for her, but it was worth making the effort. She didn't want to live in fear for the rest of her life.

Her cell buzzed again, and she smiled as Evan's message appeared

Hey you.

How's your tattoo doing? Josie typed.

Itchy.

Hang in there. It gets better.

I hope so because Dad thinks I've got lice or something and is threatening to dip me with Ben's new sheep.

Josie grinned. What's next on your list?

Isn't it your turn to pick something?

I suppose it is. Josie tapped her finger against the screen.

How about you come over for dinner at my place tonight and you can tell me all about it?

Would your dad be okay with that? Josie frowned. Even she knew that Jeff Miller wasn't known for his hospitality.

Scratch that—come to Ben's. The food is better. Meet you there at six. I'll send you the gate code.

Okay.

Evan sent through a thumbs-up and the gate code and Josie ended the call. She hadn't thought about how she would feel being alone in the ranch house for the first time at night. Evan's invitation meant she wouldn't have to deal with it—just yet.

"I don't remember asking you to dinner, Bro?"

Ben came into the kitchen and raised an eyebrow at Evan who was leaning up against the countertop, drinking a beer and chatting to Silver. He was a taller, broader, and redder-haired version of Evan and way easier going than Adam. He walked over to kiss his wife and helped himself to a glass of iced tea.

"I'm pretty sure that you did," Evan replied. "In fact, I distinctly remember you saying those words after I helped you out with your cows the other day."

"That day when you pretended to be here so Dad wouldn't know what you were up to?" Ben asked.

Evan shook his head at Silver. "Do you have any idea what he's talking about right now? Because I don't."

Silver linked her arm through Ben's. "Like, I'm going to agree with you and not my husband." She went on tiptoe to kiss his bearded cheek. "Evan asked Josie Martinez to join him for dinner."

"Ah, now things start to make sense," Ben said. "You didn't want to expose her to Dad at this early stage of your relationship."

"We don't have a relationship. We're just friends," Evan said quickly.

"Sure." Ben winked at his wife. "Do we have enough to feed everyone?"

"You know we do," Silver said. "Marta always cooks for six."

"I love Marta," Evan said fervently.

"Don't we all," Silver agreed. "If it were up to me and Ben to do the cooking, we'd be living off frozen dinners. She preps for a week's worth of fresh meals, freezes extra portions, and generally makes our life so much easier."

The oven beeped and Silver hurried over. "I need to check this."

"Must be nice being married to a rich movie star," Evan murmured to his brother whose attention was currently fixed on his wife's jeans-clad ass as she bent down to the oven.

"It has its compensations," Ben admitted, winking at Evan.

"Do you ever fight about money?" Evan asked curiously.

"Sometimes." Ben shrugged. "But we always find a way to make things work because we love each other."

"Nice," Evan said.

"Yeah, it is." Ben held his gaze and then grinned. "Look at me being all sentimental and shit. Kaiden would say I'm a true Southern Californian now."

"Luckily, he's not here." Evan finished his beer and set the bottle back on the counter.

"Danny and Faith are back tomorrow," Ben said. "Dad's planning some kind of party for them."

"So I heard." Evan fiddled with the label on the empty bottle. "He's even got Mom involved."

"Yeah, well. Danny's the second member of the family to elope to Vegas so I guess Dad's getting used to it." Ben's mouth quirked. "We got bawled out of town when we did it."

"I suppose he's trying," Evan said.

"Danny was asking how you were." Ben watched him real close, which Evan didn't appreciate. "He wondered if there was something up with your phone seeing as you're not picking up his calls."

"*Right* . . . I'm not sure why he's asking you to be his messenger or why you'd agree to it." Evan opened the re-cycle bin and tossed his bottle in with a satisfying crash. "When I have something to say to Danny, I'll say it."

Ben frowned. "I've always thought of you and Danny as a team. It's weird when you fight."

"We're not fighting," Evan said. "I just don't have anything to talk about right now."

"Not even congratulations on his marriage?"

"I said that already," Evan protested.

"You sure about that?" Ben sighed. "Look, this is obviously way more complicated than I thought and you're right, I'm sorry. I should keep my nose out of it."

Evan's cell buzzed and he took the opportunity to walk away from Ben to check the message from Josie.

I'm outside the house. Really hoping this is the right place and that I'm not about to feature in a horror movie.

Evan sauntered over to the window overlooking the circular drive and looked out.

Is that you in the black truck?

Yup.

Then you're definitely in the right place.

Evan called out to the couple in the kitchen. "Josie's here. I'll just go and let her in."

Had he congratulated Danny on his marriage? Now that he thought about his one stilted conversation with his brother, Evan couldn't actually remember saying it. He'd been too eager to get off the phone and get away to have time to make nice—not that Danny would've believed him anyway.

He opened the front door and Josie frowned at him.

"What's wrong?" she asked.

"Nothing."

"Right. You always make that face when you're welcoming guests into your home."

Evan found a smile somewhere. "It's not my house."

"I know." Josie had paused in the large hallway and looked up at the natural stone and wood pillars. "But, man, I wish it was mine."

"Don't we all." Evan took her hand and led her through to the back of the house where the large kitchen and family room took up the entire width of the building. His brother Kaiden had designed and built the kitchen cabinets, which he was certain Josie would appreciate.

"You've met Ben and Silver before, right?"

Josie smiled at his brother. "Briefly at Morgan Ranch, but you probably don't remember me."

"I do." Ben came across to offer his hand. "You're one hell of a rider."

"Oh." Josie grinned. "Was that when HW Morgan suggested I wouldn't be able to ride the horse he was breaking?"

"Yup." Ben chuckled. "You sure showed him. It's always a pleasure to see a Morgan land on his ass."

"She's a good bull rider, too," Evan added as Silver closed the oven and joined them. "I'm hoping she'll teach me some of her technique."

"Dad would hate you taking up bull riding," Ben said. "Which is superhypocritical of him because when we were young, he used to travel all over the country competing in the rodeo, leaving Mom to deal with six kids and the ranch."

Evan frowned. "I didn't remember that."

"By the time you were at school, he'd already hurt his

back and been forced to retire. Mom didn't like it at all."
Ben set his arm around Silver's shoulders. "It was one of
the reasons why she finally left him."

"Your mom had it tough," Silver agreed. "Welcome to
our home, Josie. I'm so glad Evan thought to invite you
over."

"He decided I wasn't ready for the full-on Miller experience at his place yet," Josie said.

"I get that." Silver nodded. "Things can get a bit . . .
rowdy when they all get together."

"Rowdy?" Ben asked. "That's a nice way of saying that
someone always ends up in a fight."

"Not always!" Silver protested. "When your mom and
Auntie Rae are there, things are way calmer." She patted
Josie's arm. "Jeff really is okay when you get to know
him."

"No, he's not." Evan reclaimed Josie's attention. "He's
a complete pain in the ass."

"I'm going to have to agree with Evan here, Silver,"
Ben said. "He's improved since Mom came back into his
life, but not by much."

"I hear your mom has bought a place in town?" Josie
asked.

"Yes, that's right." Ben offered Josie iced tea or beer.
"In the old movie theater that Kaiden helped restore and
redevelop into apartments. She's planning on coming
back this weekend to check in on the place and attend
Faith and Danny's wedding celebration."

"By the way." Ben turned to Evan. "Have they settled
on a venue, yet?"

"How the hell would I know?" Evan shrugged. "No one's consulting me about anything."

"I wonder why," Ben said dryly as he led them toward the table and pulled out a chair for Josie.

"I think it's going to be at the hotel." Silver set a bowl of steaming vegetables on the table and followed it up with a large pot of what looked like chicken and dumplings. "I spoke to Avery earlier and she said they could definitely do it."

"Great." Evan sat opposite Josie. "We can all crash at Mom's new place afterward."

"Like she'd let you." Ben gestured at Josie to help herself. "Although since Ellie isn't coming with her, she will have a spare room."

"Shotgun!" Evan slapped the table with his left hand and then winced. "Tell the others."

After making sure everyone had a plateful of food, Ben turned back to Evan.

"What's up with your arm?"

Evan raised his eyebrows. "I'm not sure what you're talking about."

Ben pointed at Evan's left arm. "You're moving it like it's stiff or something."

Evan glanced over at Josie who was trying to look neutral and failing dismally.

"I got a tattoo."

Ben set his fork back down on his plate. "You did what?"

"Yeah, Sonali's friend Kashvi did it for me." Evan shrugged like it was no big deal.

"She's awesome." Silver leaned forward. "She did one

for me last year in L.A. I had to wait for almost a year to get on her list. When I saw her in Maureen's in Morgantown, I thought I was hallucinating."

Evan's gaze dropped to his itching bicep. "She's like a big deal in L.A.?"

"She's considered one of the best in her field, so yeah." Silver grinned. "Have you ever watched *Inkers United* on TV? She's one of their regular featured artists."

"I don't watch much TV," Evan admitted. "She did a tattoo of Joker for me."

"Your horse?" Ben snorted. "That's so romantic, Bro."

Silver gave her husband a reproving look. "If Joker is important to Evan then he did what was best for him."

"What did she do for you?" Evan asked.

Silver blushed and pushed her long, blond hair away from her face. "Something personal for me and Ben."

"Like . . . ?" Evan paused as someone kicked him under the table. He focused on Josie, who narrowed her eyes and shook her head. "Like none of my business, right."

"Exactly." Ben cleared his throat. "Anyone want seconds?"

After their hosts declined their offer to help clean up, Josie and Evan found themselves sitting in the den with a pot of coffee between them and a fantastic view out over the foothills from the floor-to-ceiling windows.

Josie sighed happily. "This place is amazing."

"Yeah, Silver's architect did a really good job."

Evan sat at the other end of the couch, his long legs

stuck out in front of him, his heels resting on the coffee table, which Josie was sure Silver wouldn't appreciate. He wore his usual T-shirt under a plaid shirt combo and faded jeans that fitted him perfectly. There was a faint hint of stubble on his chin hiding his dimples and he seemed distracted.

"Is everything okay?" Josie asked.

"Yeah, pretty much."

"Remember, you don't have to lie to me, Miller. I'm your friend," Josie reminded him.

He turned to look at her. "If Kashvi is famous, don't you think she would've charged more for the tattoo than that?"

"Maybe she wanted to do Sonali a favor," Josie suggested.

"I asked Silver roughly how much hers cost while we were making the coffee and she said it was over a thousand bucks."

"Wow," Josie said. "Maybe it was a really complicated piece of art."

Evan still didn't look happy and Josie kept talking.

"I mean, if it makes you feel any better, I did ask her to let me know if it got too expensive so I could make up the difference, but—"

"Hold up." Evan's feet hit the ground and he swiveled around to her. "You paid for my tattoo?"

"No!" Josie met his gaze. "I just said that if it got too pricey, I'd help out."

Evan was definitely glaring at her now. "I don't want your money."

"You didn't *get* any of my money," Josie said. "Kashvi said it was cool."

"But you would've paid her if she hadn't."

"Yes! Because it was my idea for you to write a list and I encouraged you to get the tattoo with Kashvi."

"Only when Sonali suggested it."

"Yes, but when I googled Kashvi and found out exactly how much in demand she was I felt bad that I might have dropped you into something you couldn't afford."

"I'm not a pauper, Josie."

"I know that." She nodded, and hoped her expression was as serious as his was.

"And I don't need handouts."

"Got it. I shouldn't have interfered and I'm sorry."

"Okay, then." He returned to sitting, facing the window, his arms crossed over his chest.

Josie poured them both some more coffee and they sipped in silence.

"How is your tattoo anyway?" Josie eventually asked.

"It's doing good." He set his mug down on the coffee table, looked at Josie, and sighed. "I suppose I should've googled her, too."

"But then you might not have gone ahead."

"True. But there's no point being mad at you about it, is there?"

"I don't think so," Josie said cautiously. "I mean as long as I promise not to shower you with money in the future. I just feel so comfortable with you that I forgot we hardly know each other really."

He reached out his arm and drew her against his side. "I dunno. I've always wanted a sugar momma."

She rubbed her cheek against his shirt and breathed in the scent of pure cowboy.

"How about we do this?" Josie said. "I keep my money to myself and we split the bills fifty-fifty?"

"Sounds good." His fingers tightened on her shoulder. "Can I kiss you?"

She slowly raised her head to look up into his waiting, hazel eyes. "Okay, sure."

It was a nice, respectful, gentle kiss—or it was until she grabbed the back of his head and moaned his name, at which point it went wild and hot and so steamy, all she could think about was ripping off his clothes.

"Ahem." Someone behind them cleared his throat. "Just came to check if you two were okay, but I can see that you are."

Evan leapt away from her like a spawning salmon, but Ben had already left the room, murmuring something about "just friends."

"Dammit!" Evan growled. "Now Ben's going to tell everyone."

"About what?" Josie was still basking in the warm glow of the kiss, her head against the back of the couch, her body humming with anticipation. She couldn't remember the last time she'd felt so aware of someone or so safe with them.

"Us."

"What us?"

He leapt to his feet and shoved a hand through his already-disordered hair. He pointed at her face.

"*That* us."

She raised an eyebrow. "You didn't like it?"

He came down on one knee in front of her and took her hand. "You know I did."

"Then what's the problem?" She traced her fingers along the brow of his freckled nose and down to his mouth.

He held her gaze for a long moment and then smiled, which made something inside her melt into a thousand tiny pieces of lust.

"Okay."

She walked her fingers around the back of his neck, drew him close again, and kissed his mouth. She'd think about the repercussions of what she was allowing to happen later, but at this moment, and with this man, she was sure she was making a good decision.

He kissed her back and then slowly released her.

"If I go to the family thing this weekend, will you come with me?"

"As your date or as your friend?" Josie asked.

"How about both?"

She smiled into his eyes. "I like the sound of that."

He rose to his feet, bringing her with him, and kept hold of her hand. "Now, should we go and put Ben out of his misery and tell him we are a couple, or should we leave him to work it out for himself?"

Josie grinned. "*Mano,* I think even your brother got it faster than you did."

Chapter Four

Evan glanced over at Josie as they entered the lobby of the hotel. Despite the short notice, the staff had really put out the welcome mat for Danny and Faith. There were balloons and flowers and signage directing the guests toward the large dining area, which opened up into the new glass conservatory. Apparently, everyone in Morgan Valley had been invited to pop by. The celebration was slated to go on all afternoon and well into the night to accommodate all the guests.

"Are you okay?" Josie tugged on his hand and he looked down at her.

She'd braided her hair and coiled it on the top of her head like a crown. She wore long dangly earrings, her signature red lipstick, a pink dress and, currently, a concerned expression.

"I'm good."

Evan hastened to reassure her, even though it was far from true. He'd spent all morning either doing chores or out on the ranch and managed to avoid Danny completely. He wasn't proud of himself, but he needed time. Seeing his brother and Faith together in public for the first time might be easier than dealing with them over the breakfast table.

Josie searched his face. "He's your brother. He'll forgive you anything."

"I guess." Evan couldn't resist leaning down and kissing her forehead. "I'm glad you're here, though."

"I offered to help Yvonne set up the food, but she didn't need me," Josie confided as Evan reclaimed her hand and followed everyone through the door. "I was actually quite glad so that I could be with you."

"I'm glad you're here."

She hesitated and looked up at him. "It feels like things are going really fast between us. Are you okay with that?"

He rolled his eyes. "Like, duh. You're amazing, I'm totally into you and you still haven't told me what you plan to do off your list yet."

"Oh! I forgot about that after we kissed." Josie blushed.

"Me, too." Evan started moving again. "How about we stop blocking the doorway and go and get this over with?"

He set his sights on the raised dais at the end of the room where he could see his parents, some of his siblings, and most importantly, Danny and Faith. He approached from the side, appreciating the fact that he could see them before they saw him, and that he had Josie with him.

At the last moment, Danny seemed to sense his presence and looked directly at him. He smiled his usual warm, easy, smile.

"Hey."

Evan drew Josie in front of him like a shield.

"Hey, have you met Josie Martinez?"

Josie extended her hand. "Congratulations!"

Danny shook her hand. "Thanks." He touched his new wife's shoulder. "Faith? Evan's here."

Evan braced himself as Faith McDonald—now Miller—turned toward him.

"Hey, Evan." She smiled. "Sorry about the terrible wedding timing, but Danny carried me off before I really knew what was going on. I wish you all could've been there."

Evan stepped forward to give her a quick, awkward hug. "Sounds just like my brother."

"Now, you know that's not true." Danny chuckled. "I'm usually the cautious member of the family." He set his arm around Faith's shoulders. Evan didn't think he'd ever seen his brother so relaxed or so obviously happy. "Have you met Josie yet, Faith?"

"You're Rio's sister, right?" Faith smiled at Josie. "He told me all about you when I visited his place."

"All of it good, I hope?" Josie said. She'd reclaimed Evan's hand after greeting the newlyweds and Evan was surprisingly grateful for the firm clasp of her fingers.

He sensed Danny trying to get him to look at him, but kept his gaze on Faith and Josie as they swapped stories about Rio and his bull breeding program.

"Everything okay with you?" Danny eventually murmured.

"Why wouldn't it be?" Evan finally met his brother's cool, gray gaze. "Ben said I forgot to congratulate you on your marriage. Sorry about that."

Danny shrugged. "Ben's a blabbermouth."

"I thought that was my job," Evan said, aware that

there was already a line of people forming behind him, he gestured to Faith. "I'd best move along. Congratulations."

He tugged on Josie's hand and they moved away toward the bar where Evan ordered two beers and drank his down in one long swallow.

After one sip, Josie set hers on the bar. "Danny seemed fine with you."

"Yeah." Evan blew out a breath.

"You, on the other hand, aren't fine with him."

"You noticed that?"

Josie looked up at him, her brown gaze searching. "It was hard to miss. You couldn't wait to get away from him."

He shrugged. "I didn't want to hold up the line. I can see him whenever I want."

"Bullshit."

"Wow." Evan blinked. "That's direct."

"Why?"

"Why what?"

It was Josie's turn to sigh. "I'm not playing this stupid game, Evan. Either tell me what's really going on, or I'll go and talk to someone else until you get over yourself and want to be honest with me."

She picked up her beer and Evan gently caught hold of her wrist. "It's hard to explain."

"Try me."

He pointed at a secluded table in the conservatory. "Shall we go and sit down?"

They were just moving in the right direction when Evan was loudly hailed.

"Evan! Come here and greet your mother like a proper son would!"

He briefly closed his eyes and then looked at Josie. "Your call. I have to go and say hi to my parents. If you want to save that table for us, I'll get to you as soon as I can. Please feel free to walk away."

"I don't think I've met your mother." Josie linked her arm through his. "Let's go."

There was definitely more going on between Evan and his brother Danny than a simple misunderstanding. Even though Josie only had one half sibling, she'd grown up with lots of cousins and friends and had a keen eye for conflict. And what was weird was that it wasn't coming from Danny, but from happy-go-lucky, let's-all-get-along-with-each-other Evan.

Did it have more to do with Evan's sudden decision to change his life, and if so, would it help or hinder his decision making? Josie wasn't sure yet, and if Evan wasn't willing to share, she might have to bail on the whole list business. Her earlier doubts about interfering in Evan's life in a negative way resurfaced tenfold.

"Evan!"

A diminutive woman with red hair wearing a sharp cream pantsuit and lots of tasteful gold jewelry embraced Evan.

"Isn't this wonderful news?" She smiled at him and then at her ex-husband. "I'm so glad Danny and Faith finally got their happy ending."

"About time," Jeff Miller said gruffly. "I thought the boy

was going to bottle out again." His shrewd gaze moved to Josie. "And who are you?"

Josie proffered her hand. "Josie Martinez. I'm staying with Ines at my brother's place."

"You're a lot prettier to look at than your brother," Jeff said as he shook her hand.

"Don't tell Yvonne that," Josie replied, and was rewarded with a wink.

Jeff looked at Evan. "She's a nice girl."

"She's standing right here, Dad," Evan said. "And she has a name, and she can hear you."

"I know that, Son."

"It's okay," Josie said. "Thank you for inviting me to this celebration. I appreciate it."

"You're welcome." Leanne smiled at her and then looked back at Evan. "Now, why don't you make an effort to mingle while your father and I get ready for the speeches?"

"You're not going to let him talk again, are you?" Evan asked. "We haven't gotten over the last time."

"I didn't say a word out of place!" Jeff protested. "And I don't intend to do so today."

Evan looked so skeptical that Josie wanted to laugh. Even she knew Jeff Miller's idea of speaking the good plain truth was often too harsh for the majority of listeners and couched in terms that would make your maiden aunt blush.

"It was a pleasure to meet you," Josie said to Leanne.

"You must come over to the ranch for dinner before I leave."

"I'd love to—if Evan's okay with it," Josie confirmed.

"I don't think he'd object." Leanne lowered her voice.

"It's nice to see him looking so happy after everything that's happened with Danny. I was worried he'd feel at a loss without his most supportive brother always at his side."

Josie drew Evan away and waited patiently as all his other siblings, except Daisy, who was in San Francisco, checked in on him in their various unsubtle ways. Despite the joking, she could also feel the love and concern they felt for him—so why couldn't Evan feel it, too?

Eventually, they ended up at the table he'd pointed out earlier and sat down, partially obscured from the rest of the room by the large tropical plants growing in the perfumed and exotic space. Evan snagged two glasses of champagne from one of the circling waiters and handed one over to Josie.

"Your family are lovely," Josie said.

"They're okay," Evan agreed as they clinked glasses. "Sometimes they can be a bit much."

"I can imagine. I basically grew up as an only child with just my mother for company so I can't claim to understand all the dynamics of a family."

"What happened to your dad?" Evan asked.

"It's a bit of a story." Josie smiled. "Arturio married my mother in a whirlwind romance after she divorced Rio's father, Graham. She discovered just after I was born that he'd been in love with his secretary for years. She suggested they got a divorce, and he married his true love."

"And . . . he went for it?" Evan gawped at her.

"Yes. He was already quite old—I was something of a surprise to everyone—and he only lived another year or so, but *Mamãe* said he was very happy and grateful to her for setting him free."

Evan's brow creased. "Well, that's all very nice for him, your mom, and his secretary, but what about you?"

"What about me?"

"You never got to have a father."

"I survived." She took a sip of champagne. "Trust me, dealing with my mother was like having two full-time parents."

He continued to look at her, his expression unreadable. "It still wasn't fair."

"Life isn't fair," Josie said lightly. "I turned out okay. He left me enough money that I don't ever have to work, and he died happy." She reached over and patted Evan's hand. "Can we not talk about this anymore? It's really old news."

Evan didn't look convinced. He picked up his glass and drank some champagne while Josie tried to think of a new topic of conversation. Usually, when she told people about her parents' "love" story, they laughed along with her and moved on. No one thought to ask how it had affected her . . . not that it had. She'd been way too young to realize she'd lost a parent she hadn't ever really known.

"Shall I tell you about the first item on my list?" Josie asked brightly. "If I'm going to do it, I'll need your buy-in."

"Sure, shoot." Evan sat back and smiled at her.

"There's a small rodeo coming up near Jamestown in Gold Country."

"Yeah. Next week, right?"

Josie took a deep breath. "I think we should enter the bull riding event."

He stared at her for a long moment. "We, as in both of us?"

"Yes."

"Okay."

She beamed at him. "You're willing to do this with me?"

"I sure can't let you do it on your own. Rio would kill me."

"That's what I thought." She grinned. "And I propose a side bet as well."

"What would that be?" Now he looked intrigued.

"Whoever finishes lower has to take the winner out to dinner."

"That's good, because after that tattoo I'm short on funds, and I could do with a good meal."

Josie raised her eyebrows. "You think you're going to beat me?"

"*Hell*, yeah."

"Dream on." Josie grinned at him. "I've already downloaded the entry forms and filled in all the details."

"You're sure they'll let you compete?"

"I signed up as J Martinez."

"Smart woman."

"And if they try to change their minds, you'll stand up for me, won't you?"

"Absolutely one hundred percent." Evan nodded and then winced as a microphone squealed in the main room. "Time to listen to the speeches. I suppose we'd better get up there with the rest of the family just in case we need to sack my dad."

* * *

By the time it got dark outside, Evan sat on one of the seats on the veranda of the hotel in the warm, night air congratulating himself on having avoided any private conversations with either Faith or Danny. He'd talked to them in groups, laughed at the right times, and given a great performance of "I couldn't be happier for my favorite brother" even though he knew Danny wasn't buying it.

Josie had stuck with him through everything, her hand in his, her calm presence a balm he hadn't even realized he needed. He might only have known her for a short time, but she already seemed to get him in a way no one else ever had. And he felt the same about her. Her casual dismissal of the harm inflicted on her by her parents' behavior had made him want to find the dead Arturio and give him a good talking-to.

Having grown up with an absent mother and a father who sucked all the air out of a room, Evan was aware of the harm that could inflict on a person. At least he'd had the cover of five other siblings. Josie had only had Rio, who was older and not living with them for the majority of her life.

"Evan?"

Crap. He'd been so busy thinking about Josie that he hadn't noticed Danny creeping up on him. His brother sat beside him and contemplated the lights of Main Street as if he didn't have a care in the world. Evan let the silence grow. He wasn't going to be accused of starting something on his brother's special day.

"Would it help if I apologized again?" Danny eventually asked.

"You've got nothing to apologize for."

"I feel like I've let you down."

"You didn't." Evan didn't look at his brother. "I totally get why you didn't tell me."

"You think I didn't tell you I was getting married because I'm still mad at you for talking out of turn over the family dinner table?"

Evan shrugged. He wasn't about to admit he feared it was something much worse. "I know I was out of line. I already told you."

"It wasn't because of that." Danny hesitated as if trying to choose his words carefully, and Evan tensed. "Things just happened fast, and I just . . . went with it. I didn't think about anybody but me and Faith and making it happen."

"That's what Adam said."

"Then he was right." Danny turned to study Evan's averted face. "So, can we let it go, Ev? Start again?"

"Sure." Evan shrugged like it was no big deal.

"Jeez, Evan, that's all you've got?" Danny shook his head. "You're such a bad liar."

"What do you want me to say, Danny?" Even though the last thing he wanted was to antagonize his brother, he'd never known when to shut up. "I get that I talk too much, that I'm immature, and that you don't trust me, okay? I've apologized and I'll try to do better in the future."

"Way to make it all about you." Danny met his stare full-on. "This isn't just about me getting married in Vegas, is it? You've been down on me ever since Faith came back."

Evan stiffened as Danny continued speaking.

"Are you jealous or something? Because I can tell you right now that our relationship has nothing to do with my relationship with Faith."

"You think I'm *jealous?*" Evan stuttered, almost glad to be taken off on this unexpected tangent when he'd been expecting so much worse. "Like, you're going to lay that on me as well?"

Danny frowned. "I can't think of any other reason for the way you're behaving right now. I've discussed it with Faith, and—"

Evan stood up. It was way past time to put an end to the conversation. "You discussed me with Faith? Wow, thanks."

"She cares about you, and she wants to be part of our family, Evan." Danny looked up at him. "I'm not trying to make things worse, but maybe this needed to be brought out in the open."

"What? That I'm too immature to understand that my brother has found the perfect woman for him and too jealous to let him go?" Evan glared at Danny. "I get it, Danny. I'm truly happy for you, but I'm not stupid enough to think it won't change things between us, and maybe that's for the best."

Danny raised an eyebrow.

"See? You don't think I can change, do you?" Evan said. "That maybe, just *maybe* I'm trying to become a better person here, and that it really isn't about you, and I don't need you anymore."

Danny quickly looked away but not before Evan had

glimpsed in his brother's eyes the hurt he'd inflicted. If there ever was a moment for his normally even-tempered brother to really lay into him again, surely it would be now?

Evan braced himself as Danny stood up.

"I guess I should be getting back inside. Faith will be wondering where I am." Danny nodded and stepped around Evan. "Have a good night."

Chapter Five

"How am I going to get away for the weekend without my dad noticing?"

Josie eyed Evan who was standing next to her at the paddock gate as they watched Jaime work with one of the bigger bulls. It was a beautiful, clear day with just a hint of a breeze winding its way through the staggered foothills of the Sierra Nevadas.

"You need to ask his permission?"

"I need to make sure my chores get done."

"Can't you ask Danny? You must have covered for him while he was in Vegas and setting up his living arrangements with Faith."

"I suppose I could. . . ."

Josie turned to look at him. "You're not still fighting."

"Nah, we're over that. We're just not really . . . talking."

At the wedding celebration she'd seen Danny coming back into the hotel, his usual smile absent. She'd followed her instincts and gone outside to find Evan pacing the veranda. He'd made an effort to be his usual dorky self, but she hadn't been deceived, nor had she pressed him to share what was wrong. If he wanted to tell her, she knew he would—eventually.

"That must be difficult for you." Josie kept her reply light and noncommittal.

"Danny thinks I'm jealous of Faith."

"Are you?"

Evan just looked at her.

"I guess not," Josie said. "What else is bothering him?"

"The usual. He thinks I'm an immature jerk." Evan relapsed into silence as he watched the bull again. "I guess I could ask Adam to ask Danny to cover for me."

"Which doesn't make you sound immature at all, Evan." Josie rolled her eyes. "Or maybe, and trust me on this, you could just ask him yourself like a grown-up?"

"What if he says no?"

"*Then* you ask Adam." Josie nudged him with her elbow. "If the worst comes to the worst, I'll ask one of the hands from here to go and work for your dad for the weekend."

Evan frowned. "You said you wouldn't pay for anything for me again."

"I wouldn't have to." She grinned. "Two of the guys bet me I wouldn't be able to ride one of Rio's bulls for eight seconds. They both lost and they both owe me a favor."

"Convenient for you." He nodded. "Then maybe you could just ask one of them, and I wouldn't have to talk to Danny at all."

Josie met his gaze. "Evan, if you really want to change, don't you think you should do the responsible thing, and talk to your brother? You told me you'd forgiven him for going off to Vegas without telling you."

He rubbed a hand across the back of his neck, something she'd noticed he did when he was uncomfortable with the topic of conversation. "It's more complicated than that. We had a bit of a falling-out."

"Another one?"

"At the wedding thing." He grimaced. "He said some stuff about me that I didn't appreciate. I told him that if he didn't believe I could change then he could leave me alone—for good."

Josie wasn't having any of this. "Then show him that you have changed by talking to him about this weekend."

"What if he wants to know why I need time off?"

"Firstly, if you've told him to back off, I doubt he'll do that, and secondly, if he does ask, you can tell him it's none of his business."

"Okay." Evan nodded. "I'll ask him tonight at dinner."

"Great! Because I'll be there to coach you through it."

Evan groaned. "I forgot my mom roped you into having dinner with us."

"You don't want me to come?" Josie asked.

"Of course, I do." He wrapped his arm around her shoulders and dropped a kiss on her head. "It's just that at my house you usually get dinner *and* a show."

"Sounds just like home with my mom," Josie reassured him. "I can't wait."

Evan leapt to his feet and hurried down the hallway, determined to intercept Josie at the front door before anyone else got to her. He'd asked her to text him the moment she arrived. He'd received her text while he was lying stretched out on his bed, trying to ignore the fact that Danny was currently next door with Faith sorting out his stuff. He'd shared a bathroom with Danny for as long as he could remember, and now it had filled up with women's products.

From what he could tell, Danny and Faith had decided to split their time between the two houses until they could build one of their own. The McDonalds were due back from their golfing tour of Europe in a week or so, which gave the newly married couple plenty of space and time to get accustomed to each other.

Evan opened the front door so fast that Josie had only just raised her hand to knock. She pretended to topple forward into his arms and he gladly played along.

"Hey." She smiled up at him. "Nice catch."

"You're welcome. Come on in. Adam's been cooking up a storm and Mom's here."

When Leanne was at the ranch, her ex-husband tended to behave himself a lot better, which was the only reason Evan had been okay with Josie accepting the dinner invitation.

Josie took off her sheepskin-lined denim jacket to reveal a pink, flowery blouse with an open neck. She'd left her hair loose and it flowed down her back like silk.

Evan paused to appreciate the sight. "You like flowers, don't you?"

"Yes, I can't resist them on anything." She eased out of her boots and pointed at the toes. "See?"

"Pretty." Evan commented on the elaborately embroidered poppies. "Just like you."

She went up on tiptoe to pinch his cheek. "Such a sweet talker. Have you spoken to Danny yet?"

"I thought I'd do that over dinner." He clasped her hand in his and pulled her through to the large family kitchen. "Hey, everyone. Josie's here."

Leanne dusted her floury hands on her apron and came right over to give Josie a hug.

"I'm so glad you could make it."

"It was a pleasure. Is there anything I can do to help?" Josie asked.

"You can help Evan set the table, or you can come and chat to me while I finish this pie crust."

"I'll chat." Josie winked at Evan.

Fifteen minutes later, she was squeezed in between Evan and Kaiden and enjoying the roast pork with all the trimmings Adam and Leanne had cooked. Danny and Faith sat right opposite her and Evan. Josie couldn't avoid the glow of their happiness and the way they kept looking into each other's eyes at every opportunity. Evan had insisted he wished his brother nothing but good, so why was he so intent on prolonging an unnecessary conflict? Josie didn't get it at all.

She nudged him in the side. "Don't forget to ask Danny."

Unfortunately, just as she spoke there was a lull in the conversation and her voice carried way too clearly. Danny looked up, his gaze guarded.

"What do you need, Evan?"

"Uh . . ." Evan cleared his throat. "I was, um, hoping you could do my chores over the weekend."

"Sure." Danny nodded, and immediately started eating again, even as Faith's worried gaze remained on Evan.

"Thanks," Evan said awkwardly.

"Why does Danny need to do your chores?" Jeff Miller spoke from the head of the table. "What's more important than helping out your family?"

Evan went to answer, but Josie got in quicker.

"I'm afraid that's my fault, Mr. Miller. I asked Evan if he could accompany me to a local rodeo."

"You asked Evan?" Jeff frowned. "What do you need him for?"

"Maybe he's going to act as her security?" Kaiden suggested. "I mean she is Rio Martinez's sister. She might get mobbed."

"Yes, that's it." Josie grinned at Kaiden. "He's my bodyguard."

"Why are you going to the rodeo?" Jeff obviously wasn't finished questioning them and Josie got a sense of what it might be like to live with such a relentless father.

"I'm competing."

Everyone stopped and stared at her.

"Good for you!" Leanne said brightly. "I hope you win."

Jeff folded his arms over his chest. "I don't hold with the rodeo myself, but if Evan can be of any help, that's good to know."

"I do have my uses, Dad," Evan said. "I'll keep her safe."

Kaiden snorted. "From what I hear from the Morgans, Josie is perfectly capable of doing that for herself."

"True," Josie agreed. "But it never hurts to have backup."

"What time are you leaving?" Leanne asked.

"I'm planning on picking Evan up around six tomorrow morning," Josie said.

"Good. Plenty of time for him to get his morning chores done before he leaves," Jeff said. "Now, what's for dessert?"

As Josie settled in to chat with Faith, Leanne, and Lizzie, Evan allowed Kaiden to persuade him to come out to the barn to see the new calf that needed hand rearing. After exiting the low-lying ranch house, quietness enfolded them like a warm blanket. Evan slowly let out a long breath and tried to relax.

"Josie's really nice," Kaiden said as they entered the barn.

"Yeah, she is."

"You two going out?"

"I suppose you could say that." Evan flicked on the light in the feedstore, scaring a couple of mice, and automatically checked that everything had been put away properly.

"That was quick."

Evan shrugged as they continued past the horses to the pen at the end of the barn where he could see the shadowy forms of the calves.

"But I guess that's just how we Millers do things," Kaiden continued. "We rush in and out of relationships like we're scared or something."

"I wonder why," Evan muttered.

Kaiden grinned. "I guess none of us find it easy to settle down."

"You seem to have managed it."

"Well, Julia and I have a long way to go before we're

entirely on the same page," Kaiden joked. "But that's part of the fun."

Evan shuddered. His brother and his fiancée seemed to relish their nose-to-nose fights and airing of grievances, but the very thought of that made him want to hide. He much preferred the way Adam and Lizzie were quietly working through their issues.

He crouched down beside the railings to observe the newbies. "What happened to their mother?"

"She's recovering from surgery. Hopefully, she'll be back soon, but she might not be willing to feed these two if they haven't bonded."

Evan petted one wet velvety nose. "Do they need feeding now?"

"No, I took care of it before dinner." Kaiden checked the water supply and the hay. He'd always been the one with the soft spot for the orphaned calves. "I've got a lot on next week so I'd be glad if you can help out with these two."

"I'll keep an eye on them." Evan nodded. "If I survive the rodeo."

Kaiden's smile was slow in coming. "You're competing, aren't you?"

"I might be."

"That's why you've been sneaking off to Rio's place all summer." Kaiden whistled. "Good thing you didn't tell Dad the truth."

Evan straightened up. "He didn't directly ask me whether I was competing. I didn't lie to him."

"Sure," Kaiden said. "Good luck." His gaze went past

Evan back to the house. "What's up between you and Danny?"

Evan sighed. "Can't you just keep out of it?"

"He doesn't know what to do to make things right with you."

"We're good. He just doesn't like the fact that I said I didn't need him to worry about me anymore." After one last pat for the calf, Evan turned toward the entrance to the barn.

"That's not how I heard it." Kaiden wasn't one to let go once he got into something.

"Danny's complaining about me to everyone now, is he?"

"You know he wouldn't do that," Kaiden said. "You can tell something's wrong just by looking at his face."

"He looks fine to me." Evan walked away from his brother. "He's married the love of his life, he's building a new home with her, and he gets out from under Dad's thumb. I wish I had half as much wrong as he does."

"You sound jealous."

Evan set his jaw. "I'm not. Maybe he's just pissed that I won't bow down and worship him anymore. Ever think of that?"

"I get that you want to be your own person, Bro." Kaiden scrambled to catch up with him. "And I also get that sometimes the only way to break out of your usual rut is to fight your way out, but people can get hurt."

"Like we all know that." Evan kept moving. "We had front-row seats for Dad burning down his own marriage, remember?"

Kaiden sighed. "Yeah, I guess I just don't like seeing

that look on Danny's face—like he's lost something precious."

Evan stopped and briefly closed his eyes. "Can I move into Ben's old room?"

"*What?*"

He swung around. "You're hardly there and Ben's gone so I'd appreciate the space."

Kaiden studied him, his clear gaze way too knowing for Evan's liking.

"Sure." He nodded. "I guess being next to the newlyweds isn't much fun." Kaiden paused before continuing, his voice surprisingly gentle. "But Evan, you can't dance around this fracture forever. At some point, you owe it to yourself and to Danny to repair the damage."

Evan found a smile somewhere. "Yeah, I get it. I broke it so I get to fix it. Maybe I'm just not ready to do that yet."

Kaiden nodded. "I had to smash a few eggs to make my position in this family clear so I'm not going to tell you what to do."

"Thanks." Evan waited for Kaiden to draw level with him. "I appreciate that."

"So, are you and Evan dating?" Leanne asked as she refilled Josie's coffee cup. Danny had disappeared with Jeff and Faith, and Lizzie had gone to empty the dishwasher, leaving them alone to chat. "I know I'm not supposed to be nosy, but getting information from my sons is harder than breaking into a bank."

"Yes, I think we are." Josie accepted the cup back and

wrapped her fingers around it. "But it's definitely early days."

"Are you here for the rest of the year, then?"

"It depends. I mean, I do have a job at Howatch International, but I'm taking some time out—accumulated leave and that kind of thing."

"Yes, your mother told me you were having a well-earned rest." Leanne touched Josie's hand. "Working at Howatch International can be brutal."

Josie looked up. "You know my mom that well?"

"I met her when she was married to Graham and they visited New York together. Declan was already a business associate of Graham's. We hit it off immediately, and when Rio ended up in Morgan Valley, she contacted me to find out what kind of people he would be mixing with." Leanne laughed. "Don't tell Rio."

"That *Mamãe* was checking up on him? It sounds just like her."

"She is a very determined woman." Leanne paused. "But don't worry. I won't tell her about you and Evan unless she mentions it first."

"Thanks, because I haven't said a word to her." Josie grimaced. "She tends to go a little overboard and immediately starts planning the wedding, which tends to scare my suitors away."

Leanne chuckled. "Why doesn't that surprise me?"

"Not that she means any harm, but—"

"It's okay. My lips are sealed." Leanne hesitated for a second before adding, "Apparently, Evan's great fun to date, and he always stays friends with his exes."

"It's okay. We're just having fun together. I don't expect

things to get all serious," Josie hastened to reassure her. "In fact, I'm not sure if Evan is capable of being serious."

She looked up just in time to see that Kaiden and Evan had come back into the kitchen and that Evan had definitely heard what she'd just said.

"I can be serious." Evan came over to sit next to her. "Like I already think you're amazing."

"That's just your Miller charm," Josie countered.

He brought her hand to his mouth and kissed her fingers. "Nah, I mean it."

She couldn't look away from his gaze and heat crept up her cheeks.

"Now you've made me blush." She eased her fingers free.

"Which makes you even prettier." Evan wrapped an arm around her shoulders. "What time do you want me to take you home? It's already getting dark."

Josie peered out of the window and couldn't repress a shiver. There was something about the encroaching darkness that set her on edge.

"You could stay the night," Leanne suggested. "Both Daisy's and Ben's rooms are free."

"That's really kind of you, but I don't have all my gear for the rodeo." Josie reluctantly got to her feet. "I need to go back and prep for tomorrow. Thank you so much for a lovely evening."

"It was a pleasure, my dear." Leanne stood, too, and hugged Josie. "You remind me very much of your father."

"You knew him, too?" Josie asked.

"I came to the wedding." Leanne smiled. "Arturio was a quiet, charming, thoughtful man who married your mother for all the right reasons."

"Apart from the fact that he'd been in love with his assistant for decades?"

"That's also true, but remember your mother asked him to help her with a very specific thing—to free her son from Graham. Once he'd done that and she realized where his heart belonged, she gave him up again."

Leanne kissed Josie's cheek. "You're good for Evan. He seems really happy to be with you."

"Long may it last," Josie said brightly.

She walked around to say all her good-byes and then went to the mudroom to reclaim her boots and jacket. Evan was leaning up against the back door waiting for her.

"What's up?"

She considered him as she put on her jacket. "My *mamãe*."

"What about her?" Evan opened the door, took Josie's hand, and walked her out into the ink-black, star-spangled night.

"This is going to sound terrible, but it just occurred to me that she married both of her husbands within days of knowing them."

"Yeah, I suppose she did." Evan looked down at her. "She struck me as the kind of person who made quick decisions."

"Impulsive ones," Josie corrected him. "It's okay to tell me the truth."

"Okay, then yeah. She's all about the drama."

Josie unlocked her truck, but she didn't get in. "She only married Arturio because he was rich, and she needed his money to fight to get back custody of Rio."

"Hey." Evan gently took her by the shoulders and

turned her around to face him. "That's not all she got out of it. She got you."

Josie tried to smile. "I was a . . . mistake, an aberration, something that neither of them wanted or anticipated."

His expression gentled and he cupped her chin in one strong hand. "Josie, once they saw you, I bet they both fell in love with you."

"Sure, so in love that they were divorced within a year." She tried to smile but it was too hard. "I'm sorry, I didn't mean to get all sad on you. I didn't even know how I was feeling until your mom reminded me of what happened."

She only realized she was crying when Evan used his thumb to wipe away a tear from her cheek.

"Josie," he murmured as he wrapped her in his arms. "Honey . . ."

She let him gather her close and rested her face against his chest as she struggled to regain her composure. She hadn't cried since that awful night when her world had turned upside down, and to cry about something so stupid now was ridiculous.

She looked up at him. "I'm sorry for being such a mess."

"Nothing to be sorry about. We're friends, right? We can say anything to each other."

"I know my mom loves me very much."

"That's because you're totally one hundred percent lovable." He kissed her nose. "I guess we all struggle to understand why our parents did what they did sometimes. At least I get to hear both sides of the story these days, which helps a lot."

"Everyone tells the story of my mom giving Arturio

up to his assistant like it's so funny, and romantic, and everything—which it is—but no one ever thinks about what it felt like for me."

"It sucked." Evan kissed her again. "They all sucked."

"Thank you," she whispered against his mouth. He was the first person she'd ever met who had acknowledged her pain and allowed her to admit it even to herself.

With a groan, he kissed her more deeply and she responded in kind until he had her pressed up against the door of her truck, her body aligned with his from knee to shoulder. She held on to him like he was her anchor in a storm and let some of the hurt she hadn't even realized she'd been carrying flow out of her.

Eventually, when the cramp in her neck could no longer be denied, she eased away. He immediately stepped back, keeping just one hand on her hip to steady her.

"I should go." She smiled at him. "I'll be back to get you around six."

"No problem." He winked at her. "You sure you're okay driving in the dark?"

Despite what everyone thought, Evan noticed a lot of things other people missed.

"It's not my favorite thing to do, but I'll make it."

He nodded and opened the door for her. "Text me when you get in, okay?"

"Will do." She climbed up into the driver's seat, which brought her level with Evan's face. "Thank you."

"As I said, dinner and a show." With one last nod, he stepped out of the way and she started the truck. "Drive carefully."

* * *

Evan waited until Josie's truck disappeared down the driveway and then turned back to the house. The fact that she'd trusted him with such personal stuff was mind-blowing, but not as amazing as the fact that he hadn't run away or handed the problem to someone else. He'd wanted to be there for her—to help her feel better—to comfort her and tell her everything would be okay.

He took off his boots and jacket in the mudroom and made his way back into the kitchen where his mom was still sitting by the fire, checking something on her phone. He joined her on the couch and after a moment she looked up at him.

"Josie's lovely."

"Yeah, so everyone keeps telling me."

"Are you serious about her?" Leanne asked.

"Too early to say." Evan played it cool, unwilling to share feelings he wasn't even sure he understood yet himself. "Did her mom really only marry her dad to save Rio?"

"That's how the story goes."

Evan frowned. "Doesn't that seem a bit mercenary to you?"

"I suppose you could look at it that way, but I remember how frantic Isabelle was to see Rio again after Graham refused to share custody. I think she would've done anything to make that happen."

"Including marrying a rich, old guy who was in love with someone else?"

"She really didn't know that at the time, Evan, and she

didn't lie to Arturio. He knew exactly what she wanted from him. From what I remember, he'd had a terrible falling-out with Graham and was more than willing to get his revenge on Isabelle's ex."

"How nice for them both."

Leanne studied Evan's face. "What's wrong?"

"It just wasn't fair for Josie," Evan said. "She didn't ask to be born and she certainly didn't deserve to have no father in her life."

"Arturio was thrilled when Josie was born. He'd been married twice before and thought he was unable to have children. She was his little miracle."

"Such a miracle that rather than stay with her mom, he happily went off and married another woman." Evan folded his arms across his chest. "If you ask my opinion, they all made a bad situation worse, and poor Josie had to grow up without a father."

Leanne sat back. "You seem to be taking this very personally."

"Because it hurt Josie, and no one seems to care about that." He scowled at his mom as she smiled at him. "What?"

She got to her feet, came over, and dropped a kiss on the top of his head. "It's so nice to see you caring about someone, Evan."

"I care about a lot of things."

"I noticed." She ruffled his hair. "Maybe it's time you showed that side of yourself to everyone else around here."

Evan was still mulling over the evening's events when Faith came to sit beside him on the couch. She always wore her dark hair short because, as a veterinarian, the risk of it getting eaten, caught on something, or covered in shit was high.

"Hey."

Evan sighed.

"You know you're Danny's favorite brother, right?" She waited, but when he didn't respond she went on speaking. "I know this is between the two of you, but if there is anything I can do or say that will make things better—apart from divorcing him—can you tell me what it is?"

"It's all good, Faith."

"But—"

"Faith?" Danny spoke from the doorway. "He's right. It's all good."

Evan rose along with Faith, who went to stand alongside Danny who put his arm around her.

"I don't like seeing you fight," Faith said.

"We're not." Danny held Evan's gaze. "We're fine."

Evan waited until they left and then collapsed back on the couch. Surely if Danny knew, he would've said something by now? Maybe Evan was safe after all. . . .

His cell buzzed and he took it out of his pocket to find a text from Josie.

Made it home safely. See you in the morning! x

He sent her a thumbs-up, gathered up the stray coffee cups, and took them through to the silent kitchen. When Danny was out with Faith next week, he'd move his stuff into Ben's old room. He doubted his brother would even notice. It felt weird standing up for himself, but he had the sense that if he didn't do it now, he never would. Having Josie around to talk to and listen to made a huge difference. He'd always relied on his brothers to be his best friends, which sometimes meant things got too cozy, or too complicated.

Having Josie's clear-eyed perspective helped him make sense of things, and if he could be there for her as well, that would be a first. It was good to be able to do that. He'd never felt the need to protect anyone before, but she seemed to appreciate his support.

After making sure that everything in the kitchen was either turned off or supposed to be running, Evan made his way to bed. He'd need to get up at four if he was going to get his chores done before he left. He groaned at the prospect. Mornings had never been his thing, but he wasn't going to leave Danny with more than he could handle.

Was this it? Was this what being mature felt like? Evan studied his reflection in the bathroom mirror. He looked the same, but inside he felt like things were changing. He considered the spectacular kiss he'd shared earlier with Josie. Was it really possible to feel this much about someone so fast? He still hadn't come to terms with both his instant physical attraction to her and the fact that he genuinely *liked* her.

She'd been through her own shit with her parents. He didn't have to explain what had happened between his mom and dad because she already knew about the fiery divorce and the recent reconciliation. It just made everything easier somehow. She'd even had dinner with his family and not run a mile. His dad was something of an acquired taste.

Evan brushed his teeth and took a glass of water back through to his bedroom. He firmly closed the door, put his earbuds in, and refused to think about what his brother and his new wife might be doing next door. He set his alarm, turned out the light, and allowed himself to drift off to sleep thinking about how Josie Martinez felt in his arms and how quickly he could persuade her to kiss him again.

Chapter Six

"It's more of a county fair than a real rodeo," Evan explained to Josie as they shouldered their way through the crowds at the county fairgrounds. The smell of deep-fried food, caramel apples, and popcorn permeated everything and made Evan's stomach rumble. "I'm not even sure if it's PRCA sanctioned, but I don't think we care about that, do we?"

"Not really."

Josie had braided her hair down her back and looked all business in her denim shirt, blue jeans, and white, straw Stetson. She also didn't seem to be suffering from any nerves, whereas Evan was consumed with them. He glanced around the crowd but didn't recognize anyone. They were miles away from Morgan Valley and deep in California Gold Country, which suited him just fine.

They'd left their stuff at the small motel on the edge of the town and parked up near the rodeo set up at the fairground. The registration booth wasn't yet open, so they'd taken the opportunity to stroll around the attractions. There was some kind of small funfair that looked shabby in the daylight, a petting zoo, and some 4-H-sponsored contests in a big, open-sided white tent.

Evan smiled down at Josie. "This reminds me of being a kid. Even Dad let us join the 4-H club in town and attend the county fair. I won a prize for raising Joker from a foal. Did you do this stuff in Brazil?"

"Some of it." Josie was busy looking around. "I remember riding a variety of animals in junior rodeo contests, including a sheep." She hefted her bag higher on her shoulder. "If you don't want to get something to eat first, I guess we should go back and sign in. I registered us both online."

"Cool." The thought of eating made Evan want to puke. "I'm not hungry."

They turned back toward the far end of the grounds where the rodeo stand was situated. It wasn't large, but it did have proper bucking chutes and tiered seating.

"They're running a mix of roughstock events, timed events, and novelty classes," Josie said. "I did think about entering you for the greased pig contest."

"Wouldn't be the first time I've chased down a pig." Evan grinned. "Dad stopped keeping them a while back because they never liked him."

"Pigs are said to be good judges of character," Josie joked as they reached the end of the line for the rodeo registration. "I think they take same-day registrations, so this might be a while."

By the time they reached the front of the line, there were several groups of cowboys gathered around the table chatting away as they attached their competition numbers to their safety vests and caught up with old friends.

"Name?" an elderly cowboy with a badge with the name Chester on it asked.

"Martinez and Miller," Evan said, pointing at Josie and then at himself.

"Did you preregister online?"

"Yes," Josie said with a smile.

Chester looked at her properly for the first time. "You're female."

"Correct."

"And you've registered to compete in the bull riding."

"Also correct."

Chester frowned. "I don't know if that's allowed, young lady."

"Why not?" Evan asked. "The rules didn't specify you had to be male."

Chester stood up. "Excuse me a moment."

He strode over to consult with three other older men who all stared back at Josie.

"Does this happen a lot?" Evan asked her.

"I don't know, because I've never tried to enter a contest here, but I bet it happens all the time," Josie murmured.

Chester came back accompanied by one of the men who had a kind face. His name badge read Brad.

"Are you sure you want to compete, Miss Martinez? This is a very dangerous sport."

"I am well aware of that." Josie kept smiling. "All I'm asking for is an equal chance."

"I'm fine with her competing against me," Evan said loudly, aware that everyone around them was avidly listening in. "Anyone else have a problem with it?"

"I don't mind at all." One of the younger cowboys grinned at Josie. "I'm happy to beat anyone and take their money."

"How cute." Josie's smile dripped honey.

"Then know this is on your own head," Chester muttered as he sat down with a thump at the table. "And don't come crying to me if you break something."

"I won't." Josie took the proffered number and walked off, her nose in the air, leaving Evan to complete his own transaction.

He followed her through into the competitors' area beneath the stands and found her already unpacking her gear. To her right were two guys speaking Portuguese and to her left the cowboy who'd joked with her. Josie was ignoring them all as she took out her rope and started working on it.

Evan set his backpack down and copied her actions, aware that everyone else was talking about Josie and unsure what to do about it.

"You okay about all this?" he asked her.

"What? All the stupid talk?" She shrugged. "It reminds me of home. I just love it when I get to wipe the smiles from their faces." She gestured at the two guys dressed in black on her right. "These two have no idea I speak their language and are getting quite descriptive about both how I look and how spectacularly I'm going to fail in the ring."

"Do you want me to say anything to anyone?" Evan offered.

"Nope." She held his gaze. "It's much more fun to beat them in the competition."

"I appreciate your confidence." Evan kissed her nose.

"Hey, buddy!" Big, blond, and definitely stupid called out to Evan, "That your girlfriend? She sure goes the extra mile in being supportive of your interests."

His friends all laughed. Evan tried to ignore them as he took out the safety vest he'd borrowed from the Martinez Ranch and stuck his number on it.

"Like, I mean, how bad *are* you at this that you need her around to make you look good? Does she kiss everything better afterward?"

Evan went to turn toward the men, but Josie took hold of his wrist.

"They really aren't worth getting into a fight with." She looked over at the laughing men and raised her voice. "We'll do our talking in the arena, not out of it."

"Sure, sweetheart." Blondie blew her a kiss. "Can't wait."

Evan's number came up sixth in the running order while Josie was twelfth and last. She walked him over to the bucking chute and stood on the side rail, talking him through wrapping his rope, his seating position, and the knowledge she'd gained from watching the bull's earlier outing. The bucking bulls were medium size and definitely not the brutal powerhouses on the top PBR circuits, for which she was extremely grateful.

"If he's predictable, and I bet all of these guys are, then he'll pivot to the left the moment he comes out of the chute. Be aware of that and anticipate him trying to pull you off center, okay?"

"Got it," Evan said, his attention fixed on the area and the uneasy movement of the bull underneath him.

"Nod when you're ready to go," Chester, who was also in charge of the chutes, said to Evan.

"Okay."

Josie eased back as Evan nodded, and the bull exploded out of the chute and immediately veered left. Evan held on, his free arm high, his technique somewhat questionable, but good enough for him to hang in there until the eight-second buzzer went off and he was able to dismount.

Josie whistled loudly and pumped her fist in the air.

"Awesome!"

Evan picked up his rope and turned to grin at her. The ecstatic look on his face hit her right in the heart, and as soon as he cleared the ring she ran over to hug him hard. He picked her up, swung her around, and kissed her on the mouth.

"That was fricking terrifying."

"But fun, yes?"

"Kind of."

He set her back on her feet again and they walked through to the half-empty stands to watch the rest of the rounds before she had her turn. The scent of sawdust, bullshit, and sweat hung in the air like a cloud, but Josie was happy to breathe it all in. She'd missed going to the rodeo with Rio more than she'd realized.

Big Blondie was next up, and he barely managed to hang on, which gave Josie a great deal of satisfaction. She cheered when he got a lower overall score than Evan. The two Brazilians were competent. One went ahead of Evan in the rankings and the other was just below him. Everyone else either fell off or barely clung on, which meant if she included herself, there were really only five contenders. There was at least one more go-round before the scores were retabulated.

By the time she was back in the chute, with Evan taking up her former position on the side rail, she was almost enjoying herself. She'd drawn a new bull, which seemed weird, but she wasn't going to worry about it. She settled in, tightened her rope, and nodded to Chester who opened the chute.

Her body instinctively moved with the bull, and apart from one abrupt corkscrew turn and a half buck, she never felt out of control. The buzzer still seemed to take an age to come, but she had time to unwrap her rope and jump clear without even a stumble. She swaggered out of the ring past the big blond who didn't look happy.

"You looked amazing!" Evan crowed. "Best score of the night so far!"

"Thanks!" She took off her gloves and laid her rope over the railing. "Shall we go and see what we've drawn in the second round?"

"Three of the guys have pulled out and two of the others aren't looking too good, either." Evan filled her in as they walked back to the registration desk they'd moved inside. "It's really down to us, Blondie, and the Brazilians."

"Sounds like a good name for a band." Josie noticed there were raised voices at the table and the blond was pointing at her. "Uh-oh, someone's a sore loser."

"She got an easier bull," Blondie repeated as Josie and Evan drew close. "You let her win."

"I haven't won yet," Josie said pleasantly. "There's still another round to go." She addressed Chester who looked flustered. "What's the problem?"

"There isn't one." Brad, the older guy who seemed to

be in charge, leaned in and answered her. "We'll do the draw." He turned to the Brazilians. "You okay with that?"

"Yes," one of them answered. "We have no problem with anything." He turned and nodded to Josie. "You are an excellent bull rider."

"Thanks." Josie kept it brief as she waited to see where she ended up in the draw. As Evan had predicted, five of the riders had dropped out, leaving just seven of them. After a whispered conference, Brad came back with a list.

"Seeing as the weather's closing in, and this isn't an official event, we'll make this the final round rather than having a short go. Winner's score will be averaged over the two rounds, okay?"

Everyone nodded. It wasn't a formal PBR or PRCA event so no one would lose points or standing. Even Josie had noticed that the wind had picked up considerably and that there were some dark clouds gathering. She'd never been a big fan of riding a bull in the rain. She just hoped all the fair-goers would have time to take shelter before the rain came down.

The first Brazilian was competent, but his bull wasn't really into it. Because the bull was judged as well as the rider, his overall score suffered as a result. He cleared the buzzer and shrugged his shoulders as he walked out of the arena as if aware that his chances of winning had all but vanished. Two other hopefuls got tossed and then it was Blondie's turn. Josie was amused to see he'd drawn the same bull she'd ridden earlier.

She was even more amused when two seconds into the ride, the bull did the same half buck and corkscrew maneuver he'd pulled on her and Blondie fell off, facefirst into the sawdust. He got up straightaway and appeared unhurt. Josie didn't have time to watch him exit as she was next up to compete.

Evan helped her get settled and she focused in just as Rio had taught her, visualizing the ride, remembering the way the bull had performed earlier and anticipating how she would deal with each trick.

"Ready?" Chester asked.

"Go." She lowered her chin and tightened her grip as the bull rocketed forward into the arena wrenching her rope-wrapped hand off to the right. She readjusted her balance and felt time slow as she seemed to have all the time in the world to react to the bull's antics. The buzzer sounded and she released her rope and jumped clear, aware of Evan's loud cheering and that even Chester and Blondie were applauding. She smiled and waved, folded her rope over her arm, and walked out knowing she'd done her best and that win or lose, she wouldn't change a thing.

The exhilaration of it hit her as Evan pounded her on the back. There was nothing to compare to this feeling in her corporate life—this sense of life or death of being on the edge. Nothing.

"I think you've got this," Evan said.

"We'll see." She hugged him back. "There are still two riders to go, including you."

He snorted. "Like I'm going to beat you."

She took his hand and walked back to the bucking chute where the second of the Brazilian guys was already loaded up and ready to go. Josie paused as she and Evan climbed up the stand to the left side of the chute.

"Hey! Your rope's twisted on the left!"

The Brazilian ignored her as he chatted to his friend.

"Hey!" Josie shouted in Portuguese. "*Sua corda esta torcida no lado esquerdo.*"

His startled gaze met hers and then he bent down and corrected the error.

"*Obrigado*," he shouted back, and then nodded to Chester. "Go."

Josie watched intently as he entered the arena. He was a good technician but maybe not as showy as he might be; his free hand was definitely low, which might cost him style marks. He did complete the required eight seconds and landed with a slight grimace on one knee.

Josie's gaze went to the scoreboard, which took its own sweet time to display his score. She did some quick mental math as Evan got on board his bull and figured she was slightly ahead of both the Brazilians, and that if Evan absolutely nailed it, he could still beat them all.

"Good luck." She patted his shoulder as he rammed his hat down on his head. "You've got this."

Okay, so *technically* he'd stayed on the bull until the buzzer sounded, but the last couple of seconds had been dicey to say the least. He'd lost his grip, rocked around like a kid learning to post on their pony, and wrenched his shoulder. But he'd made it.

The sight of Josie applauding him like he'd won the Olympics made it all worth it. Despite the pain in his shoulder, he gathered her up and hugged her tight.

"I guess you beat me."

Even as she kissed him, the rain came crashing down, clearing the arena and the seating area as everyone made a mad dash for cover. Under the stands, the beat of the rain thrummed through the metal structure like the pounding of his heart during the eight-second thrill ride.

Brad gathered them all together and announced the results.

"In first place, Miss Martinez, second, Diego Ramos, third, Miguel Andres, and fourth, Evan Miller."

"Yay!" Evan raised Josie's hand high in the air. "Go, Josie!"

Even Blondie came over to shake her hand. "You're darn good."

"Thanks." Josie obviously wasn't the kind of person to hold grudges, which he appreciated. "It was fun."

"Maybe for you." Blondie grinned. "I need to work on a way to tell all my buddies I got my ass kicked by a female."

As he turned away, Josie leaned into Evan and whispered, "I'm fairly sure that's not the first time that's happened to him."

Evan choked back a laugh and tried to look serious as Chester and Brad shook Josie's hand and presented her with a check. He took the opportunity to get his phone out and take a picture of the historic moment. He also got a photo of Josie with the two Brazilians who were now chatting away with her in their own language.

Chester nudged his side. "Is she Brazilian, then? I hear they've got some good women bull riders down there."

"I think she just has a natural affinity for the sport," Evan said casually. "It kind of runs in the family."

"Makes sense." Chester nodded. "She could compete

professionally, and I never thought I'd ever say that about a female bull rider."

"That's progress, right?" Evan smiled at the older man. "Never assume a woman can't do anything a man can do."

Chester went to speak, and Evan held up a finger. "Don't spoil this moment of personal growth and revelation, okay? Just let it sink in."

He went to put his gear away and also packed up Josie's. When he went back, she was being photographed for the local paper and was swapping phone numbers with the Brazilians. He watched her from the sidelines, enjoying the happiness on her face and the way she dealt with people. She was as gracious in victory as he knew she'd be in defeat.

Eventually, she turned to him and grinned.

"Do you want to stay at the fair or shall we make a run for the motel so we can have an early dinner and get a good night's sleep?"

Evan contemplated the driving rain. "I say we leave, but I'm good with whatever you want to do."

She took his hand, her brown eyes shining up at him. "I'm good to go."

He nodded and, after saying a few more good-byes, they exited the arena and ran toward the parking lot. By the time they reached the truck, they were both drenched to the skin. Evan turned up the heat and headed back toward the motel that was only a ten-minute drive away.

Even so, Josie was already shivering before they got there. Evan parked up directly in front of their door, ran to open it, and waited until Josie joined him. Even though the motel looked slightly shady from the outside, it had been upgraded and the interior gave off a nice clean, modern, vibe. There were two beds, a decent bathroom, and great Internet connections.

"We can get the gear later. It's safe in the back seat." Evan heel-and-toed his boots off and gently maneuvered Josie toward the bathroom. "How about you go first? Give me a shout when you're done."

Josie was way quicker than he'd anticipated and came out wrapped in a towel, her long hair now loose around her shoulders. She pointed at the phone. "Shall I order some food? Does this place even do food?"

"How about we get pizza from that place down the road instead?" Evan suggested. "I bet they'll deliver. I don't care what kind it is." He dug into the pocket of his wet jeans and handed over his credit card. "Remember, it's on me because I lost. And if they have beer, get some of that as well."

Chapter Seven

Steam billowed out of the bathroom as Evan emerged dressed in his PJ bottoms, thick socks, and a long-sleeved gray Henley. Josie had already put on her pajamas and was lying full length on one of the beds. She'd tried to dry her hair, but the motel hair dryer was inadequate at best, supplying either as little heat as a warm breath or the fiery scorching of hell. She'd taken as much as she could bear and given up.

"I ordered the pizza."

"Great, I'm starving." Evan toweled his hair dry. "At least it's warm in here."

"I jacked the heat up." Josie pointed at the thermostat.

"I didn't know you could do that." Evan wandered over to look at the panel on the wall. "I haven't stayed in many hotels."

"Lucky you. I travel all the time with my job." Josie handed him a cup of coffee she'd made in the room machine. "Did you have fun today?"

"Yeah," he said, then smiled as he sat on the end of her

bed. She pointed her toes and settled them against his hard thigh. "Chester thinks you should be a professional."

She chuckled. "I think one Martinez on the bull riding circuit is enough for now."

"I thought Rio retired after he won that second title?"

"He did, but he's still involved. I wouldn't want anyone thinking I'd only been allowed in the club because of who my brother was."

"Could you use your dad's name instead of your mother's?" Evan asked.

"Not really. It's never felt like it belonged to me." She sat up against the headboard. "And the chances of being successful and getting out without any serious injuries is hard to do."

"Your brother managed it."

"Only because he had a choice about when to leave." She sighed. "He might have his differences with his father, but he's always had the knowledge that he's got options, career-wise. Most bull riders don't, and they go on until they've ruined their bodies and just can't compete anymore. Rio was able to walk away on top. Literally."

"It's a dangerous sport," Evan agreed, and reached out to wrap his fingers around her ankle. "I'd rather not see you get hurt."

"Which is weird because the worst injury I've ever had—" Josie stopped and recalibrated. "Well, it wasn't when I was riding a bull."

She looked up to find Evan regarding her closely and decided to trust him with at least some of the truth. She touched the scar on her left cheek. "A mirror smashed in my face. It took a while to get all the tiny shards of glass out."

"Shit." Evan breathed. "That must have hurt."

"Yes." She sighed and got off the bed. "I'll just check my phone. The pizza should be here soon. The store is only up the street."

To her relief, there was a knock at the door. Evan went to check who it was while Josie made sure she'd added a tip for the delivery. Six boxes of various sizes were handed over along with a liter of soda. It had stopped raining. In the distance, Josie could just about hear the crowds at the county fairgrounds getting things going again at the funfair.

"Are you sure you got enough?" Evan set the boxes down on the small table between them. "I mean there are two of us."

"I thought if we had any leftovers, we could eat them before we leave tomorrow, or take them with us."

"Good thinking. I'm totally cool with cold pizza." Evan whistled as he opened the boxes. "You got wings and Parmesan bread. I love them!"

Josie sat opposite him and found the pepperoni pizza. "We hardly ate anything today. I'm starving."

"Me, too." Evan took a slice of pizza, pinched the two sides together until it was half the size, and put the whole lot in his mouth.

"Wow." Josie stared at him. "I don't think I've seen that technique before."

"It stops you getting sauce on your clothes," Evan said when he finished chewing.

"I suppose it does." Josie tried it, and while she didn't succeed in cramming the whole slice into her mouth, she did appreciate the benefits. "It's basically a calzone."

As they ate, they regaled each other with tales of their

rides, critiqued the other contestants' techniques, and generally laughed themselves silly. Josie couldn't remember ever feeling so in tune with another person who wasn't direct family. There was just something about Evan's easygoing manner that appealed to her. It didn't hurt that he was also hot to look at.

"How's your tattoo?" Josie asked.

Evan raised an eyebrow. "Wanna see it?"

"Yes, please."

He grabbed hold of the hem of his Henley, yanked it over his head, and turned to one side. "I think it looks great."

"Hmm . . ." Josie breathed.

"You're not looking at it."

"I'm just taking all of it in," she said as she admired his flat stomach, lightly haired chest, and tight biceps. "The tattoo is merely the icing on the cake."

"Yeah?" He stood up, came around to the other side of the table, and held out his hand. "May I kiss the winner?"

Josie hastily wiped her mouth on her napkin and jumped to her feet. "Sure!"

He drew her into his arms, and she raised her head to meet his steadfast gaze.

"Thanks for making me do this."

"Right back at you."

She kissed him lightly on the lips. "I really mean it. I think I'd forgotten how to have fun."

"Fun? That's what you call that terrifying experience?"

"It was for me. And having you right alongside me made it even better."

"Truth." He brushed his mouth over hers. "You look damn good on the back of a bull."

She slid her fingers into his damp hair and locked her mouth against his, her other hand on his bare shoulder. He groaned her name and kissed her back with a direct fierceness that surprised and intrigued her. She forgot everything except the taste and scent of him as she explored his body and leaned right into all that hard, warm flesh.

A few minutes later, he was walking her back toward the bed. As soon as the backs of her legs hit the mattress, she sat down. He knelt in front of her and continued to kiss her as his hand traced the waistline of her pajamas.

"May I?"

Josie nodded and breathed out with pure pleasure as his strong hands cupped her bare ass, bringing her PJ's down past her hips. He pulled them off and dropped a light kiss on her belly.

"No panties. Nice."

He nudged her knee to one side with his shoulder and bent his head. "Good that I always leave room for dessert."

Josie surrendered to the subtle lick of his tongue against her most sensitive flesh, the rasp of his stubble on her inner thigh, and when things really got out of hand, the controlled scrape of his teeth against her already-throbbing bud. She came hard against his mouth, her fingers tightening in his hair until her nails dug into his scalp.

"God . . ." She finally managed to breathe normally

as he raised his head and grinned at her. "That was . . . fantastic."

"You're welcome." He kissed her knee and eased away from her.

"Where are you going?" Josie asked.

"I just—"

"Thought we were done?" She pointed at his groin. "Something sure needs attention."

He glanced down at himself. "Nah, I'm good."

Josie sat up. "Evan . . ."

"I just didn't want to assume."

She patted the bed with the palm of her hand. "Come here right now, or else."

He grinned at her. "Or else what?"

"Do you want me to fetch my ropes from the truck?"

He considered her for a long moment. "I've never thought being roped and tied like a steer would be fun, but I'm reconsidering."

He sat beside her, and she pushed on his chest until he lay on his back and she could attack the cord holding up his pants.

"Nice," she breathed as she uncovered his hard length.

"Mmm." Evan's attempt at speaking ended as she licked him like an ice cream, her palm gently cupping his balls as she explored him.

She took her time sucking him into her mouth, aware that she hadn't touched a man so intimately in ages and that the fact that she could was something to savor in itself.

"Josie," Evan said hoarsely. "If you keep that up, I'm going to—"

Even as he spoke, his hips bucked upward and he

came, his hand cupping her head as he swore a blue streak.

Josie gave him one last kiss and sat up to study his dazed expression.

"Good?"

He nodded and reached for her, drawing her down to lie against his side. Even in their shared silence, Josie had never felt so safe before in her life. She spread her fingers over his chest and felt his heartbeat gradually return to normal. Her eyes closed and she couldn't seem to open them again. . . .

The next thing Josie remembered was light shining in through the open drapes and the faint hint of coffee. She woke up to find Evan coming back in the door with a pink box and two cups balanced on the top of it.

"Morning, Sleeping Beauty." He set everything down on the table. "I went and got us some fresh coffee and donuts for breakfast."

Josie yawned. "What time is it?"

"About nine." He shrugged as he took off his Stetson and jacket. "We've got plenty of time before we need to head out."

She got out of bed, ran to the bathroom, took a very quick shower and got dressed before returning to the main room where Evan had already started on the donuts. She couldn't remember the last time she'd slept through the night without taking a pill.

"Hey, leave some for me."

He grinned at her. "I got a dozen. I think we're good."

"I've seen how much you eat," Josie reminded him as

she took the seat opposite, relieved that there was no weird vibe in the air after their night together.

"Yeah, I suppose you have." Evan winked at her.

Jeez . . . now she was blushing like a schoolgirl. She took a donut at random and crammed it into her mouth and experienced a moment of pure, sweet bliss. She licked her lips and took another huge bite.

"This one is basically a malasada. My favorite kind."

"Cream filled?" Evan nodded. "I asked them for a selection. I knew there would be something you'd like." He pushed the cup of coffee over toward her. "Don't forget this."

Keen to think of something to talk about that didn't involve going over what had happened the previous night—although to his credit, Evan didn't seem to think that needed discussing either—Josie drank some coffee.

"So that was the first thing off my list. What's next up on yours?"

Evan set his cup on the table and leaned back, his hands behind his head. "Well, there is something I've been wanting to try for quite a while."

"What's that?"

He looked down at the table. "Sex."

Josie blinked at him. "You mean like sex with me?"

He finally met her gaze. "No, like sex."

"You haven't?" Josie made a vague gesture at his groin. "I mean you seemed very proficient in other departments, and—"

"I've just never met anyone I've wanted to have full-on sex with before." Luckily, Evan kept talking before she made an ass of herself. "I've spent years living with the consequences of people making bad life decisions usually centered around 'love.' It hasn't inspired me to want to get into it before now."

"Are you sure that this was really on your list and you didn't just make it up after last night?" Josie asked suspiciously.

Evan handed her his phone. "Here's my list. It's right there."

She handed the cell phone back. "Why me?"

He shrugged. "I just know you're the right person to be my first."

"That's one heck of a responsibility you're putting on me," Josie said. "Like what if I get it wrong, or have weird tastes, or—"

Evan chuckled. "You don't have to take me up on this. You can say no. I'd be okay with that."

"But I guess what I'm trying to say is—if you've waited this long, don't you want to wait until you find someone you love?"

"I'm not sure I believe in love. I just know that this feels like the right thing to do with you." He held her gaze. "I trust you, I like you, and I have this weird sense that whatever happens between us we'd still be friends."

Josie stared back at him for a long moment as a thousand questions and objections flew through her usually orderly mind. But what if he was right? What if they had the unique ability to give each other something special? Wouldn't that be wrong to ignore such an opportunity?

Evan grinned. "That's the first time I've managed to stop you talking." He paused. "Scratch that. The second. You went pretty quiet last night apart from screaming my name."

She threw a piece of donut at him, which he easily dodged.

The logistics of them ever getting together were daunting to say the least. . . . Josie only realized she was seriously considering the idea when she attempted to work out where they could meet when they both lived in other people's houses.

She reminded herself that after the incident in San Francisco she'd promised herself that she'd live her life to its fullest and that helping Evan with this particular matter on his list wouldn't exactly be a hardship.

"I don't want to hurt you," Josie blurted out.

"Does it hurt?" Evan opened his eyes wide. "Like, really?"

She contemplated throwing her last bit of donut at him and ate it instead. "You know what I mean. If you're already convinced that relationships don't work, us having sex might only complicate things."

"Only if we let it and don't go in with our eyes wide open." Evan reached across the table, took her slightly sticky fingers in his, and batted his eyelashes at her. "I don't want to die a virgin."

"Don't be ridiculous," Josie said. "Look at you! Any woman would be thrilled to have sex with you."

"Apart from the one I want, apparently." Evan squeezed her fingers. "Come on, Josie. I think we would be great together."

"And when I go back to work, you'll be okay with that?" Josie asked. "That we're done?"

He shrugged. "I can't see why not, and I guess you'll still be coming back to see Rio from time to time, so we'd have that to look forward to."

"What if I had another relationship?"

"At the same time?" He frowned. "I wouldn't do that to you, and I bet you wouldn't do it to me either."

"I wouldn't," Josie assured him. "I'm a one-guy-at-a-time kind of person. I just wanted to make sure we're on the same page."

His smile emerged. "So, you're considering it?"

"Maybe." She sighed. "I just keep worrying that we're going to end up hating each other, and I don't want to lose our friendship."

"I'll never hate you." He met her gaze, his expression serious. "I couldn't."

"Don't ever say that," Josie said. "You never know what might happen. My mom and Graham were totally in love when they got married."

"The way I see it is we try it out. If either of us thinks it's changing us too much, we stop." He looked at her expectantly. "No questions asked."

"Sex complicates things," Josie reminded him. "It just does."

"I get that." He nodded and took a sip of his coffee. "Or it might make things between us even better."

Josie blew out a breath and contemplated his face. If such a ridiculous arrangement was going to work with anyone, it would be with Evan—a man, she instinctively trusted. She also had to admit that the thought of being his first was incredibly arousing.

"Okay." She checked her phone. "What time do we need to be on the road, because if you're ready maybe we could make a start right now?"

* * *

Evan almost choked on his coffee as Josie answered all his prayers with one brisk sentence. The idea of asking her if she'd have sex with him had genuinely been on his list from the get-go, but convincing her that he meant it was another matter entirely. He should've known that she'd understand and that the honesty between them would make things easy.

"I didn't give Dad a set time for my return, so as long as I'm back before midnight I guess I'm fine." He cleared his throat. "How about you?"

"I'll text Ines and Yvonne to give them an estimated arrival time once we've decided what we want to do." She looked at him expectantly. "What do you think?"

He glanced around the motel room. "What time are we supposed to get out of here?"

"Twelve, but I can always ask for a later checkout."

"You can do that?" Evan knew that at some level he was prevaricating, but Josie didn't seem to mind. "I always thought it was set in stone."

"It never hurts to ask." She picked up her phone. "What do you want to do?"

"I want to stay here—with you—and have sex."

"Okay." She smiled at him. "I'll talk to Reception."

Evan nodded and strolled off to the bathroom as if he didn't have a care in the world. He brushed his teeth, took another quick shower, got dressed and went back through to find Josie busy cleaning up the room.

"I put the DO NOT DISTURB sign on the door to keep the housekeeper out, double-locked the door, and Reception says we can stay until three, which means even if we leave then we'd be back in Morgan Valley in four hours at worst."

"Sounds good." Evan cleared his throat and wondered why he'd bothered to put clothes on after his shower when he was fairly certain he'd be taking them right off. "Where do you want me?"

She turned to grin at him. "Wow, you sound like you're getting another tattoo. You don't have to do this if you don't want to."

"Oh, I want to," Evan reassured her. "I *really* want to."

She pointed at the bed. "How about you go and lie down there?"

"Naked?"

"Not yet. I rather thought I'd like to unwrap you slowly like a birthday present."

Just the thought of that made everything male in Evan stand to attention. He was just about to lie down when he had another thought.

"Do we have protection?"

"Yes," Josie said as she stacked their mugs and empty cups on the small countertop next to their recharging phones. "In my backpack. I also have an implant."

"Like a boob job?" Evan regarded her with interest. "I wouldn't have guessed that. Everything felt very natural to me."

"Not that kind of implant, dummy." She pressed her upper left arm. "A hormone thing. It lasts for three years."

"Oh, right!" Evan stretched out on the mattress and put his hands behind his head as if he didn't have a care in the world. "Got you."

She came to stand at the bottom of the bed, her hands on her hips, her teeth tugging at her lower lip. "You sure you're okay about this?"

"Yes! Seduce me, woman!"

"Okay."

He nearly swallowed his tongue as she stripped down to her bra and panties and crawled up the bed to straddle his lap.

"Would you like me to leave my hair braided or let it out?"

"Out, please," Evan said hoarsely as he forced his eyes to meet hers and not drop to the generous curves of her breasts. "Can I touch you?"

"No." She set her hands on his shoulders and carefully pulled his T-shirt over his head. "Mmm . . ."

"What?"

She trailed her fingers down over his collarbone to his chest and the ridged muscle of his abs.

"This is nice," she murmured. "So kissable and lickable."

She suited her words with action. For a while, Evan let her have her way until he was fidgety with lust and had the need to touch her in return. Her teeth lingered on his flat nipple, making him groan as his hard dick pressed against the front of his boxers.

"Josie, let me—"

"Nope. I'm doing the seducing here." She sat back, her loose hair curled around her breasts—breasts he wanted to touch and kiss more than he wanted to breathe right now.

She knelt up and released his pants, leaving him in just his boxers, which were already tented and clinging damply to his shaft. She took off her bra and panties and he almost stopped breathing.

"Jeez, you're pretty," Evan murmured. "And, hey, there's that tattoo you were telling me about. I should've known it would be a bucking bull."

"Oh, Evan." She sighed and leaned down toward his groin, her breasts grazing his skin along with the curls of her hair. "You're such a beautiful man." She licked the damp fabric of his boxers and he groaned and rolled his hips. "I can't wait to feel you inside me."

"Then don't wait," he encouraged her. "Take it all."

She set her lips around the first inch of his cotton-covered cock and sucked him into her mouth. His hands fisted against the sheets. "Josie . . ."

She took one of his hands and placed it between her legs. "Touch me; make me wet for you."

He'd never obeyed a command so eagerly in his life as he thumbed her bud and pressed his fingers deep inside her, feeling her body clench around him, fantasizing how it would feel when it was his dick being squeezed like that.

"Please." He was totally good with begging right now.

"Okay." Her voice sounded shaky, which somehow made him feel better.

She eased him out of his boxers and retrieved the condom packet she'd set on the bedside table.

"Do you want to put this on, or shall I do it for you?"

"You." He gestured at his overexcited dick. "I don't want to mess things up."

He loved her serious expression as she carefully covered his shaft, and the way she bit down on her lip as she concentrated. He felt like he meant something to her and that she wanted to make his first time the best she could.

"Are you still okay with this, Evan?" she asked, her fingers stroking his hip as she stared down at him. "Because we can stop whenever you want."

"Got it." Evan had no problem sounding as serious as she did, which was kind of weird. "I want this."

Her smile made every anxiety left in him disappear as she straddled his hips and gently lowered herself over his way-too-excited dick. For a moment, all he could do was clench his teeth and breathe as the exquisite sensation of her flesh against his hardness threatened to make his first time over before it had even begun.

"Evan?"

He slowly opened his eyes to reveal her concerned expression.

"Yeah?"

"How do you feel?"

He slowly rolled his hips upward and almost bit his tongue.

"Absolutely amazing," he breathed. "You feel . . . fantastic."

"I'm so glad. For a moment there I thought I'd ruined it."

"God, no." He tried another experimental thrust. "I think I've got this."

"Oh, good, so I can move." She fitted her words with actions and rose over him and then sunk down.

He immediately picked up her rhythm, grabbed hold of her hips, and rolled with it. Within seconds, his over-excited dick was coming too fast for him to do anything but hang on and deal.

"Sorry," he gasped as his head fell back on the pillow. "I just lost it."

"It's okay." Josie climbed off him and dealt with the condom. "Next time."

He came up on one elbow and stared at her, his expression stricken. "You didn't get to come, did you?"

"I didn't even notice." She shrugged as she walked back to the bed. "It was much more fun watching you."

He reached for her hand and drew her down to lie next to him. He kissed the top of her head as he enfolded her in his arms.

"Thank you."

"You're welcome." She pressed her mouth against the taut skin of his muscled chest. "Wanna try again?"

Chapter Eight

"We still good?" Evan asked as they drove through the quiet streets of Morgantown and out the other side toward the Miller and Martinez ranches.

"Yup." Josie turned to smile at him.

They'd shared the driving back with him taking the middle section over the high mountain pass where the snow still lingered. She was going to drop him home and then continue on alone. His body was still humming from the sex and he knew he had a ridiculously goofy grin because Josie kept mentioning it. The thought that he'd screwed things up with her had only gradually resurfaced the closer he got to home.

"Awesome," Evan said. "I wish—"

"That we could spend another night together?" Josie suggested.

"How did you know?"

"Because I feel exactly the same way." She sighed. "But I can't just turn up at my brother's house with you. It wouldn't feel right."

"And I can't imagine my dad's face if you just casually

appeared at the breakfast table." Evan groaned. "How on earth are we ever going to get together again?"

She patted his knee. "We'll find a way."

"I damn well hope so. I don't want to be skulking around like a teenager. I saw enough of that when Danny—" Evan stopped speaking. "Anyway, I don't want to be that person."

Josie opened the window to punch in the gate code to his family ranch and they continued up the drive. They'd left the motel around three in the afternoon and it wasn't that late. Evan could see lights on in both the barn and the house, which meant his father would expect him to get on with any outstanding chores. His mother's rental car was still in place as was Faith's veterinary truck. The sudden return to reality was sobering.

Josie cut the engine as they pulled up in front of the barn.

"Do you want to come in?" Evan offered.

"I think I'd like to get back before it gets too dark," Josie said. "I can call you when I'm home."

"I'd like that." Evan let out a breath. "I don't want to leave you."

"I know."

He stared at the lights in the windows until they blurred. "You could just come in and go to bed with me."

"Evan . . ." It was her turn to sigh. "I'm not ready for that amount of drama right now. I haven't even told my mother or Rio that we're dating."

"Okay." He released her hand and turned toward the door, suddenly feeling like a dumb fool. "I guess I'm being the stupid one here."

She grabbed the sleeve of his jacket. "That's not what

I meant. This is about me and the stuff I'm dealing with right now—not you."

"Okay, what you're saying is that you need your space." He eased out of her grip and opened the door. "I'll just get my stuff out of the back."

She followed him out and stood in his way and he hefted his gear over his shoulder. She looked so worried, that he cupped her cheek.

"Look, ignore me, we're good. Maybe we both need a moment." He leaned in and kissed her. "Call me when you get in. I'll be up for a while doing whatever my dad comes up with to punish me for being away."

He waited for her reaction, hoping to God that he hadn't trashed any chance he had with her, and was relieved to see her smile.

"Okay." She kissed him back. "I had the best time with you this weekend."

"Me, too." He stepped away before he got too handsy and nodded. "Call me."

He didn't wait for her to leave but marched right on up to the back door and let himself into the mudroom. The washing machine and dryer were both in use, heating the space and giving him cover. He dumped his dirty clothes in a hamper and took off his boots and jacket. He was halfway down the hallway to his bedroom when his mother called his name.

"Evan? Is that you?"

He sighed. "Yeah."

"Come into the kitchen and tell us how the weekend went!"

"Do I have to?"

He heard Kaiden laugh. "I assume you didn't win, then."

"Win?" his dad asked. "He wasn't supposed to be competing!"

An argument broke out and Evan made his escape to his room where he hastily changed his clothes that didn't smell like Josie, sex, or anything that would give him away to his nosy family. Even as he bundled everything into the laundry basket, there was a knock on his door.

"Can I come in?" His mother peeked her head around the door.

"Hey!" Evan smiled at her. "I'm just sorting out my stuff. I'll be there in a minute." His fingers caught on something in his discarded jeans pocket and he paused to take it out. "Hell, I've still got Josie's cell phone. I used it to text Ines while she was driving." He glanced over at his mom. "I've got to get this to her, or she'll be frantic. I'll be right back."

"Evan . . ."

"Sorry, Mom. I'll be back before you know it."

He squeezed past her and hotfooted it back to the mudroom where he put on his boots and grabbed the keys to Adam's truck, which was boxing his in. Josie wouldn't be far ahead of him on the road. If he hurried, he might catch her before she even got into the house.

Josie kept her speed down as she carefully navigated the twisty county road that went from the Millers, past a couple of other ranches, and then to swung back toward the outskirts of the town where Rio's place sat between

Morgan Creek and the foothills of the Sierra Nevadas. She was almost home when headlights appeared in her rearview mirror approaching faster than she appreciated.

She checked the side of the road, but there was nowhere to pull over. The idiot behind her would have to slow down because she had no intention on speeding up. Just before she made the turn to Rio's, the truck behind flashed its lights at her. It was close enough for her to see the silver-gray cab but not the driver. She resisted giving the finger as she turned on her indicator, slowed down even more, and made the left turn across the road into the already-opening automatic gate.

Even as she let out a breath of relief, the truck behind her made the turn as well, slipping in through the gate she'd opened seconds earlier. Josie gripped the steering wheel even harder. Either the guy worked at the ranch and she'd give him a piece of her mind for scaring the bejesus out of her when she got out, or she'd picked up a crazy, intent on forcing a fight with her for not driving fast enough.

Neither scenario made her feel good, and for once she prayed that Rio might miraculously have returned home so she could count on his help if things got ugly. Fear iced her veins as the feeling of being pursued, of being hunted, crept over her, shortening her breath and making her feel like she was going to pass out.

She forced herself to concentrate on the road ahead and ignored the too-close lights behind her. There was a solitary light on in the house and she stared at it like a beacon. There was nothing in the truck she cared about. The guy could take it all as long as she got out of it alive.

The edge of the barn jumped out at her from the darkness and she had to swerve violently to avoid hitting it. By now she was struggling to breathe as she skidded to a halt, switched the engine off, and clambered clumsily out of her seat.

"Hey!"

She ignored the shout and ran for the light, her legs like jelly as she hammered on the door like a madwoman before remembering she actually had a key. She got it out and turned it in the lock.

Someone touched her shoulder and she screamed and fell to the ground, curling up in a ball just as the door fell open, and she rolled awkwardly into the hallway.

Josie screeched so hard, she thought she was going to black out. Above her there was a confused sound and then someone picked her up. She punched out, connecting with a stubbled jaw.

"Ouch," Evan grunted. "That hurt."

She forced her eyes open and realized he was carrying her to her bedroom.

"What the hell, Martinez?" he said as he gently lowered her onto the sheets.

"I thought—" She could hardly bear to look at him. "That was you in the truck *behind* me?"

"Yeah, what about it?" Even as he rubbed his jaw, he was delving into his pocket.

She sat up still shaking, but this time for a different reason. "You scared the crap out of me!" she shrieked. "*What were you thinking?*"

"You left your cell phone in my pocket! I thought you'd need it." He set it on the bedside cabinet. "I sure as hell didn't mean to freak you out like this."

"Well, you did!" Josie burst into tears and pointed at the door. "Go *away!*"

Evan frowned and then hunkered down beside the bed until his gaze was level with hers.

"I'm not going anywhere until you calm down."

"Calm down?" Yeah, she was still shrieking. "This is all your fault! If you hadn't behaved like a complete and utter idiot, I wouldn't need calming down."

He rubbed a hand over the back of his neck. "You know that doesn't make sense, right?"

"I don't care," she hissed. "Go. Away."

"I can't do that."

"Sure, you can. Just stand up, turn around, and march your stupid ass right out of here."

He did stand up. "You don't think you're overreacting a tad here?"

She glared at him until he held up his hands.

"Look, how about this? I'll wait in the kitchen until Ines or Yvonne can get here and take over. How does that sound?"

As her rage disappeared and was replaced by the hollow of despair, she drew her knees up to her chest and wrapped her arms around them.

"Okay, I'll do that." Evan still hesitated. "Is there anything I can get you? Some warm milk? A stiff drink?"

She managed to shake her head, the weight of it almost too much to bear as she dropped her face onto her knees. It seemed to take forever for him to actually leave, but eventually even he seemed to get the message.

* * *

Evan sat at the kitchen table, texting like the wind as he tried to work out exactly what had happened. There was something he was missing—something that had turned the woman he thought he was beginning to understand into someone entirely different. He'd obviously scared the shit out of her, and he didn't know why. Sure, he'd driven a bit close behind her on the way up the drive, but he'd assumed she would've worked out who he was by then.

"Shit." Evan breathed. "She didn't recognize Adam's truck."

He spoke to the empty kitchen. He'd made himself some coffee to settle his own nerves and applied some ice to his jaw. He stood up as lights traveled across the ceiling and down to the floor through the window and steps crunched through the gravel.

The back door opened, and Ines and Yvonne appeared together.

"What happened?" Yvonne demanded. Her gaze went to his face. "Did you two fight?"

"No!" Evan recoiled. "She clocked me one when I tried to pick her up from the floor!"

"And what was she doing on the floor in the first place?" Yvonne still didn't look happy.

Ines came to stand between them. "How about you let Evan tell his side of things before you speak to Josie? I'm sure he meant her no harm."

Evan squared up to Yvonne. "Josie dropped me home and came on here. Five minutes after I got in, I realized I'd been using her phone to text you and Ines while she was driving, and it had ended up in my pocket. I didn't want Josie worrying about where it was, so I turned around, grabbed Adam's truck, and followed her home."

"Okay." Yvonne nodded. "And then what?"

"I caught up with her near the bottom gate, flashed my lights to let her know I was behind her, and followed her up the drive." He swallowed hard. "She . . . started driving erratically and almost hit the barn. When she stopped, she ran for the house. I was worried about her, so I went after her. The moment I touched her shoulder, she started screaming and tried to get away from me."

Ines and Yvonne exchanged a quick glance.

"Go on," Yvonne said.

"She curled up in a ball and I bent down to pick her up. That's when she punched me. I carried her through to her bedroom and put her on the bed where she finally seemed to realize it was me and not some rando crazy." He blew out a breath. "Then she went off on me. When I suggested she calmed down because I'd only been trying to return her phone, she told me to get out."

"Okay." Yvonne's expression relaxed slightly.

"It didn't occur to me until just a couple of minutes ago that I borrowed Adam's truck because mine was boxed in and that she might not have recognized it," Evan confessed as he shoved a hand through his already-disordered hair. "So, if she really doesn't want to talk to me ever again, can you apologize to her for that at least?"

Ines set a pan of milk on the stove. "I'll make her some hot chocolate. Would you like some, Evan?"

Evan looked at Yvonne. "I guess you want me to leave as well."

"No," Yvonne said thoughtfully. "Let me talk to Josie first, okay?"

"Is there something I'm missing here?" Evan had never known when to keep his mouth shut. "I understand that I might have scared her, but her reaction . . ." He shook his head. "She was *terrified* of me and—" His voice caught. "I can't get that out of my head."

"I'll go and see how she's doing." Yvonne came over and gave him a side hug. "How about you take Ines up on that hot chocolate?"

Evan sat down again and stared at his boots. He hadn't felt this sick in years. Her face when she'd looked at him—like he was some kind of killer . . .

"It's all right, Evan." Ines patted his shoulder.

"No, it's not. Josie hates my guts."

"I doubt that," Ines said. "I think you need to give her some space right now."

"Then maybe I should just go home." Evan went to stand up. "I really don't want to make things worse."

"You're in no state to drive right now when you're upset." Ines set a mug under his nose. "Stay where you are and drink your hot chocolate."

Was he upset? Evan tried to think through all the noise. "I need to let Mom know where I am, but I don't want to mention what happened with Josie."

"Leanne will be fine for a while. You can tell her when you get back." Ines's voice and words were very soothing. "At least wait until you hear what Yvonne has to say about Josie."

It seemed to take forever for Yvonne to return, giving Evan plenty of time to finish his drink and text his mom some lame excuse. He looked up as she came into the kitchen.

"Is Josie okay?"

"She's getting there." Yvonne smiled at him. "She's embarrassed at how she behaved toward you."

"I don't care how she behaved." Evan waved that stupid notion away. "I just don't get why I scared her so much."

"I'm sorry." Yvonne bit her lip. "It's not my explanation to give. Maybe when you next see Josie you can ask her about it yourself?"

Evan rose to his feet. "I guess that means she doesn't want to talk to me right now."

"She's taken something to calm her anxiety and help her sleep. She was already half-gone when I left the room." Yvonne hesitated. "I suggest you call her tomorrow, okay?"

"Sure." Evan nodded, like he'd be bothering her anytime soon. "Just make sure she knows how sorry I am." He picked up his jacket and car keys. "I'll be off, then."

Ines came to give him a hug. "Now promise you'll drive careful. You've had a bit of a shock and I don't want you crashing on the way home."

Evan bent to kiss her cheek. "I'll be careful." He looked over at Yvonne who still looked worried. "Take care of Josie, won't you?"

"Absolutely," Yvonne said. "And don't worry. I'm not going to say anything to Rio before Josie decides what she wants to tell him."

A minute later, Evan found himself outside in the dark walking toward Adam's truck, his mind in freefall. He hadn't had much sleep for forty-eight hours and had gone through more emotions in one weekend than he normally did in ten years. He got in the truck, gripped the wheel, and gently banged his head against the rim.

"Good job screwing everything up, Miller," Evan muttered to himself. "Josie's never gonna let you near her again."

Unfortunately, when he got home everyone was still up. He braced himself as he went into the kitchen. Adam went off first.

"You took my truck."

Evan set the keys on the countertop with something of a bang. "Yeah, sorry about that. Mine was behind yours and I needed to get out fast."

Adam came over to reclaim the keys. "Just ask next time, okay?"

Evan nodded and turned toward the table where his parents and his brother Kaiden were sitting.

"What?"

"Well, firstly did you get Josie's phone back to her?" Leanne asked.

"Yeah."

"Why did it take you so long?" his dad demanded. "You've been gone over an hour!"

"I didn't realize you were timing me, Dad. I'm not on the clock." Evan remembered he needed to tell them something before he blurted out that he'd scared his first proper girlfriend half to death and that she probably hated him now. "Ines and Yvonne insisted I stay and have hot cocoa with them."

"Makes sense." Leanne nodded. "How are they doing?"

"They're both good," Evan said. "And they were asking after you."

Leanne patted the seat next to her. "Come and sit down and tell us all about your weekend."

"Do I have to?" Evan complained as he reluctantly took a seat. "I mean—it wasn't exactly riveting."

"How did Josie do in the barrel racing?" his dad asked.

"She didn't enter that class. She competed in the bull riding."

For once Evan had managed to make everyone around the table speechless. He gloried in the rare and precious moment.

"The *bull* riding?" Jeff sat back. "That's a man's sport."

"Not anymore." Evan found a smile somewhere. "And guess who beat out eleven other competitors?"

"Well, probably not you or else you'd be doing a victory lap around the kitchen," Kaiden mused. "So—Josie won?"

"Yeah, by a mile. Even the crusty old judges said she was good enough to compete in proper PBR tournaments."

Evan remembered her triumphant grin and the way she'd felt in his arms when he'd swung her around and kissed her. It already felt like that had happened a hundred years ago.

"Well, I never." Jeff tutted. "I'm surprised Rio allowed it."

Leanne poked him in the arm. "Like he gets to tell her what to do. This is the twenty-first century, Jeff. Women don't need to ask permission from their menfolk to do anything."

"Yeah, you tell him, Mom." Kaiden punched the air and Jeff groaned.

"So, how about you?" Kaiden turned his attention to Evan.

"How about me, what?"

"Where did you place?"

Evan shrugged. "Fourth."

"Not bad, little brother." Kaiden grinned. "Not bad at all for a rookie."

"Better than you could've done," Evan retorted.

"I'm not arguing with that." Kaiden leaned in and gave Evan a brotherly punch on the shoulder. "Nice job."

Jeff cleared his throat. "I seem to remember I expressly forbade you boys from competing in the rodeo."

"I don't remember hearing that," Kaiden said. "Did you, Adam?"

"Nope." Adam offered Evan his slow smile. "Never heard a word. Well done, Evan."

"Thanks."

His father scowled. "I hope you're not going to make a habit of disappearing to compete in rodeos. You're needed here." Leanne made a snorting sound and Jeff stared at her. "What?"

"Says the man who left me alone on this ranch with six kids to do the very same thing."

Jeff reached for her hand. "Which is why I'm telling Junior here not to do it. It's not fair."

"Wow, Dad." Evan tried his hardest to be as normal as possible. "Talk about growth."

"We can all learn, Son." Jeff was now smiling into Leanne's eyes. "Even me."

"It's a miracle," Kaiden muttered. "Make it stop."

"Nothing wrong with appreciating your better half," Jeff said. "And learning from your mistakes. If you and Adam were half as quick, you'd both be married by now."

"We're both working on that in our different ways," Kaiden protested. "And, by the way, you took about twenty years to work out your mistakes and make things right."

"*And* you were lucky Mom forgave you and let you make it up to her." Evan couldn't let that go. "Without her you'd still be your old, miserable self."

"I can't disagree with you there," Jeff said. "Leanne coming back was the best thing that ever happened to me."

Kaiden caught Evan's eye and made fake retching sounds, but for the first time ever, Evan was totally caught up in the idea that maybe everything was forgivable—if both parties were willing—and that things between him and Josie might somehow improve again.

"It's cute," Evan said to Kaiden. "They are cute."

"Did you bang your head hard at that rodeo, Evan? Because you're sure talking a crock of crap right now." Kaiden frowned as he studied Evan's face. "What happened to your jaw?"

Evan shrugged. "I can't remember."

"Sure, you can't," Kaiden said. "I'll have to ask Josie about that."

Evan just smiled. The chances of that ever happening were fairly low. He faked a yawn. "It's been a long day. I think I'll turn in."

"Did you eat?" Leanne asked.

"Yeah, we stopped in Bridgeport to get gas and had

an early dinner." Evan rose from his chair. "Where's Danny?"

"He's at Faith's place tonight."

"Cool." Evan nodded at his family. "I'll get up early to do my chores, Dad. 'Night, all."

He only realized how tired he really was when he went through into the bathroom. He stripped down to his boxers, contemplated taking a shower, and decided he'd just have a good wash instead.

He frowned at the suddenly clear countertops. All his brother's and new sister-in-law's stuff was gone. Kaiden tapped at the door and came into the bathroom through Danny's room.

"I forgot to tell you. There's no need for you to move. Danny and Faith have taken over Daisy's old room. It's got its own shower and gives them and us a little more privacy."

"Was this Danny's idea?"

"No, I think Mom checked in with Daisy and she said she was okay with it—why?" Kaiden studied Evan carefully.

"Just wondering." Evan set his shaving kit out on the tiled surface.

"Nice ink, by the way."

Evan glanced down at his bicep. "Thanks. Don't tell Dad."

"Like I'd do that to you." Kaiden paused. "You might want to do something about your neck before Mom gets to sit on that side of you."

Evan frowned at his brother. "I told you I don't know how my jaw got hurt."

"I wasn't talking about that." Kaiden pointed lower. "I meant that massive hickey."

Evan stared into the mirror and slapped his hand over the purple bruise.

Kaiden was already chuckling as he left the room. "'Night, Bro, and don't worry, I'll keep all your secrets."

Chapter Nine

"*Como vai?*" Rio asked, his concern radiated even through the screen. "Yvonne said you hadn't been too well."

"Everything's *bacana*," Josie answered automatically.

It was several days since she'd come back from the rodeo. She'd slept through most of them and missed her regular chat with her brother the day before.

"Josephina Maria Isabella . . ."

"Don't try that full-name Mom crap on me, *mano*." Josie frowned at him. "It's not going to work."

"Then tell me what's going on. You look like shit."

"*Obrigado*."

Josie considered her options. If she didn't share some version of the truth with her brother, she'd be putting Yvonne in a difficult position if Rio asked her what had really happened.

"I competed in a rodeo on Saturday."

"You did?"

Josie shrugged. "Just the informal county fair kind. I went with Evan."

"Were you injured?"

"No, I won." She smiled at him. "It was fun."

"So, did you like have some kind of reaction when you got back?" Rio asked carefully.

"I had a full-on anxiety attack, yes, but it wasn't because I won the bull riding at the rodeo. That was the good part." Josie cleared her throat. "I thought someone followed me home and freaked out before I realized it was just Evan trying to return my cell phone, which I'd left in his pocket."

Put like that, it sounded even more stupid.

"Trust Evan to scare the pants off you." Rio frowned. "Do you want me to have a word with him?"

"It wasn't his fault." Josie leaned toward the screen. "Believe me, I absolutely freaked him out, too."

"But still—"

"If anyone owes someone an apology or an explanation it's me, and I'd rather do it myself."

"Okay, if you're sure." Rio nodded. "Have you seen that therapist yet?"

"My first appointment is today, actually."

"Good. Let it all out, *irmã*. Get your money's worth."

Josie smiled properly for the first time. "Spoken like a true businessman." She paused. "I don't have to tell you not to share any of this with Mom, do I?"

"My lips are sealed." He drew a line across them. "Now, speaking of *Mamãe*, can I ask for your help with something?"

"Like what?"

"Can you persuade her to visit you at the ranch next month?"

"Why would I ever want to do that?" Josie joked. "I'm enjoying my drama-free life."

"Well, Yvonne and I have this idea to get married in Vegas and, obviously we'd like you, Ines, and *Mamãe* to be there."

Josie pressed her hand to her mouth. "Finally!"

Rio grinned, displaying his dimples. "About time, eh? Took me a long while to convince Yvonne I was sincere. But we don't want Mom to get into a big fuss about the arrangements and everything. If we can get her here and then spring it on her in Vegas at the last minute, things will go much more smoothly."

"I can't argue with that approach," Josie said. "Of course, I'll ask her to come here."

After her brother signed off, she sat there smiling at nothing for a while, glad that her big brother was finally going to marry the woman he loved. After her first disaster of a marriage, Yvonne had been justifiably skittish of entering into another one, but Rio's steadfast love and devotion had obviously worn her down. Josie couldn't think of any two people who were as well suited as Rio and his pastry chef.

Her cell buzzed and she checked her messages. There was nothing from Evan and only a reminder of her appointment in town with the therapist at Dr. Tio's clinic. With a sigh, Josie took herself to the bathroom to shower and get ready. After days of hiding in bed, it was definitely time to woman up and get back to living her life.

Evan hadn't contacted her since the night she'd screamed in his face and told him to leave. Yvonne had relayed his message about being sorry for not realizing she didn't recognize Adam's truck and for frightening her. But she could hardly blame him for what had happened. Sure, he'd scared her, but she'd definitely overreacted.

* * *

She got out of the shower and wrapped herself in a towel, wondering how he must be feeling. Talk about the worst timing ever. He'd probably decided she was way too kooky to be his girlfriend, and who could blame him? She certainly didn't. But up until that point, their weekend together had been so special. . . .

Josie dried her hair and got dressed. Perhaps this new therapist would help her figure out how to deal with the panic attacks, keep her demanding job, and make sure Evan continued to be her man. She snorted as she turned to leave. Even she knew the counselor was a medical professional, not a miracle worker.

"So, Evan, I was thinking . . ." Leanne's voice trailed off and she poked Evan in the arm. "Are you actually listening to me?"

"Sure!" He nodded as he climbed the stairs to the new apartment she had bought in the old movie theater Kaiden had helped renovate. "You said something about having my own space."

She paused on the top landing and fixed him with a very momlike stare. "And the rest of it?"

He grinned apologetically. "I kind of zoned out after that."

She took a key out of her pocket, and instead of turning right to her apartment, she unlocked the only other door on the other side.

"Come on in." She gestured for him to follow her.

"What do you think of this apartment? It's one bedroom, one full bath, and a combined kitchen and living space."

Evan walked into the nicely proportioned family room that looked out over Main Street. The whole space smelled like fresh wood and plastic. There were two small couches, a coffee table, and high stools at the kitchen counter that divided the room. All the appliances in the kitchen were still in their wrappers and included a nice big refrigerator and a dishwasher. The bedroom was at the rear of the apartment right next to the bathroom. It had been simply furnished with a large pine bed and chest of drawers and had a walk-in closet.

"Kaiden did a great job on the kitchen cabinets and new wood framed windows," Evan said. "Are you thinking about adding it to your place?"

His mom walked over the original plank floor to stand beside him. "I already did. I originally thought it might be nice to use it as an office or for guests, but I was wondering whether it might suit you better."

"Me?" He frowned at her. "Why?"

"Because I think you need your own space away from the ranch."

"I can't live here and work up there," Evan pointed out.

"I know."

"So, what's the point?"

She went to sit on the wide window seat overlooking the street and he followed her.

"Adam's going to inherit the ranch from your father. Ben has his own place now, Kaiden and Danny have options, and Daisy is spoiled for choice. That just leaves you."

"You don't think I'm ever going to meet someone who wants to set up home with me?"

Leanne patted his hand. "Of course, you will, but you might as well make use of this space while it's empty. You'd be doing me a favor because you could keep an eye on my place next door when I'm in New York visiting Ellie."

Evan considered everything she'd said. "It's very nice of you to offer, but I'm still not sure I'd get much use out of it. You don't need to waste this place on me."

"But I want to." She paused. "You know that I inherited a considerable sum of money from Declan?"

"Yeah, sure, but that's for Ellie. She's his daughter."

Leanne chuckled. "Oh, don't worry about Ellie. She's set for life. The money Declan settled on me is just for my own use. He knew about my situation with Jeff and all my regrets about abandoning my kids. Originally he established the fund so that I would always have the money to go to court to get access to you kids—access your father had denied me." She smiled. "It was actually his wedding present to me."

"That's kind of cool," Evan said. "Although, I have to say that back in the day, Dad would probably have ignored any court in the land before he would've let us see you again."

"Which is one of the reasons why I didn't use the money," Leanne said. "Your auntie Rae said that if I moved against him, Jeff would probably take you all and run for the hills. I couldn't bear to think that you'd all lose the only home you'd ever known along with your mother."

"That would've sucked," Evan agreed.

"I tried to explain that to Declan and give him the money back, but he wouldn't hear of it." Leanne smiled again. "The fund just sat there and grew interest until Declan died, and it was eventually released to me."

"Nice."

"Bittersweet." Leanne sighed. "When I decided it was time to see your father again, I came prepared for litigation and found him surprisingly amenable."

"Which meant you got to keep the money." Evan nodded.

"After talking to your father about it, I decided to split it up into equal amounts for all of you regardless of how well you were doing."

"So, Daisy and Ben get the same as me?" Evan asked, intrigued. "That's good. I wouldn't want them to lose out."

"Oh, Evan." Leanne kissed his cheek. "You are such a sweetheart."

His gaze settled on the patches of sunlight coming through the large windows and he took one of her hands between his. "You don't owe me anything, Mom. You know that, right?" He looked into her worried eyes. "I don't have any beef with what you did when you left Dad. I was six, it didn't impact me the same way it did the others because I was young enough to be babied by the whole family and already had too much parenting all round."

She sighed. "I'm not trying to buy you off, Evan. I realized long ago that money can't buy happiness or love. But I truly think it's important for every one of us to have our own little refuge. A place where we can just be ourselves. And we both know that your dad makes that hard to do up at the ranch."

"Yeah, he does." Evan took another slow look around the apartment. "Okay. I'll take you up on your offer and keep an eye on your place while you're not here."

"That's . . . wonderful," Leanne said. "Thank you."

"I could pay you some rent?" Evan offered.

"No. If you're going to be looking after my apartment, that makes us even."

"And if you need the space back, just let me know, and I'll get the hell out."

"I sure will." She cupped his chin. "I love you, Evan."

He grinned at her. "I know."

"Shall we celebrate with lunch at Yvonne's?"

"That would be awesome."

Josie was afraid that she might have slammed the door on her way out of Dr. Tio's clinic, which wasn't fair when everyone had been so kind to her. Well—apart from the therapist who had asked her way too many uncomfortable questions and sat there in silence while Josie tried and failed to answer her. She'd come out feeling even more confused than before she went in. She wanted to talk about the break-in and all Rashida wanted to ask about was her relationship with her family.

Okay, so her mom could be difficult, and she had problems establishing boundaries with her, and Rio hadn't been there much, and her father . . .

Josie let out her breath and realized she had no idea why she'd ended up standing outside the post office, glaring at everyone who went in or out. Her gaze shifted to the pink-and-black-striped frontage of Yvonne's patisserie. She'd go in there, claim family status, and stuff her face with cake so she could ignore her feelings.

She had a sense that Rashida wouldn't approve, but that somehow made it even better. She reminded herself that not every therapist was a good fit for everyone and that even though she was happy to go again, she had the ability to back out if things weren't working for her.

The smell of coffee wafted out of the café as someone exited and Josie followed it like a siren call. Lizzie looked up as she headed for the counter.

"Hey, you, did you want to see Yvonne?"

"No, I just came in for coffee and cake." Josie smiled at Adam Miller's fiancée who was genuinely one of the nicest and most open people she had ever met. "I bet she's busy creating that wedding cake for the weekend."

"Yeah, but I'll let her know you're here anyway if I get a chance." Lizzie handed over the coffee. "What kind of cake would you like?"

"Surprise me."

"Will do."

Lizzie waved her off to a table and dealt with the next customer while Josie sat down and took out her phone. There was a message from Rio asking how her appointment had gone but not much else. Even her office had stopped calling her, which meant either Rio had put his foot down, or they didn't think she needed to be involved anymore. She didn't like either of those scenarios.

"Here you go." Lizzie set a plate in front of her. "I

thought you needed chocolate so here's our mini sampler of six different things."

"That's perfect." Josie breathed in the complex scents of sugar, chocolate, and caramel. "Yvonne is amazing."

"Say that louder so they can hear you at the back." Yvonne came toward her, wiping her hands on her apron. "It's good to see you out and about."

"I had an appointment with that new therapist."

Yvonne sat next to Josie. "How did it go?"

"Okay, I guess." Josie shrugged. "Hard to tell after just one visit."

"Will you go back?"

"I booked another appointment in a week's time, so yes, I suppose so." Josie sighed. "I've got to try something to get me out of this funk."

"Maybe you just need to go with the flow," Yvonne said gently. "There's no timetable for recovering from trauma, Josie."

"Well, there should be. It would make everything so much easier." Josie studied her plate. "I think I want to tell Evan why I reacted like that."

Yvonne nodded. "If you're comfortable doing so, I'm sure he'd appreciate it. He was very worried about you."

"But what if he thinks I'm a complete disaster and dumps me?"

"I don't think Evan's the kind of guy to do that. He's got a good heart. All the Millers do." Yvonne hesitated. "Do you care what he thinks?"

"Yes."

"Then take the risk. Better to know where you stand early in the game than when you're all committed and stuff." Yvonne pulled a face. "Ask me how I know."

"I'll call him when I get back," Josie said. "Thanks for the advice."

"You're family, Josie. No need to thank me for anything."

Josie blinked back sudden tears. "I understand I need to lure my mother here so that you and Rio can get married in Vegas."

"Only if you want to." Yvonne grinned. "All Rio would have to do is say he's sick and she'd be on the next plane anyway."

"She sure would." Josie was well aware that Rio had always been her mother's favorite. "But if the request comes from me, she won't be so suspicious if our plans change."

"That's what Rio thought." Yvonne sat back. "I can't wait to finally make everything official."

"I'm glad to hear it. *Mamãe* has never been happy with him 'living in sin.'" Josie tried to look pious and failed miserably. "The only thing she'll regret is you two not having a big wedding so she can show you off to everyone."

Yvonne shuddered. "I can't think of anything worse. If we have our way, it will just be us, Ines, Graham, Isabelle, and you and HW Morgan as witnesses."

"Sounds good to me," Josie agreed. Yvonne's parents had died years before and she was an only child.

"Now, I'd better get back to work." Yvonne stood and smoothed down the skirt of her black dress. "Tell Ines I'll be late tonight so don't wait on dinner. As usual, I'm in the middle of decorating a wedding cake."

"Will do." Josie smiled at her future sister-in-law. "Thank you."

Yvonne had barely disappeared behind the kitchen door before someone called out to Josie.

She looked up to see Leanne advancing toward her with a big smile.

"Hi!" Josie smiled back even though her stomach dropped.

"May I join you?"

Even as Josie nodded, Leanne was already slipping into a chair. "Evan said you won the bull riding contest at the fair! How cool is that?"

"It definitely was fun," Josie agreed. "And Evan was great company."

"Yes, I think he enjoyed getting out of Morgan Valley for a few days. He's definitely been moping around since he came back." Leanne looked up as Lizzie approached. "Hi, Lizzie, sweetie. Can I get coffee for two and some of those delicious-looking cakes Josie has?"

"Coming right up!" Lizzie said.

Just as Josie started to relax with the knowledge that Evan obviously hadn't said a word about what had happened between them to his mother, the man himself came in, did a double take, and balked at the sight of her, which wasn't encouraging.

"Hey." He offered her a wary smile as he finally got moving again in the right direction. "What's up?"

"Nothing much." She smiled in return. "I was just telling your mom about the fun we had at the rodeo."

Leanne pulled out a chair and Evan folded his long, lean body into it—a body that Josie had licked, kissed, and thoroughly explored only days before. He wore his usual T-shirt-and-shirt combo with his work jeans and boots and looked totally comfortable in his skin. His hair needed trimming and there was a distinct glint of red stubble on his chin, which gave Josie all kinds of wicked ideas.

So, despite everything, she obviously still found him hot. But did he feel the same about her? Did she even want him to? She eyed him under her lashes as he replied to something his mom said. The ease between them warmed her heart.

Leanne's cell phone buzzed, and she took it out of her pocket. "Drat, it's Henry. He needs me to come in and sign the final papers for the apartments."

Evan set his coffee down and went to rise, but Leanne set her hand on his arm.

"There's no need for you to come with me, sweetheart. It won't take long. How about I come back here when I'm finished?" She smiled at Josie. "I'm sure you two have plenty to talk about."

"Are you sure?" Evan asked.

"Quite." She put her cell away and rose to her feet. "I'll tell Lizzie to keep the coffee coming, and if you both want to get a proper lunch, it's on me."

Evan watched as Josie ate a chocolate éclair and then a macaron flavored with lemon and hummed with plea-sure. He still couldn't work out if she was pleased to see him or not, but then he'd never been the best at reading the room. The purring sound she was making made him horny, and at first, he couldn't think why until it finally clicked.

"You make that sound when you're having sex," Evan said.

Josie finally looked at him properly. She wore her hair in a plain ponytail, and although her lipstick was still red, she wasn't shining as brightly as usual. She looked tired and vulnerable and that made his heart hurt.

"Did you just say that out loud, Evan Miller?"

"Yeah, sorry." He waited as she licked her lips free of crumbs. "You've got to stop doing things like that in public."

"I'm not exactly in public right now. I'm sitting with you."

"In public." Evan folded his arms across his chest and regarded her. "Because if it was just us right now . . . I'd be all over you."

This time she deliberately licked her lips as she stared at him.

"I take it my screaming fit hasn't tamped down your desire to have sex with me?"

He frowned. "Why would it? We all have our bad days."

"Bad days? Evan, I completely lost it and told you to get out!"

"But that's my fault." He sat forward and took her hand, his brow creased with concern. "You were upset. I scared the *crap* out of you. It didn't occur to me that you wouldn't know I was driving Adam's truck and that you'd think I was a stranger coming after you. I should've called out and kept my distance."

She met his gaze, her brown eyes wary. "I way overreacted."

"Josie, I've got a sister. Daisy's told me how unsafe she's felt in situations like that. I forgot and behaved like an inconsiderate ass."

"Okay."

He continued to look at her. "Anything else we need to say before we put it behind us and both stop apologizing to each other?"

"Yes," Josie said, and glanced around the crowded café. "But maybe not here."

"Got it." Evan kissed her fingers before he released her hand, the tight band around his heart easing slightly.

Lizzie came by to refill their coffee and Evan ordered himself a burger while Josie opted for a sandwich. Leanne reappeared and helped herself to Evan's fries while she chattered about the apartment.

"I need to talk to Yvonne about something," Leanne said. "Evan, why don't you take Josie over and show her the apartment?"

"Mom . . ." Evan rolled his eyes. "Can you be any less obvious?"

She winked and pressed the key into his hand. "It's all official now. I put your name in as tenant on the documents I just signed for Henry. Take your time. I'll text you when I'm ready to leave."

Evan turned to Josie. "Would you like to see my new place?"

"You're moving off the ranch?"

"Nope." Evan stood and offered her his hand. "How about I explain on the way over?"

Leanne waved them off and went into the back of

the café to find Yvonne in the kitchen. Nodding ami-
ably to his neighbors, Evan led the way back out into
the sunshine and across the street to where the old movie
theater stood in all its restored glory.

"Kaiden did this?" Josie shielded her eyes as she
looked up at the fake front that had been repainted just
like the movie theater in its prime. They'd also restored
the cast iron exterior and glass foyer.

"Not all of it, but he did do the woodwork, the window
frames, and the kitchens," Evan said. "I helped out sometimes when he needed extra labor. He's a pain in the ass
to work for and a real perfectionist, but I enjoy the work."
He pushed in a few keys on the security pad and let her
into what used to be the ticket office. "Come on up."

There was a discreet elevator at the rear, but Evan took
the stairs and Josie was happy to follow him up to the
third floor. There were two doors off the narrow landing
and Evan turned to the left and unlocked the door.

"We're here."

Josie stepped into the fabulously light apartment that
looked out over Main Street.

"It's so cool." She spun around. "Now, how on earth
did you get it?"

"Can we talk about that in a minute?"

As she completed her turn, she slammed right into his
chest and his arms came around her.

"I feel like I've got some apologizing to do," Evan
murmured as he bent his head and kissed her gently on

the mouth. "And I can't think of a better way of doing it than this."

She went up on tiptoe to kiss him back, her sense of relief at being in his arms more intense than she'd anticipated.

"I thought we'd agreed to let that go?" she whispered against his lips and kissed him again.

He reluctantly eased back and looked into her eyes. "After you'd talked to me. Maybe you'd better do that before I get carried away and embarrass myself or something."

She took his hand and they both sat on the couch.

"Okay." Josie took a steadying breath. "Someone broke into my apartment in San Francisco. I ended up crouched in the bottom of my closet while they ransacked the place."

"*Shit*," Evan breathed.

"I can't seem to get over it," Josie admitted. "I kind of get panic attacks right out of the blue and I'm hypersensitive about loud noises, people, the dark . . ." She tried to smile. "Everything actually. After the attack, I couldn't function at work because I was too scared to fall asleep at night. I started screwing up even the simplest things."

Evan put his arm around her shoulders. "And then I tailgated you, and jumped out at you in the dark. No wonder you screamed in my face." He shook his head. "Jeez, I'm so sorry, Josie."

She leaned against him and put her head on his shoulder.

"I just thought you should know what was going on with me."

"Thank you." He kissed the top of her head and stayed quiet for a while, which she appreciated.

"I'm trying to work through it. I actually saw a therapist today."

"Good." Evan gently squeezed her shoulders. "I guess it's going to take some time to get your head on straight. I know Jackson, Daisy's husband, still struggles with PTSD after his career in the Air Force, as does Sam Morgan after her tours in Afghanistan."

"What happened to me is hardly on a line with their service," Josie objected.

"I didn't realize it was a competition," Evan said gently. "Trauma's trauma."

"Well . . ." She eased out of his embrace and crossed her arms. "Now you know."

He angled his head to one side and studied her. "You look like you expect me to get up and leave."

"I could see why you might do that." She shrugged as if she didn't mind either way. "I mean, not everyone wants to deal with something like that in their personal life."

"I'm not planning on going anywhere." He met her gaze. "If that's still okay with you."

"I can't always predict what will set me off," she said desperately. "It could be the most stupid of things, and sometimes I get way too emotional, and—"

"Hey." He reached out and stroked her cheek with his forefinger. "I don't care about any of that. All I care about is you."

"Are you sure this isn't just because I'm the first person you had sex with?"

His brow creased. "Like I'd stick with you because I was so desperately grateful or something?"

"Maybe."

His smile was slow in coming but still incredibly hot. "I could've gotten laid when I was fifteen if I hadn't minded who was offering. I waited to find the right person and I chose you."

"Maybe I'm trying to give you an out." She bit down on her lip. "But you're making it incredibly hard for me not to like you, you know?"

"Good, because as I said, I'm not going anywhere." He leaned over, picked her up, and set her on his lap. "Now come here and let me hold you, okay?"

Chapter Ten

"My darling!!"

"*Mamãe.*"

Josie opened her arms wide as her mother rushed toward her and was enveloped in a familiar perfumed hug. Isabelle was only five foot two and made even Josie feel tall. Yvonne got out of the truck and beamed at the two of them.

"Come and get settled in, Isabelle. Rio's due back in a couple of hours."

Josie picked up her mother's monogrammed hand luggage and followed her into the house where Ines awaited them. Isabelle uttered another shriek and hugged Ines and chattered away in Portuguese as they walked down the hallway to the newly redecorated guest room, which had once belonged to Ines's daughter, Louisa.

Yvonne sighed. "I guess I really should learn Portuguese."

Josie smiled at her. "Only if you want to know what they're really saying about you."

"Ha! Maybe ignorance is bliss." Yvonne hefted the two big suitcases. "How long is she planning on staying anyway? I thought she said she could only make a quick trip?"

Josie cast an experienced eye over the bags. "This *is* a quick trip. If she was really planning on staying, you'd need a truck to deliver all her bags. Mom never travels light."

"So, I see." Yvonne lowered her voice. "You good for the weekend ahead?"

"Yes. I plan to avoid her as much as possible, so I don't give the game away."

"Me, too," Yvonne said. "Luckily, I've got a whole lot of orders to get through at the café before I can leave, including decorating my own wedding cake."

"How exactly are we going to get to Vegas without Mom noticing?" Josie asked.

"Rio's commandeered one of the Howatch International private jets, so we'll be going on that. He'll be parking up at the Morgan Ranch airstrip anytime now. HW's already in Vegas and he'll meet us there. How we actually persuade her to *get* on the jet is another thing completely. I'm expecting Rio to come up with a plan for that."

Laughter came through the open door into Isabelle's room. Josie paused in the doorway to admire her mom in her full glory. She wore her dark hair piled high on her head, four-inch heels, and a pink pantsuit with shoulder pads that Joan Collins would've envied. Her jewelry was chunky and mainly gold, and she still wore both of her wedding and engagement rings on her slim fingers.

She not only looked like a character from an eighties soap opera, but also lived her life on a somewhat dramatic scale. She'd met Graham Howatch at the age of

seventeen as a contestant when he was judging a beauty
contest, married him days later, and divorced him in
spectacular style when she found him banging Rio's
nanny. Even after that horror show, she'd remained un-
defeated and had returned to Brazil to marry and extract
her revenge on her ex. Josie sometimes felt like her
unwilling partner in crime as she watched from the
wings while her mother dominated the stage like the star
she was.

Eventually, Ines and Yvonne departed, leaving Josie
to help her mother unpack.

"You look so much better, darling." Isabelle patted
Josie's cheek. "Less . . . stressed. Rio said you'd been bull
riding."

"Yes, it was great fun." Josie hung up two of her
mom's favorite Chanel jackets in the closet. Even though
she lived on a ranch, Josie didn't think she'd ever seen
her mom in jeans. "I won."

"Of course, you did." Isabelle beamed at her. "You get
that from my side of the family."

"Arturio wasn't a fan?"

"He enjoyed the sport, as did most Brazilians, but
soccer held his heart." Isabelle walked into the new attached bathroom, her voice echoing back to Josie. "This
is lovely."

"Yes, I think you're the first guest to use it." Josie finished with the closet, lining the shoes up on the floor.
She'd been given the old guest room to the left of the
family bathroom. "Rio said it had to be fit for a queen."

"Such a sweet boy." Isabelle set her large makeup case
down on the new marble countertop. "I think I'll take a

nice bath to relax so that I'll be ready to greet *meu filho* when he arrives."

"Okay." Josie prepared to depart. "Do you want coffee or anything to eat?"

"Just a large glass of water, darling. I'm so dehydrated." Isabelle studied her reflection in the mirror. "I'm looking quite haggard."

"Nonsense," Josie said robustly. "We still get mistaken for sisters."

Her mom laughed and drew her into a hug. For a moment, Josie studied their reflections, noting both her similarities to her mother and her differences. She loved Isabelle dearly but sometimes felt more like the mother than the child.

"Do you have any pictures of Arturio's family?"

"I'm sure I do somewhere. Why?"

Josie shrugged. "I'd just like to see them."

"I'll check when I get back home. And if I don't have any, I'm sure his widow will. You can always contact her."

Josie nodded. Like she'd be getting all friendly with the woman her father had chosen to marry after divorcing her mother.

"She's very nice, Josie," Isabelle said gently.

"So everyone tells me." Josie headed for the door. "I'll see you later, okay?"

Evan checked his phone and read the short message Josie had left him.

Mom's arrived. Rio expected soon. Looking forward to seeing you tomorrow x

Shame I can't see you right now. He texted back.
Was hoping to get your help picking some new
sheets for my bed.

I wish.

They'd managed to spend one glorious evening together at the apartment so far where Evan had learned
lots of new ways to please his woman. He was dying to
find out more, but the arrival of Josie's mom had put all
his plans on hold.

"What's wrong?"

Evan looked up to see his mom watching him from
the other side of the table. She'd come up to the ranch for
lunch and to make sure Jeff went to his appointment with
Dr. Tio at the clinic.

"Nothing. Josie's mom's in town."

"Isabelle's here? How lovely!" Leanne picked up her
phone. "I'll ask her over for dinner tomorrow night. Then
you'll get to see Josie, too."

"Hmph."

Evan finished his coffee and rose from his seat to go
and rinse out his mug. If his dad passed his final physical
with Dr. Tio today, he would be released back on the
range, which meant that Evan's hours of freedom to plan
his time and do his job the way *he* wanted were likely to
come to an end. His dad had very set ideas about everything and usually wore people down into doing things his
way because he was so exhausting to deal with.

His mom's phone buzzed.

"Isabelle wants to know if we'd like to come over to
Rio's place for dinner tonight?"

"What—all of us?"

"No, just you, me, and Jeff."

"Why me? What did you say to her?" Evan asked suspiciously.

"I didn't say anything. It was her suggestion." Leanne looked innocent. "Do you want to come or not?"

Six hours later, Evan showered, put on his best shirt and jeans, and drove his parents over to the Martinez Ranch. His father's glee at his release from home confinement made him a mellow companion for once. Evan knew it wouldn't last, but he intended to enjoy the moment. His mom spent the whole trip lecturing her ex about what he could and couldn't do out on the ranch and still didn't start a fight, which must have been a first.

He pulled up behind an assortment of trucks and opened the back door for his mom.

"Thank you, Evan."

He waited as they walked ahead of him to the well-lit house, savoring the chill of the night air and the sharp cut of the breeze coming off the foothills.

"Welcome!" Ines let them in and immediately hugged Leanne and Evan. He tended to forget that his parents and Ines had once been in-laws and still considered themselves family.

He walked through into the kitchen and zeroed in on Josie who was chatting away to Yvonne as they both peered at something cooking on the stove. Rio was setting the table with Isabelle's help. There was a mixture of Portuguese, English, and something in between, which didn't faze Evan at all. He'd picked up quite a bit over the summer while hanging out with Rio's cowboys.

He wanted to go over and kiss Josie, but he wasn't sure what she'd told her mom and didn't want to drop her in anything, so he compromised by wandering over and smiling down at her.

"Hey, what's cooking? You look hot." He offered her an exaggerated wink.

"We're making a traditional Brazilian meal, but we're also trying not to go too hard on the deep-fried stuff because Jeff doesn't need another heart attack."

Josie pushed her hair away from her flushed face. She pointed at the two large enamel pots sitting on the back burners of the large stove.

"We've got *feijoada,* a pork and black bean stew served with garlic rice and collard greens in that one. And *baião de dois,* which is a rice- and pork-based dish over there. I'm about to start frying up the *acarajé* balls, which we'll split open, and add the *vatapá* in the middle."

"So, I guess you're telling me to get out of the way," Evan said.

"Correct." She smiled up at him. "I'm so glad you came. Why don't you help yourself to something to drink while I finish up here?"

He leaned in closer. "Have you told your mom we're going out together yet?"

"I haven't, but seeing as you got an invitation here tonight, I'm guessing someone did." She went up on tiptoe and kissed him right on the mouth. She tasted like spices and shrimp. "Now, that makes it official."

Evan was still smiling when he turned around and saw not only Josie's mom, but his parents, were staring at him. He sauntered over to the refrigerator and helped himself to a beer before going over to say hi to Isabelle again. She patted the seat beside her, and he sat down.

"I hear you entered the same rodeo as Josie."

"Yeah, and she beat me fair and square," Evan admitted. "She's a really good bull rider."

"So, I hear, although I don't think she's quite ready to give up her position in Howatch International and take it up full-time like her brother did." Isabelle chuckled. "At least, I hope she isn't. I don't think my heart could take another bull rider in the family."

"It's a dangerous sport," Evan agreed. "But if anyone could be successful, Josie could. She's just that kind of person."

"I have to admit that I've never thought of her like that," Isabelle said. "She's far too down-to-earth to want to risk everything for the chance of fame and fortune."

Evan considered and discarded several replies before he settled on something noncommittal. The last thing he wanted to do was upset Josie's mother.

"I guess we all have our dreams. I wouldn't stop anyone following theirs, especially Josie." Evan picked up his beer. "Did you have a good flight?"

"Yes, indeed." Isabelle was now studying him intently. "I'm lucky enough to have access to the Howatch International private fleet."

"Cool. I've never been on a private jet."

"It certainly makes travel more convenient, but as Josie is always reminding me, it is terrible for the environment. I tell her I just plant more trees on my ranch to make up for it."

"We're doing a lot of that in Morgan Valley," Evan said. "In the last century the silver miners chopped down almost everything to power the stamp mill and prop up the shafts, leaving half the valley treeless. We're going to repair that damage."

"That's good to know." Isabelle hesitated. "I hope you don't mind me asking, but are you going out with my daughter?"

"Yeah." Evan smiled. "She's great."

Isabelle took his hand, her tone indulgent. "And she deserves to have some fun while she's here. Your mother says if anyone can cheer her up it'll be you."

"Thanks, I think." Evan looked over to the kitchen where Josie was now filling the *acarajé* with the shrimp paste. So, his role was the class clown making the princess feel better?

"She's had a tough time recently," Isabelle said carefully.

"So she said." Evan gently removed his hand from hers.

"She *told* you?"

"Yeah." Evan stood up. "I'd better go and help her out. She looks as if she needs it."

The whole idea that he was too dumb to realize he was just a temporary aberration in Josie's rise to stardom in Howatch International was annoying as hell. He knew she wasn't going to hang around. Why would she? But he certainly didn't need anyone pointing it out to him, especially her mother.

"What did she say to make you look like that?"

Josie didn't even glance up from what she was doing as Evan approached her.

He shrugged as he found her another serving dish and put it on the counter beside her. "Nothing much."

"Evan, I know my mom. She loves to meddle in other people's lives. What did she say?"

"Just the truth—that I'm a nice little distraction for you while you get better."

Josie stopped what she was doing and looked up into his guarded hazel eyes. "She actually said that out loud?"

"It's okay, because my mom apparently agrees with her."

She knew him well enough to realize he wasn't as unfazed by the comments as he appeared. Her annoyance with both their mothers grew.

"I mean, like you'll be going back to San Francisco or Boston at some point, right?" Evan asked. "We both know that."

She put her hand on his arm. "I haven't decided what I'm going to do yet, and I certainly haven't told my mom or given her permission to tell you what role you currently do or do not play in my life. She was out of line, and when I talk to her, I'm going to—"

He cut across her. "There's no need to say anything. I get where she's coming from. She's your mom, she's worried about you."

"You are a much better person than I will ever be, Evan Miller," Josie said fervently.

His wry smile made her heart hurt. "I think you're the first person who's ever said that. I'm usually known as the irresponsible family screwup."

"You're far more than that."

Ignoring the hum of conversations and bustle in the kitchen, she flung one arm around his neck and brought his head down to meet hers.

"I mean it." She kissed him twice just to make sure everyone saw. "Now, let's serve up this dinner before everything gets cold."

Even as she chatted and laughed with her mother, brother, and the rest of their guests, Josie was still steaming about her mother's decision to intervene in her relationship with Evan. The thing was, should she try and have it out with her mother? They were due to leave for Vegas in a day or so for Rio and Yvonne's wedding and the last thing she wanted was to cause any bad feelings before that happened. And Isabelle could be very dramatic when called on her behavior.

But if she didn't say anything, her mom might take it as permission to say even worse things, and Evan didn't deserve that. He didn't deserve any of it. Josie set down her fork. The thought of going back to work curdled her stomach. She'd always had a plan and her current indecisiveness appalled her almost as much as the physical effects of the break in. Evan wouldn't fit in with her old life—she knew that—but he already meant far more to her than as just some convenient, low-key stand-in.

Her gaze went across to the table to where he sat between Leanne and Yvonne. He was smiling at something his mother was saying, his profile full of life. As if conscious of her stare, he suddenly looked at her and raised an eyebrow. She hurriedly studied her plate and took a hasty slug of wine, which made her cough.

"Too strong for you, *filha?*" her mother joked. "Perhaps you should drink some water."

"That's a great idea." Josie stood up and headed for the kitchen.

"There's water right here. . . ." Yvonne called out, but Josie was already moving on through the mudroom door.

She slid her feet into the first pair of boots she found, grabbed her jacket, and headed out into the night. Since her anxiety attack, Rio had installed floodlights between the barns, the outbuildings, and the house, which illuminated her path. There was no chance of anyone sneaking up on her now. It also meant it was hard to see the beautiful night sky.

The back door shut again, and she looked over her shoulder to see Evan coming after her. She waited, her arms wrapped around herself, until he reached her.

"Hey." She turned into him and rested her head against his chest. He put an arm around her shoulders. "What's wrong?"

"I'm just still mad at my mom," Josie confessed. "And I don't know how to deal with her right now."

He persuaded her to walk toward the shelter of the barn where they couldn't be seen from the house.

"There's no need for you to be mad. As I said, I get what's she's saying." He hesitated. "And she's not wrong, is she? We both know you're not based here permanently or anything. There's no point fighting with her about something that can't be changed."

It seemed like Evan had come to the same conclusions she had, which for some reason made her even madder. She moved out of his embrace.

"But I don't know what I want to do! I'm incapable of making that kind of decision right now!"

"Okay."

She glared at him. "That's supposed to be helpful?"

He smiled. "It's not my job to tell you how to live your life, Josie."

She walked away from him for a few paces and then spun around. "I've *always* had a plan. I don't know how to function without one."

"Maybe you just need a new version?"

"That's even less helpful than your first suggestion."

"Then I might as well go for a strikeout. How about you just play things by ear? Your brother basically runs the company, and he's not going to kick you out on your ass anytime soon. Why not take advantage of that and just let things ride until you *are* ready to make some decisions?" He held her gaze, his voice gentle. "You've been through some difficult things, Josie. Don't be so hard on yourself."

She walked toward him. He slowly straightened and held one hand out in front of his face.

"Now, don't—"

She stopped and looked into his eyes. "Will you kiss me?"

"Anytime you want."

"Now?"

"Sure." He drew her close into the shadow of the barn wall, bent his head, and took her mouth in a voracious kiss. "I've been wanting to do that since the moment I saw you in the kitchen."

Josie slid one hand behind his neck and joined in until they were both breathing hard, and she'd somehow managed to untuck his shirt from his jeans and her fingernails were scratching his back. He bucked his hips against hers, the thick line of his shaft pressing against her stomach through his jeans.

"I want you," Josie whispered.

"Like right here and now?"

"Yes." She bit down on his lip, making him groan. "Please."

His hand slid up her thigh past the hem of her dress to her lace panties. "We'll have to be quick."

"I don't think that'll be a problem." Josie wrestled with his belt and the button of his fly. "Thank goodness I wore a dress tonight."

"Yeah," he groaned as his fingers slid past her panties to the slick, wet heat of her need. "You know this place better than I do. Where's the safest place for us to get this done without being interrupted and me getting shot?"

"The feedstore has a lock. It's just inside the barn on the right."

"Okay." He picked her up, her thighs straddling his hips, which made her gasp. "Let's go."

Even with the short distance he carried her, the delicious friction of his jeans against her lace panties made her writhe against him. He set her down momentarily as he wrestled with locking the door, and then sat her on the countertop, pressing himself between her thighs as if he belonged there.

"No condom," he murmured as he disposed of her panties and thrust his fingers inside her. She fumbled to unzip his fly in the darkness.

"We're still good. Implant, remember?" She pushed down his jeans and boxers in one motion and sunk her nails into his muscled ass. "Please hurry."

"I'm on it."

She felt the flex of his hips and then he drove his shaft deep inside her in one sure thrust. She immediately climaxed and hung on to him like the champion bull rider she was for barely more than the eight seconds needed before he came hard.

"Way too fast." Evan nuzzled her throat. "Sorry."

"That was perfect," Josie breathed. "Just . . . perfect."

He eased free of her, his gaze caught by the wetness he'd left behind, and bent to kiss her bud. She shivered and his dick twitched, ready to do it all over again—but better.

"Glad there's a sink and plenty of hot water in here." Evan snapped on the light and paused to take in the stunning sight of Josie, her head thrown back, eyes still closed, and her arms braced on the countertop. He'd never actually seen heaving breasts before. Apparently, they did exist outside the romance novels he'd secretly borrowed from Daisy, which to be fair, had given him some amazing pointers about how to sexually please a woman.

He washed himself before zipping everything up and patting down his hair.

"I've got you." He returned to Josie with a warm soapy cloth and towel. She took them off him.

"If you clean me, we'll never get out of here."

"Especially if I just use my tongue." He winked at her, handed over her panties, and stood back to let her get straightened out.

She slid down from the countertop. "How do I look?"

He considered her. "Very fuckable."

"Evan Miller!" She shook her head. "I meant, do I look presentable?"

He took in her flushed cheeks, sensual eyes, and bee-kissed lips.

"Nope."

"Dammit." She sighed. "How about we take a walk around the paddocks to see the bulls before we go back in? Half an hour out in this weather will soon take care of my happy glow."

Chapter Eleven

Evan frowned and stared out of the kitchen window at the horses in the paddock below the house. It was a windy morning, and tails and manes were flying as the horses played, ran, and swayed together like a school of fish. It was two days since he'd last seen Josie. If he was a betting man, he'd be putting money on her mom keeping her too busy to see him.

"What do you mean you can't tell me?"

He was talking to Josie on the phone about the weekend, his cell jammed under his chin as he made his breakfast. He had a sense she wasn't being straight with him.

She sighed. "Look, I've got plans."

He remembered to be reasonable. "Like with your mom?"

"Exactly."

"Cool." Evan set his empty coffee mug in the sink. "Then why not just say that?"

"Because it's complicated."

"What—she's taking you to Vegas to marry you off to another man?"

His joke seemed to fall flat as she went very quiet.

"Josie? You still there?"

"Yes."

"Look, it's fine, okay? Have a good weekend and text me when you get back."

"Evan . . ."

He ended the call. He was not going to be the kind of jerk who expected his girlfriend to account for every second of her time to him. They were both adults, and if she had plans that didn't include him then that was fine. The problem was that was all well and good in theory, but he wondered whether she didn't want to tell him what she was doing because she didn't trust him.

After checking the time, he went back out to the barn to finish up the rest of his chores. Danny and Adam were around somewhere, but they all knew their jobs and wouldn't get in each other's space. As he went into the feedstore, he met Adam coming out.

"Hey," Adam said. His faint smile disappeared as he looked over Evan's shoulder. "Hell, *no*."

"All right, then!" His father called out from behind them. "Where do you want me to start?"

For a moment, Adam and Evan shared a look of horror, and then his big brother turned to their father.

"It's entirely up to you, Dad."

"Nope, you're the boss now and I'm sure you've got a new system in place already. Just consider me like a special team or backup."

"Are you sure you're feeling okay, Dad?" Evan asked, eyeing him suspiciously.

Jeff frowned. "Yes, or I wouldn't be out here, Son."

"I mean it's not like you to offer to help rather than order us all around."

"As your mother reminded me last night, things have changed. I'm taking a back seat and Adam's making the decisions now."

"Well, yeah, you *said* all that, but none of us thought you actually meant it." Evan glanced at Adam who nodded.

"I meant it!" His dad's frown was rapidly turning into a scowl. "Now, stop your blathering and give me something to do!"

Adam cleared his throat. "You can, um, start letting the rest of the horses out into the pasture and check they've got fresh water in their stalls."

"Good. Then I'll get on with that."

Jeff stomped off down the center aisle of the barn and Evan whistled.

"I wonder how long that's going to last? I bet he's going to be complaining about something you've changed before lunch."

Adam groaned. "I figure it'll be less than an hour."

Evan held out his hand. "Winner has to do the other person's evening chores?"

"Deal." Adam shook his hand.

Evan was still grinning when he came around the corner of the barn and almost ran into Danny.

"Hey."

"Hey." Danny paused. "What's so funny?"

"Dad taking orders from Adam."

"You're kidding." Danny draped the lunge rope over his arm. "I missed that?"

"Yeah." Evan couldn't stop smiling. "He said he was taking a back seat."

"Like, sure."

"I know! I mean—" Evan suddenly remembered who he was talking to. "We've got a bet going as to how fast Dad loses it."

"I should get in on that."

"You should." Evan nodded and went to move past Danny. "Talk to Adam. Winner doesn't have to do their evening chores."

"I will, and . . . Evan?"

Evan looked over his shoulder. "Yeah?"

"It's good to see you smile."

There was nothing he wanted to say to that, but maybe, just maybe, things would get easier between him and Danny as time went by. He was whistling by the time he reached his truck and checked he had the necessary tools to repair one of the gates in the lower pasture. Dealing with stuff head-on was obviously the way to go.

He pulled out his cell and flicked through his contacts until he found Josie's number and called her.

"Hey."

Not surprisingly, she didn't sound very pleased to hear from him.

"Hey, I just wanted to clarify something." Evan took a deep breath. "I know you don't want to see me this weekend, but is it because *a*, you're doing something you think I won't approve of, not that I have the right to approve or disapprove of anything you do, obviously, or *b*, my famous inability to keep a secret?"

She took so long to answer, he thought he'd lost the connection.

"It's kind of *b,* but it's not about you, Evan, and it's not my secret to share."

Evan tried to work through the ins and outs of her reply.

"Okay, so you can't share because there is a secret, but it isn't yours to tell, and you don't want me blabbing it to the wrong person. Makes sense. Thanks. Have a good one."

He ended the call and walked back to the storeroom to get some more nails. His cell rang again, and he put it to his ear.

"You're such an idiot, you know?"

"Yup," Evan agreed even as he started to smile.

Josie lowered her voice. "I can't tell you because if my mom finds out it would be a disaster."

"Okay, and you're right. I shouldn't assume that everything is about me."

"Correct." Josie paused. "I could meet you at the Red Dragon for drinks tonight?"

"Only if you have time."

"I'll find it." Josie spoke with conviction.

"Text me when you're on your way, or do you want me to swing by and pick you up?"

"No, I don't want you anywhere near my mother. I'll meet you there."

"Who are you talking to?"

Josie jumped and almost dropped her cell phone as

her mother spoke from right behind her. She was in the kitchen making a fresh pot of coffee after helping muck out the stalls earlier in the morning, and her mom had obviously just gotten up.

"It was Evan."

Who was absolutely and completely a huge dork who made her smile.

Isabelle raised her eyebrows. "I know you're going out with him. You don't have to hide it."

"It's not that. You just startled me."

She hoped to hell that her mother hadn't overheard her conversation. It would be kind of ironic if she was the one to give everything away after basically telling Evan he was incapable of keeping a secret. Although, to be fair, her reluctance to tell him where she was going also had a lot to do with his current sensitive spot about hasty marriages and Las Vegas.

She poured her mom some coffee and offered her the jug of cream.

"I'm meeting Evan at the Red Dragon tonight for a drink. We were just finalizing our plans."

Isabelle took a seat at the table. She wore a cream bathrobe with feathery collar over her pajamas and high-heeled slippers with jewels on them. She'd already put on her makeup, which she did regardless of where she was or what her day would look like. Josie had watched her drive a herd of cattle looking as glamorous as someone on a photoshoot. It was a skill and a mindset she envied.

"Everyone tells me he is a nice boy—if a little immature."

"He's definitely nice." Josie stirred her coffee and then shared the spoon with her mom.

"He certainly seems keen on you."

Josie smiled serenely, and her mother chuckled.

"You can talk to me about him. I *love* to hear about your boyfriends."

"I know." Josie sipped her coffee.

The last thing she wanted to do right now was get into any chatty mother-daughter conversation. Isabelle was an expert in worming things out of her, and this time for some reason, her feelings for Evan were too new and unsure for her to want to share them with anyone.

"He won't inherit that ranch," Isabelle said. "Leanne says Jeff has left it to Adam."

"It makes sense not to break it up," Josie mused. "I'm sure Evan will be just fine."

"I suppose he will since Leanne isn't short on money. Declan left her very well provided for, indeed."

"Lucky Leanne, but I'm fairly certain Evan would rather have his parents and Adam around for as long as possible rather than wishing they were dead so he could inherit something. He's a good person."

"Who probably needs to get out into the world a bit more." Isabelle laughed. "Leanne said he's never been out of the country! Can you imagine that?"

Josie set her mug down on the table and met her mom's all-too-innocent gaze.

"If you've got something to say, why don't you just go ahead and say it?"

Isabelle reached for her hand and spoke in a rush. "I'm just worried about you, *minha filha*, that you might make choices you regret while you're not feeling quite yourself."

"Choices like Evan Miller, you mean?"

"Yes! Obviously, he's a dear, sweet, boy and the son of one of my best friends, but he's hardly your *type,* is he, darling?"

"My type?" Josie asked.

"Yes, a businessman—someone who has aspirations beyond working on a ranch for the rest of his life."

"You own a ranch. You know how much work and dedication is needed to keep it going."

"Yes, but that's not what I envisioned for you, darling—l . . ."

"Can we stop this?" Josie gently removed her hand from under her mother's. "I'm not a child, *Mamãe.* I'm perfectly capable of making my own decisions about the men I date."

"But—"

Josie stood up. "I have to get changed. I'm meeting Rio over at the bull breeding pens."

"But we've always shared everything." Isabelle pressed her palm to her heart, her eyes filling with tears. "I meant no offense—"

"None taken." Josie smiled down at her. "I just need some space right now, okay?"

Isabelle nodded and waved her hand at the door. "Then please go ahead. I wouldn't want you to be late to help your brother."

Josie ran—there was no other polite way of putting it. One of the things she'd promised herself after waking up in the hospital after the break-in was that she'd make her own life—that she wouldn't share everything with her mother—that she needed to be herself.

It was hard. Josie brushed away a tear as she went to change. It wasn't as if her mom was unkind or trying to influence her, she just liked to be involved in everything. They'd spent so many years as just the two of them supporting each other against the world that sometimes Josie felt like her mother's shadow or her younger sister rather than her daughter.

And they weren't even that alike. Isabelle was charming, outgoing, emotional, and made up her mind instantly whereas Josie was . . .

She wasn't even sure who she was, which was part of the reason why she needed time to be herself and work it out. Something that Evan had reminded her of just the other day.

He wasn't a lightweight. He saw things very clearly— sometimes too clearly—and had never learned to hide what he thought.

Josie changed quickly into her oldest pair of jeans, a faded T-shirt, and a fleece before braiding her hair down her back. She had to go through the kitchen to get to the mudroom where her boots and hat were. There was no sign of her mother, just the lingering scent of her perfume. Ines and Yvonne had gone into town much earlier with wedding plans on their mind, leaving Josie to deal with Isabelle.

Rio glanced up as Josie came to stand beside him by the bucking chute. He hadn't been back to the ranch for a while and Jaime was eager to show off the progress of some of their new bulls. Breeding bulls fit to be used in the PBR was a long-term, expensive, often heartbreaking, and time-consuming process.

"*E ai?*" He frowned. "You're upset."

"Just *Mamãe*." She tried to smile as he put his arm around her shoulders and led her away from the others. "She was asking all kinds of intrusive questions about Evan, and I just . . . didn't want to get into it with her."

"She means well."

Josie sighed. "I know that, and I love her to pieces, but I'm not willing to dissect my relationship with Evan right now. I know he's not my usual kind of guy, but who cares? Maybe he brings something to the table that all the others were missing?"

"Maybe he does." Rio looked thoughtful. "Are you serious about him?"

She met her brother's brown-eyed gaze. "I can't answer that."

His smile was slow but worth waiting for. "*Mana*, I know you. If you can't say no, then I think the answer has to be yes."

"But—"

He kissed her cheek. "You'll work it out, okay? Now, how about talking me through these bulls you've been riding literally behind my back?"

"You again?" Nancy called out to Evan as he came through the door of the Red Dragon.

"Nice to see you, too," Evan said as he took a seat at the bar. "I'll take a beer when you have a minute."

It was already getting busy at the bar. Friday night was when the cowboys, ranchers, and townsfolk came out to mingle with the tourists staying at the local hotel and the Morgan Ranch dude ranch farther up the valley. Jay, who owned the bar, had organized live music on Friday nights along with a highly contested darts contest and billiard league. Not that anyone got too rowdy in the Red Dragon with its owner being a retired Navy SEAL.

The local band hadn't yet arrived and most of the attention in the bar was on the four TV screens airing various sports.

"Here you go." Nancy put the beer bottle in front of him. Her short hair was dyed bright neon blue and her piercings were silver and black.

"Thanks." He gestured at the restaurant end of things. "Busy in there?"

"Getting busy. Do you want me to snag a table for you?"

Evan checked his cell and sent a text to Josie. "I might get takeout."

"Yeah?" She winked at him. "And where exactly will you be taking that out to?"

"I have my own place in town now."

"So I heard. What do you want to eat? I can get that going for you while you wait for Josie."

He checked his phone and saw that Josie had replied that she was running late and to get her the ribs.

"Two orders of ribs, fries, and corn on the side to go, please."

"Coming up." Nancy put the order through on her tablet. "Sonali says fifteen minutes."

"Perfect."

"So . . . you and Josie, right?" Nancy asked, giving him an amused grin.

Evan raised an eyebrow. "What about it?"

"You look good together." Nancy wiped the bar with

a cloth. "I've seen a lot of couples come and go through this bar and I know what I'm talking about."

"She's only here for a few weeks." Evan shrugged. "It's not going anywhere."

"Things can change, Ev. Don't ever think they can't."

Dammit, he didn't want hope entering the arena. He liked Josie way too much already, and the thought of her leaving—of leaving *him*—already felt like a punch in the gut. But why would she stay? She had a career, a future, and a life that could never include him. They were like two different species and yet somehow, they clicked.

Just as the food arrived in a sturdy paper bag, Josie came into the bar and waved at him from the door.

"Gotta go." Evan slid off his stool. "Thanks, Nancy."

She blew him a kiss as he weaved his way through the packed tables, nodding and smiling at familiar faces along the way.

"Hey." He bent to kiss Josie's cheek. "I got dinner."

"Awesome." She pushed the door open wide and walked out onto the street. "Sorry I was late."

"Everything okay?" Evan took her hand as they crossed the corner and headed for the old movie theater.

"I was trying to pack without my mother noticing and working out if I could fit my bags in my closet in case she came into my room while I was out and saw them."

Evan tutted as they walked into the building. "I guess my dad was right about something for a change. He always said that once you start lying it's hard to stop."

"I'm hardly lying." Josie poked him in the ribs. "I'm

just trying to make sure my mom doesn't know what's going on until the last possible moment."

He paused at the top of the stairs to get his key out and she caught hold of his shirt and looked up at him.

"Can we not talk about this?"

"Sure." He unlocked the door. "I'm starving. I stocked the refrigerator with beer, so I think we're good."

By the time they were sitting up at the countertop next to each other with a fresh beer and a plateful of the best pork ribs in the state, Evan wasn't thinking about anything but eating.

After a while, he wiped his fingers for the umpteenth time on his napkin and pointed at Josie.

"You know it's your turn, right?"

"For what?" Rather than using her napkin, she was licking each finger with an attention to detail that made his dick come to attention.

"Next item on your list."

"Oh!" She paused to fully insert her thumb into her mouth and lovingly licked it clean. "This sauce is so good."

Evan shifted uncomfortably in his seat. "Stop doing that."

She grinned and swirled her tongue around the tip of her finger. "This?"

"Focus." He mock scowled at her. "I don't want barbeque sauce all over my new sheets."

"There was something I've always wanted to do here in Morgan Valley."

"Apart from meeting me, you mean?"

"Of course." She grinned at him. "You know there's a ghost town on Morgan Ranch?"

"Yeah, Morganville. It's the original settlement. The townsfolk moved down here when the silver mine went out of business about a hundred years ago."

"I've heard that there's a long-standing tradition of daring to spend the night up there without running away screaming."

"Correct."

"Did you try it?"

"Nope, I was too young when my older brothers did it. I had to stay home and keep an eye on Daisy."

"Did they make it through the night?"

"They came back around four in the morning. Adam said it was because they remembered they had to get back to do their chores, but they all looked terrified." Evan chuckled. "Danny told me later that he'd definitely seen a ghost."

"Really?" Josie's eyes lit up.

"Knowing Danny, it was probably a stray cow, but it was enough to send them all running for home."

"Then I'd definitely like to try it." Josie wiped her fingers on a napkin. "And maybe you could come as well? We can go when I get back from my trip."

"To keep you safe?"

She leaned in and flicked his nose. "We both know who'd be the one screeching, don't we?"

"Yeah, probably me." He took hold of her wrist, drew one of her fingers into his mouth, and slowly sucked. "Now, Miss Sticky Face, how about we finish up here, take a shower, and go and christen those new sheets of mine?"

"How about we just head for the sheets and forget the shower until afterward?"

He slid his arm around her waist and picked her up, making her shriek.

"Sounds good to me. I just remembered my mom has a pretty good washing machine right next door."

Chapter Twelve

"That sure is a great view." Kaiden shielded his eyes and looked out over the valley floor.

Adam had persuaded Evan and Kaiden to meet him, Ben, and Danny at the proposed site for Danny's new house. Evan had only gone because he didn't want to get into it with Kaiden, and with Josie away with her mom, he was at a massive loose end. It was amazing how much of his free time she'd already consumed without him being aware of it or resenting it.

"Yeah," Danny said. "And it's halfway between our place and Faith's parents so we'd have roughly the same commute." He glanced over at Evan. "What do you think?"

"It's great," Evan agreed. "You won't even have to make a fancy garden when you've already got so much nature around you."

The two-tiered pad was surrounded by pine trees and exposed knolls of rock covered with climbing plants. Below them ran Morgan Creek, the sound of the rushing water amplified by the hollowed-out channel of rocks it threaded through at this point in its journey. Evan already knew how cold and clear the water was. It ran right off the snow bed up in the Sierra Nevadas and fertilized the whole valley.

He pointed at the slope. "Garages and offices below and living on the top—a bit like Faith's parents' place."

"Yeah, we're thinking about getting the same architect in, but I don't want exactly the same house," Danny said.

"You could ask May Chang to take a look," Kaiden suggested. "She was great to work with on the old movie theater and she's local."

"That's a good idea." Danny nodded. "I'll see what Faith thinks when I see her tonight."

Adam settled his Stetson more firmly on his head as the wind strengthened. "Well, at least we've cleared and prepared the lot. All you need now is to build the house."

"Our thanks to Adam Miller for stating the obvious as usual," Evan murmured under his breath. "What would we do without our fearless leader?"

Beside him, Danny choked back a laugh, and even Adam smiled.

"While I've got you all here, Lizzie and I have decided to get married."

"Cool!" Kaiden slapped his brother hard on the back. "When?"

"When Roman's next out of school." Adam cleared his throat. "We've decided to take him to Disneyland for our honeymoon."

Everyone stared at him until Evan spoke up.

"Wait—Disneyland? You in a pair of mouse ears?"

"What about it?"

"Just . . ." Evan tried not to laugh. "Must be true love,

Bro, because nothing else would make you fall for that shit."

"Have you told Dad and Leanne?" Ben, always the peacemaker, asked quickly.

"Not yet. I wanted you guys to be the first to know." Adam looked pointedly at Evan. "Can you all keep it to yourselves today? Lizzie and I plan to take Mom and Dad out to dinner tomorrow night and tell them then."

"Where are you planning on having the ceremony?" Ben asked as they all strolled back to where they'd left their collection of trucks and horses.

"Here on the ranch, if we can," Adam said. "In the backyard with our families and friends around us."

"So many weddings right now," Kaiden said. "And no, Julia and I aren't ready yet—hell we can't even decide where we're living month to month." He nudged Evan. "You'll probably get hitched before I do."

"I doubt it," Evan said. "Not really on my agenda right now."

"I dunno. You and Josie look pretty good together."

"And like Julia, Josie has a career in the city that she loves and will be going back to," Evan said firmly. "There's no way she'd want to stick around here with me."

"But would you like her to?" Danny asked.

Suddenly, Evan didn't like the way his other three brothers were all looking at him.

"Stop," he ordered. "You're all getting way ahead of yourselves. I'm the family screwup, the baby brother, the irresponsible one, remember?"

"People can change," Ben said slowly. "Most of that used to be my job until I sorted myself out."

"With a lot of help from Silver," Kaiden reminded Ben. "She wouldn't let you fail."

"True." Ben smiled. "But all I'm saying is that our baby brother might be growing up."

Evan rolled his eyes, gave them all the finger, and marched over to where he'd tied up Joker. He could still hear them laughing and hollering as he rode away.

"Come on, *Mamãe*."

"But Josie . . ."

Josie linked her arm through her mother's and tried not to give the impression that she was hurrying her along the hallway toward the bank of elevators. If she did that, Isabelle might get suspicious and balk again. Josie couldn't believe how long it had taken her mother to get ready for what had been billed as a simple family dinner to celebrate Yvonne's birthday after a hard day's shopping in Vegas.

She tried not to look at her phone while they waited for an elevator that seemed to be taking an age to arrive. She knew her brother's texts had probably reached full-on caps and exclamation marks by now, but there was nothing she could do about it. At least they were on the move and her mother was still oblivious.

"Where are we meeting Yvonne and Rio?" Isabelle asked as Josie ushered her into the elevator, her high heels clacking on the tiled floor.

"At the entrance to the dining room. We're already twenty minutes late."

"They'll wait." Isabelle waved a regal hand.

"I'm sure they will," Josie agreed, breathing a sigh of

relief as they reached the lobby level and the doors slid open. "It's just over here."

She spotted Rio immediately pacing the entrance to the dining area, immaculate in a black suit, white shirt, and blue bowtie. The glare he shot her behind their mother's back was not reassuring.

"I did my best," she mouthed at him. "She's impossible."

He gave her an imperceptible nod and trained all his considerable charm on Isabelle, who chatted away apparently unaware that she was being led beyond the dining room into a separate suite of rooms.

"Oh!" Isabelle pulled up short as Rio closed the last door behind her. "What's going on?"

Josie smiled for the first time as she spotted Yvonne, resplendent in a dark blue silk flapper-style dress with flowers in her hair. Ines was majestic in brown stripes and HW Morgan had gone for the dime-store cowboy look, complete with a white straw hat and skull and crossbones boots. Slightly in the background and sitting in his wheelchair was Graham Howatch, Rio's father, and her boss who was currently fighting cancer.

A woman stood on a slightly raised podium in front of them with thick crimson curtains at her back.

"Are we ready to proceed now, Mr. Martinez? I do have another appointment in half an hour."

"Yes, of course. I do apologize." Rio kissed his mother's hand and placed it in Josie's. "Yvonne and I are getting married, *Mamãe*."

"Right now?" Isabelle asked.

"Yes." He gestured at the woman and went to take Yvonne's hand. "Please. Go ahead."

Josie drew her mother to one side beside Ines and Graham and took her place beside HW who winked at her as he took off his hat to uncover his thick, blond hair.

"Hey, beautiful."

"Right back at you," Josie said.

HW, his twin Ry, and Rio had competed together on the rodeo circuit. Rio had told her that the twins had been both welcoming and encouraging when he'd first arrived back on the PBR scene and that he'd never forgotten their kindness. And, if he hadn't come to lend HW a hand at Morgan Ranch, he would never have met Yvonne and fallen in love. That was the main reason why Josie put up with HW's somewhat loud personality. He was a good man at heart, and she could never forget that.

The ceremony was short and sweet, but Josie still found herself shedding some tears. For a crazy second, she wished Evan had been beside her to lean on, but HW proved to be up to the occasion as he handed over a tissue.

"I knew you'd cry. Sam always swears she won't, and she does anyway, so I always come prepared."

"If they put pockets in women's dresses, we wouldn't have to rely on the kindness of strangers," Josie murmured under her breath.

"Strangers? I thought we were friends these days."

"It's a figure of speech."

He winked at her and then went over to offer Rio a hug. "Congrats, *mano*. You owe me."

"I sure do."

Josie didn't think she'd ever seen her brother look so happy before in his life. Apparently, even winning two world bull riding championships wasn't as amazing as marrying the love of his life, which was just as it should be.

She hugged Yvonne, who looked incandescent, and then her mother and Ines. She paused in front of Graham who had sat back in his wheelchair the moment the ceremony ended.

"Mr. Howatch."

"A pleasure to see you, Josie. The monthly financial reports I'm getting from your department aren't as expansive or as well prepared as when you were delivering them. I hope you will be back to work soon."

"I'll do my best," Josie replied even as her stomach rolled over.

"Good." He nodded and effectively dismissed her as he turned the angle of his chair toward her mother who was gesticulating and exclaiming about something in a stream of excited Portuguese.

Rio clapped his hands. "We're going to have some pictures taken and then we'll have dinner together next door, okay?"

He nodded at the waiter who had appeared at the internal double doors and opened them to display the circular table inside with the wedding cake in the middle. There were flowers in various shades of white, blue, and purple. The theme was echoed in the candles and the table settings. Josie was amazed Yvonne had managed to organize everything so quickly.

"Champagne will be available shortly," the waiter said.

Thinking of pictures . . .

Josie took her phone out of her purse and held it in front of her face to take a selfie with Yvonne and Rio holding hands behind her and the rest of the wedding crowd milling around. After deciding that the photo would do, she texted it to Evan.

Surprise wedding!

She waited a moment to see if he'd reply immediately and saw the bubbles forming in the corner of the screen.

Your mom does know HW is already married, right?

She had to smile. **You know this is Rio and Yvonne's big day, right?**

Jeez, everyone is getting married. LOL

Josie smiled. I've got to go. Speak to you later, ok? x

She slipped her phone back in her purse and headed over to the raised dais where the photographer was already attempting to arrange their small group in some kind of order. She noticed Rio draw him aside and point at his father who already looked exhausted.

The first dozen photographs were taken with Graham, and then he left with his caregiver and a wave of his hand. Josie went over to Rio who had escorted his father to the door while the photographer started with Yvonne. He was staring after Graham, his expression troubled.

"Is he okay?"

"Not really. He wanted to be here despite his doctor's advice." Rio grimaced. "He just told me that watching me get married was the last thing to check off his bucket list."

"I thought that would be you running his empire full-time," Josie reminded him.

"Yeah, that as well." He sighed. "I guess he's an expert in pulling my strings because one of the reasons I asked Yvonne if we could schedule it sooner rather than later was because I kind of wanted him to see us get married before he died. How stupid is that?"

"Not stupid at all." Josie hugged him. "He didn't want you to marry her and you proved him wrong again. No harm in that."

"I suppose that's one way of looking at it." Rio's smile reemerged as he took her hand. "Come on, let's get these photos out of the way. I'm starving."

Three hours later, Josie was back in the large suite she was sharing with her mother and Ines. She'd left the two ladies chatting in the sitting room and found refuge in her bedroom where she was happy to kick off her high-heeled sandals and call Evan.

"Hey."

He accepted her Facetime request and she got to see him stretched out on his bed at home wearing just an old blue T-shirt and PJ bottoms. His smile made her smile in return.

"Having fun?" Evan asked.

"It was pretty cool," Josie acknowledged. "The hard part was getting Mom on the private jet without giving everything away."

"How did you manage that?"

"Rio told her he'd booked a table at a Michelin-starred restaurant for Yvonne's birthday, and that it was a surprise, and that she wasn't to say anything to her, but to pretend she wanted to go shopping in Vegas and see a show."

"Ah, a double bluff. Sneaky."

"It worked. She thought she was keeping Yvonne's secret; meanwhile, everyone else managed not to say anything to change that belief. She didn't even realize she was attending a wedding until it was just about to begin."

"Awesome." He grinned at her. "You look nice."

"Yvonne got me this dress." Josie held the phone higher so he could appreciate what it did to her curves.

"Nice boobs."

"Thanks."

"Any chance you could shimmy out of that dress right now?"

"Evan Miller, are you asking me to put on a show?" Josie faked outrage.

"Only for me."

"Hang on then. I need to find a good angle to place my phone." She studied the space around her and opted for the top of the padded headboard. "Can you still see me?"

"Oh, yeah."

He settled more comfortably back against his pillows, one arm behind his head, the other obviously holding up the phone.

"If I put my earbuds in, I'll still be able to hear you clearly."

"Great idea," Evan agreed.

Josie scooped them up from her bedside table and put them in her ears, which made Evan's voice sound stronger and more intimate than ever.

"Okay, take that dress off for me. Slowly."

Josie took her time easing the zipper down and then slid one shoulder off followed by the other to expose the top of her strapless bra.

"Man, that's pretty." Evan sighed. "I wish I was right there to cup your breasts in my hands and tease your nipples nice and tight." He paused. "Maybe you could do that for me, sweetheart?"

"Like this?" Josie lowered the dress to her waist, gently placed her hands under her breasts, and stroked her nipples through the taut silk.

"Hell, yeah." Evan's voice deepened. "I'm getting hard just watching you."

Josie smiled as she pinched her nipple and shivered. "How hard?"

"Enough to want your hands on me." She heard the slight rustle of clothing being disturbed. "I guess I'll have to make do with my own."

"Oh, God," Josie whispered. "I've never done anything like this before, and I'm kind of loving it. Shall I take my dress off completely?"

"Yes, please."

She tried to remove her dress in a slow and sultry way, but it was a lot harder to do in real life than it was in the movies.

"That's better." She tossed the dress onto the floor.

"Good." He groaned. "Slide your hand inside your panties."

Josie did as he suggested and almost moaned at her slick readiness. "Oh, Evan, I wish . . ."

"I was there? Not half as much as I do right now."

He hesitated. "Can you . . . would you make yourself come for me?"

"Evan . . ." Her breath was coming in uneven gulps as she touched herself more vigorously. "I want you to do the same, okay? With me? Together?"

His breathing fractured along with hers as she climaxed with a high-pitched sound muffled instantly by her hand over her mouth. The last thing she needed was her mom rushing in to see what was wrong with her. She heard Evan's guttural groan as he came along with her.

She reached forward, still panting, and held onto the headboard as she stared at his image on the phone.

"I miss you."

"Me, too." Evan's hand was still tucked inside his pants. "When I see you again"—his slow smile held a load of sensual promise—"we'll take that foreplay as a given and get right down to the main event."

"We'll see about that." Josie smiled at him. "I like all of it."

"You're so demanding, woman."

"You wouldn't have it any other way," Josie reminded him.

"True." He winked. "I bet you're tired after your long day."

"I am now, but I think I'll sleep a lot better thanks to you."

He blew her a kiss. "Always glad to be of service, ma'am. Looking forward to your return more than I can say."

Josie signed off with a kiss of her own and walked through into the bathroom in something of a sensual daze. She hadn't had that many boyfriends in her busy life, but she already knew that none of them had ever come close to making her feel the way Evan Miller did. Even though Graham Howatch had made it plain that he expected her back at her desk as soon as possible, she still wasn't sure she was ready. And it wasn't just because she'd lost her confidence at work.

Josie studied her flushed reflection in the mirror. Before, there had only been negative reasons not to do things with her life. For the first time, she'd found someone positive, and whatever happened next, that would always be a good thing when she'd feared she'd never feel hope again. Evan Miller made her feel alive, and that was far more precious than she had ever anticipated.

The problem now was—what was she supposed to make of all of it, and what on earth was she supposed to do?

She had a quick shower and wrapped herself in the fluffy hotel-supplied robe before going out to speak to her mother. She hoped the flush on her cheeks would be ascribed to the heat of the water and not to what she and Evan had been up to.

Isabelle smiled at her as she approached the couch where she sat with Ines.

"What a wonderful day, *minha filha!*"

"It sure was." Josie grinned at her mom and Ines. "I thought we weren't going to make it at one point, and that I'd just have to pick you up, run out of the room, and dump you in front of the happy couple."

"You knew all along?"

"Of course!" Josie took an elaborate bow. "Why do you think I asked you to join me at the ranch?"

Isabelle's smile dimmed slightly. "I thought you wanted your mother with you during this difficult time."

"That as well," Josie hastened to agree with her. "I mean, you always cheer me up." She changed the subject. "Rio and Yvonne looked so happy."

"Oh, yes, they did. So in love." Isabelle sighed. "They reminded me of my wedding with Graham."

Josie wasn't sure quite what to say to that, seeing as she'd been frequently told it had been a disaster from start to finish.

"I just came to tell you that I'm going to bed and to say good night." She went to kiss Ines and then her mother. "We're leaving at ten by the way, Mom, so please be ready."

"I am always ready," Isabelle declared as she kissed Josie's cheek.

"I'll make sure you are," Josie said sweetly. "See you in the morning. I'll probably go to the gym around eight if you want to join me?"

Isabelle shuddered. "I need my beauty sleep, darling. I'll see you when you return."

Josie went back into her bedroom and spent a few minutes packing her things. She was fairly certain she'd have to help her mom pack in the morning because time management wasn't Isabelle's strong point. If they stood any chance of getting on the plane by noon, her mom would need to be coaxed and cajoled to participate.

Just as Josie was about to switch off the light, her cell buzzed with a text.

I know where you are, bitch. Watch out.

Josie's entire world slowed down, and she froze in place as she stared at the message. She almost went to delete it before a spark of self-preservation stopped her.

With hands that shook, she scrolled through her contacts to find her attorney and pressed connect.

"Hey, Ruth, sorry to call you so late."

"Josie!" Ruth said, and hesitated. "I was just about to call you. I had a message from the court to say that your attacker has been released early."

The room started to spin, and Josie forced herself to breathe deeply.

"*Why?*"

"He was let out for exemplary behavior and his assurance that he will honor the terms of the current restraining order."

"Really."

"How did you find out?" Ruth asked.

"Because he just sent me a threatening text from a new phone number."

"*Shit.*" Ruth breathed. "Sorry for cursing."

"Yeah, well, maybe you could get back in contact with his parole officer and let them know that it's going really well so far," Josie said.

"I'll do that first thing tomorrow morning when his office opens." Ruth hesitated. "Are you at home right now?"

"No, I'm currently in Vegas at my brother's wedding. I haven't been back to my apartment since I got out of the hospital."

"That's good, I think." There was a rustle of papers.

"You're based at your brother's California ranch right now, correct?"

"Yup."

"Would it be hard for someone to get to you there?"

"I can make it hard." Josie was amazed that instead of crying she was absolutely furious. "I'm also a very good shot."

"Then I'd head back there. By the time you're settled, I hope I'll have him off the streets again."

"Thanks."

"I'll speak to you tomorrow."

"Looking forward to it." Josie ended the call, put her phone on charge, and climbed into bed. She went to turn out the light and hesitated. Maybe she'd leave the light on just in case.

Chapter Thirteen

Josie had been home for two days and Evan still hadn't managed to see her in person. The first day was on him because he'd been needed to move part of the herd out of a field where Morgan Creek had burst its banks. It had been raining for three days straight now, which wasn't typical, and made everyone as miserable as hell.

Sure, they'd texted each other regularly, but he was beginning to wonder whether something had happened in Vegas to make her lose interest. Had a weekend away from the sameness and smallness of Morgan Valley made her realize she was done with it? He'd heard that her boss, Graham Howatch, had attended the wedding. Maybe he'd made her an offer she couldn't refuse.

Evan hated all this stupid worrying. It wasn't his thing.

His cell buzzed and he took it out of his jacket pocket as he strode toward the post office in town.

Want to meet in Yvonne's? I just got there.

He sent Josie a thumbs-up, collected the family mail, and hightailed it back along the boardwalk to the café. He spotted her immediately sitting toward the rear of the room facing the door.

"Hey." He searched her face as he approached the table. "What's up?"

She sighed. "Stuff."

"Bad stuff?" he asked, taking a seat. "You look like you haven't been sleeping much."

"I haven't." She pushed her dark hair away from her face, her fingers lingering on the small scar on her cheek.

"Did something happen at the wedding?" Evan had never minded being the one to ask all the awkward questions, but sometimes getting information out of Josie was hard work.

"The wedding went great."

Lizzie appeared and set a mug of coffee made just as he liked it in front of Evan. He winked at her.

"Congrats."

She blushed. "About time, right?" She showed him her left hand. "Look what Adam got me."

Evan pretended to blink at the sparkling diamond. "Now I know where all the profits from the ranch are going."

"Don't be silly." Lizzie grinned. "This was Leanne's engagement ring."

"Not from my dad," Evan pointed out. "I bet he didn't even buy her one."

"He did, and she still wears it on her right hand," Lizzie said. "But this one was definitely from Declan. It's kind of cool of her to hand it down to Adam, although, I'm terrified I'm going to lose it."

"Mom wouldn't care."

"But I would." Lizzie smiled and went out to help another customer. Evan turned back to his silent companion.

"Adam and Lizzie have set a date?" Josie asked.

"Yeah, next month at home in our backyard." He smiled at her. "You're invited, obviously."

"I'm not sure if I'll be here then."

Evan's smile faded. "Oh, yeah, of course. I forgot." He sipped his coffee, for once at a loss for words—or for once maybe he was just afraid to ask all the right questions.

Josie seemed to gather herself. "Evan . . ."

He held up his hand. "It's okay. I know what you're going to say. We had a great time together, and I'm always going to be your friend whatever happens."

Her brow creased. "You think I'm breaking up with you?"

"Sure sounds like you are."

"Is that what you want?" She regarded him seriously. "I mean, maybe it would be for the best, because I'm not sure if I want you to have to get involved in what might happen next."

He frowned. "Hold up. What are you talking about now?"

"The thing I was going to tell you before you decided to break up with me!" Josie folded her arms over her chest.

"I'm not the one bailing here." He held her gaze. "Can we have a redo?"

"You two lovebirds fighting?" Kaiden slid into the

empty seat between them and grinned. "Mind you, putting up with Evan must be a full-time job."

"Go away, Kaiden," Evan said through his teeth. "This isn't a good time."

"I need the key to your apartment. Mom said the sash window in the front is sticking or something. She has the spare, but she's out with Dad in Bridgeport today, and has it with her."

"Fine." Evan dug in his pocket for his key and handed it over. "Don't forget to give it back."

"I won't." Kaiden stood and tipped his hat to Josie. "Nice to see you."

Kaiden had barely left before Yvonne came out of the kitchen and headed straight for Josie.

"Are you okay? Rio said—"

"It's getting way too crowded in here." Josie stood up. "I have to go." She turned to Evan. "You know that thing on my list? I think we should do it as soon as possible."

"I hear ya." Evan nodded. "I'll text you."

He got what she was trying to say. Having a conversation in a town where everyone knew your name and your business was never going to be easy.

Yvonne sighed as Josie exited the shop. "Dammit, I didn't mean to freak her out. I'm just worried about her."

"Me, too." Evan looked up. "Anything I need to know?"

"Nothing I can tell you without betraying her confidence," Yvonne said. "I'm sorry."

"That's okay." Evan finished his coffee and stood up. "If I can get her alone for five minutes, I'm sure she'll tell me herself. Have a good day, Yvonne, and congrats on your marriage. Rio's a good guy."

He picked through the mail as he walked back to his

truck. He didn't like the feeling of being excluded, which was stupid seeing as he and Josie had only been together for a few weeks. Now that he knew she wasn't planning on dumping his ass, he'd do everything in his power to support and help her through whatever the hell was going on. And if that meant planning a midnight trip to Morganville to stir up a few ghosts just so he could get her alone, then that was what he would do.

"Hey, you're Josie, right?" Nate Turner came out of his office at the rear of the sheriff's office and shook her hand. "Rio's sister."

"Correct."

After rushing out of the café as if someone was chasing her, she forced herself to slow down and made her way along the boardwalk to the sheriff's office, which was right next door to Daisy's flower shop.

Nate ushered her into his sparsely furnished office and offered her a seat before returning to sit behind his desk.

"What can I do for you?"

Josie steadied her breathing. "This is probably going to sound way over the top, but the guy who trashed my apartment in San Francisco and attacked me has been released early from prison for good behavior."

Nate made a face. "That's not good."

"The problem is that he's already contacted me and says he knows where I am."

"Do you think that's true, or is he just trying to scare you?"

"One of the problems with having a very famous brother is that finding out where he lives is easy." Josie grimaced. "And, seeing as the only two places I'd probably be right now, if I'm not at work, would be with my mother in Brazil, or with my brother in Morgan Valley, it's highly likely he's worked it out."

"So, you are justifiably worried that he might turn up here and try again." Nate nodded.

Josie tried to control an instinctive shudder. "Yes, and thanks for not making me feel like a hysterical idiot."

Nate frowned. "You're certainly not that. Did you report the new threat to the authorities in San Francisco?"

"I told my attorney that Rob had already violated the conditions of the existing restraining order. She called me this morning to let me know that she'd contacted his probation officer and that he hadn't turned up for their first meeting."

"Damn." Nate frowned. "He's already running."

"They've sent out a statewide alert, but he's not exactly a high priority." Josie shrugged. "It's not like he murdered someone or anything."

Only because he was unlucky. . . . The thought wouldn't leave Josie's head. *He'll be way more careful next time.*

Nate wrote some notes. "Do you have contact details for your attorney and the relevant department dealing with this in San Francisco?"

"Here you go." Josie had already written out the pertinent information and she handed it over to Nate. "I know there's probably very little you can do, but—"

He looked up at her, his gaze steady. "I'll do everything I can to keep you safe, Josie. One good thing is that strangers stick out around here. Once I send out an alert with his picture on it . . . ? Everyone in the valley will be on your team and looking out for him."

"Thank you," Josie said as she rose to her feet. "Rio's obviously beefed up the security around the ranch as well."

"Good to know." Nate nodded as he tidied his notes and stood up. He handed her a business card. "And keep in touch. My personal number is on there. Don't ever think you're bothering me if anything feels wrong. Just let me know, even if you feel stupid doing it."

"Thank you, Nate." Josie smiled for the first time in days. "I genuinely feel better with you knowing what's going on."

"All part of my job." He walked her through the main office and to the front door, which led onto Main Street. "Take care now."

Josie had parked Rio's truck right outside the sheriff's department and hopped up into the driving seat, her gaze immediately checking the back seat just in case. She should've known that trying to talk to Evan in public wouldn't have gone well, but she'd wanted to give him an out if he'd balked at what she was going to tell him.

Well, that hadn't worked. Josie carefully backed out of the parking spot and headed home to the ranch. Hopefully, if Evan was half as resourceful as she knew he was, he'd already be busy arranging their midnight adventure for two.

She stopped at the stop sign and took a left past the Red Dragon Bar onto the county road. Even if her attacker did come to Morgan Valley, she doubted he'd find her in a ghost town. She was no longer prepared to live her life in fear. Coming so close to the thought of her own death had taught her something vital. If Rob did turn up, he should be prepared to face a whole new woman.

* * *

"Where are you going?"

The hushed whisper made Evan freeze in his tracks and slowly turn his head back toward the kitchen door where Adam was standing, his eyebrows raised. It was ten-thirty at night, the moon was full, and Evan was all locked and loaded for his trip.

"Got something to do," Evan said vaguely. "I'll be back in the morning. You won't even notice I've gone."

"Like what exactly?"

"Nothing criminal."

Adam sighed. "That's not actually as reassuring as you might think it is."

"Look." Evan met Adam's gaze straight on. "I'll be up at Morganville with Josie. She wants to spend the night there."

"Okay." Adam nodded. "Don't do anything stupid."

"I'm not intending to."

"That never seems to matter with you, Bro. You attract trouble like flies on a corpse. Are you riding up there?"

"Yeah. I've got Joker and Milly all packed with supplies and ready to go, so don't freak out tomorrow morning if they're still missing."

"But you said you'd be back before I'd notice."

"I'll certainly try." Evan hedged his bets. "I've got my phone. I'll call if there are any problems."

"Good." Adam smothered a yawn. "Now get out of here before you wake up the whole house."

Evan, who had only made the trip back to the house because he'd forgotten to grab his back-up ski jacket, skedaddled. When he reached the barn, he attached a leading rope to Milly's bridle and mounted up on Joker. Both horses carried large packs filled with all the things Evan had decided Josie deserved to have up at Morganville, which was in his opinion one of the saddest, most barren places in the universe.

He'd even checked in with the Morgans to make sure the family knew they'd be out there, and they wouldn't get shot for trespassing. The local teens who still made the annual pilgrimage up there at Halloween were also allowed but were definitely kept a discreet eye on. No one wanted a repeat of the near disaster when some of the ranch guests had almost ended up inside the collapsing abandoned silver mine.

With the moon being full and the skies clear, Evan had no problem navigating his way through the local ranchlands until he arrived on the hill overlooking the slumbering Martinez spread. There were lights between the barns, the house, and the outbuildings, but most of the main house was dark. Evan took out his phone and texted Josie.

Within minutes, he noted a small figure detaching itself from the shadows and coming toward him. He was pleased to see she'd heeded his advice and had wrapped up well. Despite the milder weather during the day, the nights could be extremely cold due to the stiff breezes coming off the still-snow-laden peaks of the Sierra Nevada mountains.

He clicked to Joker and eased his way down the slope toward her.

"Hey," he whispered. "You good to go?"

Josie nodded and walked around Evan who was barely recognizable in all his dark gear to meet and greet Milly, her horse for the night. She'd snuck a carrot in her pocket and offered it palm up to the mare who took it with a whicker of thanks, a gentle lipping of Josie's skin, and a brush of feathery whiskers.

"She's a great horse. You won't have any problem with her," Evan said.

Josie adjusted the stirrups, checked the girth, and mounted up before gathering the reins and releasing the leading rope.

"How long will this take?" she asked as Evan coiled the loose rope up and secured it on the back of his saddle.

"We're approaching from the top of the valley, which means we're closer to the old town than Morgan Ranch is. It shouldn't take more than an hour even at night."

He showed her his cell. "I even got the gate codes from Ruth Morgan, so I don't set off their security alarms."

"Good for you." Josie settled into the saddle, glad for once of the warmth steaming off Milly's body. "I'm ready when you are."

Evan turned Joker's head toward the slope and Josie followed him. The silence around them was only broken by the grasshoppers, the occasional howl from a pack of coyotes in the distance, or the grazing cattle. For the first time in several days Josie regained a modicum of peace inside herself. There was something about listening and watching nature that made her realize how very small and insignificant her problems were.

As they climbed higher, the faint lights of the outlying ranches and the glimmer from the county road faded as did the sounds of life. Evan stopped ahead of her and waited until she caught up. He turned on his flashlight to reveal high barren walls of stripped-back white and gray chalky rock.

"This is where it all gets a bit weird. The channel was cut and blown through by the miners and comes out just above the old stamp mill where they used to process the ore. It's wide enough for a mule and a cart or two iron rails so stay behind me. I'll keep my flashlight on."

"Why is it so different up here?" Josie asked.

"Deforestation. They stripped the whole hillside of wood, lost the topsoil, and created a mini-desert." Evan grimaced. "There were sequoia trees here once. Can you even imagine that?"

"Not now." Josie fought an urge to cross herself. "It looks like pictures of the moon. No wonder no one likes coming up here anymore."

"You wait until you see the town."

Josie followed Evan through the echoing passageway. The walls were so high, she could only see a slim patch of the dark, night sky above her head. She was glad she wasn't claustrophobic because it seemed to take forever to get through the channel. She emerged onto a flat plane and the ruins of a stone structure that sat on the side of the creek.

"There's not much left of the stamping mill," Evan said. "The townsfolk basically took everything that wasn't nailed down and used it to rebuild lower in the valley."

Josie studied the low stone walls and patches of rusted metal that were all that remained of the structure and tried and failed to imagine it as a bustling busy enterprise.

"The silver got too expensive to be worth mining, the

creek dried up, and changed course, which meant they were screwed," Evan continued. "But I kind of admire the fact that rather than giving up and going back to wherever they'd come from, they regrouped and rebuilt."

"That is admirable," Josie agreed. "They were tough people."

"Yeah." Evan flashed her a smile. "Much tougher than I'll ever be. Can you imagine being a Miller or a Morgan and traveling halfway around the world just to follow the dream of getting rich from mining gold?"

Josie shook her head and Evan gathered his reins. "Let's move on. Morganville is just around the corner. There's an actual parking lot at both ends and a shelter where we can safely leave the horses."

"You seem to know a lot about the history," Josie commented as she followed him. There was no need to raise her voice in the complete absence of sound.

"I did some reading up today," Evan admitted. "Although we all grew up with the old stories. I used to think they were boring, but I've changed my mind. I mean, I work hard, but it's nothing compared to what these people went through." He stopped again and held up his flashlight even though with the full moon it was quite easy to see the layout of the town. "This is a good place to get an overview of what's left before we head on down."

"It looks like the buildings were dropped out of the sky," Josie said softly. "And they look almost eerily perfect."

"It's very dry up here. It takes a long time for anything to fall down, but they aren't structurally sound. One of the things the Morgantown Historical Society is doing is shoring up each building without it being too obvious."

Josie's gaze moved from one low building to the next. "There's no . . . context. I mean, apart from them being in one straight line. There aren't any gardens or trees or anything really."

"All disappeared in the dust," Evan agreed. He pointed at a large structure at the end of what was left of the street. "That was the bank. The metal safe is still in the back wall since no one could get it out of there. If you walk down to the other end of the street, you'll get to a second parking lot, which is right next door to where the original Morgan family livery stables was built."

Josie shivered. "I'm beginning to understand why no one feels comfortable up here even in the daylight."

"Do you want to go back?" Evan asked. "I mean, technically you've ticked this one off your list. You don't have to actually stay here."

"It's as if everyone just up and went outside and never came back," Josie continued her thoughts out loud. "Like a movie set."

"Hey."

She looked back at Evan who was regarding her intently. He was really good at noticing when she wasn't comfortable, which still surprised her.

"We don't have to stay, Josie."

She gathered herself and smiled in return. "Did you say there was somewhere to stable the horses? I can't wait to get in there and explore on foot."

He didn't answer her directly, but he did click to Joker and move off, leaving Josie to follow behind. To her surprise, both the parking lot and the stalls for the horses were well maintained. There were glass framed poster boards detailing all the relevant structures with their histories and the names of the people who had lived there.

"Any Millers up here?" Josie asked.

"Not as far as I know." Evan dismounted and spent a moment petting Joker. "We were second-wave immigrants and came for the land rather than the gold. I *think* we have some connection with the Morgan family because someone wrote to my great-granddad and suggested he come out here."

"I should imagine that happened a lot," Josie said. "I mean, how else would you even know this valley existed?"

"I'm glad it's not overrun with people," Evan said. "I like it just the way it is."

Josie dismounted and led Milly toward the fenced-in paddock. "It's good that we can keep the horses safe up here."

"The Morgans worked out that people were always going to want to come and see this place and that the best way to try and preserve it was to stop four-wheeled vehicles on the site, allow horses, and just let people walk around."

Evan pointed out some metal posts with boxes on the top and waved. "There's some twenty-four-hour high-tech security cameras up there. If anyone tries to make off with anything substantial, they'll be caught before they get off Morgan land."

"They know we're here, right?" Josie asked as they dealt with the horses.

"Yup. I got the Ruth Morgan seal of approval." He hoisted one set of the saddlebags over his shoulder. "Would Madam like to choose which dwelling she wishes to reside in? And can you make it close by, so I don't have to lug everything too far?"

She grinned at him. "I can help with the bags, you know. Where do most people end up?"

He pointed at a clapboard house about three doors past the bank. "That's the original Morgan family house. It's got a fairly decent floor and the walls are stable."

"Then let's set up in there."

"Best to go in through the back," he advised her as they walked along the eerily quiet street. "It's more open."

She took his advice and walked around to the rear of the property, which wasn't as closed in as the front. Stepping over some debris, she found herself in what she assumed had once been the Morgan family parlor. There were still strips of wallpaper visible on the walls and a rusting cast-iron grate still fronted the crude, stone-built fireplace. As Evan set down his bags, the stillness descended again. The velvety darkness was so thick, Josie could almost taste it on her tongue.

"I'll get the lanterns out." Oblivious to the elements playing through Josie's head, Evan was already on the move again. "Do you want to stay here and unpack while I get the second load?"

"Alone?"

Evan grinned at her. "You scared already?"

"No, I'm—"

His grin faded and he stepped toward her. "Hey, I didn't mean that you shouldn't be scared. I was just kidding, which was stupid of me, but what do you expect? I'm—"

She pressed her gloved fingertip to his lips. "I'm fine. Why don't you go and get the other bags?"

For some reason it did actually feel safer inside the old house than it had outside. There was still a sense of something—a warmth and echo of the people who had once lived and thrived there until it became too difficult to continue.

Evan came back in with his second load of bags and grinned at her.

"You look pretty in the lamplight."

"Not as pretty as you." She went over to give him a kiss. "What can I do to help?"

"You can roll out the mats and put the sleeping bags and pillows out while I make a fire in the old hearth. Ruth said the chimney still works." Evan was already busy taking things out. "I've got hot soup and coffee somewhere."

"No hot chocolate?" Josie unrolled one of the mats.

"Like I'd forget your favorite." He set three large flasks on the wide windowsill. "I even wrote on the lids so that we wouldn't get a nasty shock when we tasted something."

"I'm impressed," Josie said.

He shrugged. "I wanted to make it a great experience for you."

"You always do."

Their eyes met in the lamplight and Josie couldn't look away.

Outside, the wind rattled the front of the building, making them both jump. Evan knelt down in front of the fireplace.

"I'll get the fire going. My theory is that if we stay in the light then no ghosts are going to turn up and get us."

Josie plumped up the pillows and put them next to each other. "Not all ghosts are bad, you know. I can already sense that this place is full of happy memories."

"You can?"

It was her turn to shrug. "I've always had a strong reaction to places. If it had felt bad in here, I would've been out that door in a second."

"Good to know."

Evan returned his attention to the fire and soon coaxed it to life, despite the unhelpful drafts that continued to run through the structure. Josie sat down on one of the fold-out chairs Evan had also managed to bring with him. She appreciated the silence and the complete absence of background noise she normally only realized was missing when there was a power outage.

She tried to imagine living with the constant howling winds, the bitter cold, and the constant fear that you had made a terrible mistake moving west and that your livelihood was disappearing in front of your eyes. But the Morgans and the other townspeople hadn't given up. They'd made the best of it, voted to move their entire existence to a different location that was lower in the valley, and hoped for the best.

There was a lesson to be learned from their resilience, and Josie was more than willing to learn it. For some reason it felt very real to her right now.

Evan stood up and dusted off his hands. "That should burn okay for the rest of the night." He glanced over at Josie. "Do you just want to sit for a while or are you ready to turn in?"

"I think I'll sit," Josie said. "I'm wide-awake now."

"Then I'll join you." Evan drew up the second chair and sat at an angle to her, his body blocking some of the gusts from the cracked windowpanes. "I can't exactly say I like this place, but I've always found that if I want to think about something with no distractions it's kind of like a blank canvas."

"That totally makes sense." Josie nodded.

"When my mom decided to come back to Morgan Valley after all those years away from us, I wasn't sure how I felt about it. Dad wouldn't talk about her often, and when he did, he made it sound like she'd died." He half smiled. "And for a long while, I was okay with that because if she was dead, it meant she hadn't been able to come back rather than choosing not to.

"But when Dad said she was coming home, all hell broke loose." He sighed. "Adam wasn't talking, but I knew he was furious; Ben went quiet and Kaiden and Danny were fine about it. I was so young when she left, that I didn't really know how I felt." He looked over at Josie. "I knew I was supposed to feel 'something,' but what? There was no one I could talk to about it at home. I came up here and stared into space for an afternoon to get my head around it."

"Did it help?" Josie asked.

"Yeah, with no one around to influence my way of thinking, I realized I was okay with her coming back. I guess I really wanted to hear her side of the story because I was sure as hell that Dad wasn't being fair on her. She loved us like crazy, and if she hadn't died there had to have been a really good reason why she hadn't returned."

"And was there?"

"Dad." He grimaced. "He did everything he could to

stop her from seeing us, contacting us, or even writing to us. We only got to see the birthday cards she'd lovingly sent us every damn year after Adam made a big deal about her silence and Dad finally brought them all out. When she'd threatened to take Dad to court to get access to us, he told her he'd take us away and she'd never get to see us again in her lifetime."

Josie reached for his hand and held it tight. "I didn't know any of this. I'm kind of surprised that everyone's still talking to your *father* not your mother."

"He was a complete ass," Evan agreed. "But he did stick around and raise us."

"Because that was his *job*," Josie said. "You were his kids, too."

"I know that. Maybe it just made me realize that people are complicated—that no one's one hundred percent right or wrong—and that sometimes people make mistakes for all the right reasons."

"And sometimes they're just complete jerks," Josie muttered.

Evan squeezed her fingers. "Hey, don't start on my dad next time you see him. He's changed a lot recently, admitted his mistakes, and taken responsibility for screwing us over on the mother front."

Josie still wasn't happy. "As I've mentioned before, Evan, you are definitely a much nicer person than I'll ever be."

He chuckled. "I'm the baby brother of the family. That's kind of my job description." Josie stood up and he looked wary. "What did I say?"

"I want to kiss you, but I'm worried that if I sit on your lap that chair will collapse."

"How about I just stand up and make it easy for you?"

She went into his arms, pulled his head down to meet hers, and kissed him as fiercely as she could.

"Wow." He eased slightly back. "I feel kind of possessed here."

She glared at him. "Your family sucks."

"I know that."

"You are a saint!"

"Far from it." He sighed. "I've always gotten away with murder. I've skipped out and let everyone else deal with all the shit and I let my favorite brother down bigtime."

She kissed him again. "Okay, maybe you're not perfect, but I like you."

"Yeah?" His smile warmed her soul. "Well, that's good because I like you a lot, too."

It was his turn to lower his mouth to hers and kiss her while the wind wrapped itself around them and the house creaked, groaned, and swayed above their heads.

"We were supposed to be talking about you," Evan reminded her when they finally drew apart.

She grimaced. "I was trying to forget that."

"Do you want to get comfortable in the sleeping bags while we talk? We can zip them together for warmth."

"I'm not getting completely undressed," she warned him.

"Neither am I. I'm just taking off my coat and boots and going in fully clothed." He removed his thick ski jacket and stepped out of his boots. "Gah, it's cold."

Josie did the same and rushed to get inside the sleeping bag that was farthest away from the window.

She propped herself up against the two pillows. "You did great on the supplies, Evan. I'm totally impressed."

"I aim to please, ma'am." He reached for the flasks. "I guess you want the hot chocolate?"

"Maybe some soup to start with." She sighed. "I haven't felt like eating much since I got back from Vegas."

"That bad, eh?" He poured some of the soup into a cup and handed her the flask. "It's tomato. Adam made it for lunch yesterday."

"He's such a good cook."

"Someone had to help Auntie Rae after Mom left."

"What was your job?" Josie sipped the excellent soup.

"As I said, as the youngest boy I pretty much got away with looking pathetic and doing nothing—except with my dad, who wasn't as easy to fool as Rae. He had us all working before and after school. He said it cut down on the ranch hand salaries."

"Child labor, right." Josie sniffed. "What a shocker."

Evan nudged her. "You know as well as I do that if you live on a ranch you pretty much have to pitch in the moment you're capable of getting on the back of your pony."

"Not at my mother's place."

"Well, your mom is superrich, to be fair," Evan reminded her. "We were barely surviving, and everyone had to help." He put his arm around her shoulders. "And, hey, you wouldn't be procrastinating right now by getting all bent out of shape over my family rather than telling me what's going on with you?"

She scowled. "Maybe, but still, your family situation does need discussing."

He set down his empty mug on the floorboards. "Are you done?"

"With the soup or the procrastinating?" Josie asked.

"Both?"

"Okay." She sighed, handed over the flask, and settled back down, her head on his shoulder.

"So, what's up?"

"Remember when I told you about my apartment being broken into?"

"Yeah."

"Well, I didn't tell you everything." She took a hasty breath. "The guy who broke in. He found me hiding in the closet, dragged me out by the hair, and smashed my face into a mirror."

"*Shit*," Evan breathed.

"I was lucky because by the time he found me, I'd already called nine-one-one and my building security so they caught him before he did too much damage to the place."

"I don't care if he trashed your place." Evan eased his finger under her chin and gently touched the scar on her cheek. "He damn well hurt you. That's way too much damage for me."

"Yes." She tried to smile. "He said that if I wouldn't go out with him, he'd make sure no one else would want to go out with me ever again."

She remembered his blank face and wide, black pupils over her shoulder in the mirror, the excruciatingly painful grip of his fist in her hair as he smashed her face into the glass.

"He was your ex-boyfriend?"

"That's the weirdest thing. He worked in my office building. I'd said hi to him a couple of times in the elevator or in passing, but I barely knew his name, let alone that he'd developed some crazy fixation about me being his next girlfriend."

She shivered and Evan drew her even closer. She wanted to curl up in his arms and just forget everything, but she had to tell him the rest of it.

"He was arrested and charged, and a restraining order was put in place, but apparently he's been let out of prison early for good behavior." Josie tried to lighten her tone. "He ghosted his parole officer and sent me a text saying he's coming after me."

For a long moment, Evan didn't react as she remained frozen by his side. When she dared to look up, all traces of the man she thought she knew had disappeared.

"Are you okay?" Josie asked tentatively.

He finally looked down at her, a muscle working in his jaw. "I'm going to find him and kill him."

"No, you are not!" She thumped his chest. "If anyone gets to kill him it's going to be me!"

Chapter Fourteen

It was still only five in the morning when Evan let himself back into the house, took off his boots, and shed his many layers of clothing. He'd taken Josie back home, dealt with the horses, and was looking forward to something substantial to eat to keep him going through another day of hard work. He was still trying to figure out how he felt about what Josie had told him earlier. He'd never considered himself a violent man, but if he ever met that sleazeball up close and personal, he'd have no compunction in introducing the guy to his fist.

He tiptoed through the unusually quiet house into the kitchen and stopped short when he saw Danny sitting at the table.

"I made coffee. It's still hot," Danny said.

Evan helped himself to a mug and leaned up against the countertop to survey his brother who wasn't looking his normal happy self.

"Why are you up so early?"

Danny's smile was brief. "Couldn't sleep."

"Where's Faith?"

"She's gone to pick up her parents from the airport." He cradled his mug in his hands and stared into his coffee as if it held all the secrets of the universe.

"You didn't go with her?"

"She didn't want me to." He drank a slug of coffee.

"Okay." Evan sidled closer and sat down on one of the chairs.

"I guess they have things to say to each other that she doesn't want me to hear." Danny shrugged. "It's no secret that the last person they wanted her to get involved with again was me."

Evan considered what to say. Last time he'd offered his older brother advice, he'd been shot down in flames and was still reeling from the blowback.

"That's a tough situation," Evan agreed, and sipped his coffee again.

"Yeah, and Faith's kind of stuck in the middle."

"I'm sure she'll set them straight. I mean, I don't think she's going to be calling you to say she's decided to get a divorce anytime soon because they can't be happy for their only daughter."

Danny's head came up and he stared hard at Evan.

Even as he'd finished speaking, Evan wanted to take the words back. He was getting way too personal again. Hadn't he learned anything? He held up his hand and said hastily, "Not that I know anything about anything of course, so feel free to tell me to shut up."

"Evan, I'm just glad you're sitting here talking to me right now."

"Really?" Evan tried to keep the skepticism out of his voice.

Danny looked down at his mug again. "The thing is—and I definitely can't say this to Faith. I'm not sure I want to see her parents—*period*. They lied to her and to me and I'm not in a very forgiving place right now. What if I see them, they say something stupid, and I lose my temper? That wouldn't help them accept our marriage."

Evan nodded. "So, maybe letting Faith handle it is the best solution?"

"Maybe." Danny finished his coffee. "How was Morganville?"

Evan accepted the abrupt change of subject with alacrity. "Creepy as hell and so cold, I thought my dick might freeze off."

"Shouldn't have got it out, then."

"I was speaking metaphorically. Josie and I were just . . . talking."

"Did you see any ghosts?"

"Josie said she did, but I went right to sleep and only woke up at three in time to pack up and leave."

"She's really nice."

"She's one of the strongest people I've ever met." Evan finished his coffee. "I might as well give you a heads-up before you hear it from Nate. Josie had some stalker guy after her in San Francisco who tried to kill her because she wouldn't be his fake girlfriend."

"Come again?" Danny blinked at him.

"The guy's out and about and apparently headed this way. If you see him, shoot him right between the eyes, okay?"

"You're the best shot in the family." Danny winced.

"Poor Josie. I guess that's why she came to stay at Rio's place."

"I guess." Evan stood up. "I'm getting some breakfast. Do you want anything?"

"Mom said she left some healthy overnight oat pots in the refrigerator if you want one of those."

"Cold, wet oats?" Evan screwed up his face. "*Hell,* no. I'm making bacon, eggs, and pancakes."

Danny rose, too, and smiled for the first time. "When you put it like that, I think I'll join you."

"Any news?"

Rio came into the kitchen where Josie was having a late lunch with Ines. After returning from Morganville, she'd taken a long nap and had only just woken up.

"I haven't checked my phone. I forgot to charge it last night," Josie said.

Rio helped himself to some coffee. "I've spoken to my father. He's making sure everyone in your old department knows about what's happening with Rob. They will keep an eye out for him hanging around the building and report any suspicious activity to the police."

"Good to know." Josie ate some more eggs. "I doubt he'd risk being seen back there. He wasn't stupid."

"True." Rio sighed and reached over to take her hand. "I'm so sorry about this, Josie."

"It's not your fault or your problem, *mano,*" Josie reminded him.

"You're still my baby sister and I tend to take it personally when someone I love gets hurt." He studied her carefully. "You're a lot calmer than I'd be in this situation."

"I doubt it." She smiled. "Maybe I just got better at holding it together. This time I know who he is, and what he's capable of, and I'm not going to be paralyzed with fear if he dares to come near me again."

Even as she said the words, Josie hoped they were true, but she was angry now rather than afraid and she much preferred that feeling. Last time when Rob had talked his way past security at her apartment block and knocked on her door, she hadn't been expecting him or his uncontrollable rage when she'd refused to let him in. Her fear had turned to blind panic, and rather than using the time to run down the fire escape at the rear of her apartment, she'd spent precious moments frozen in the hallway watching in disbelief as he steadily smashed down her door with a fire extinguisher.

When she'd finally managed to run, she'd hidden in her closet like a five-year-old playing a game—not a woman facing a delusional man who was primed to be violent. Even as law enforcement had spoken all the right words about her not being to blame, she'd absolutely blamed herself.

"I'll just get my phone." Josie stood up and went to her bedroom, the mellow feeling she'd gained at Morganville talking and being with Evan rapidly dissipating in the harsh reality of the day.

She brought her cell back into the kitchen where Rio was still sitting at the table talking intently to Ines in Portuguese.

"You know I can understand you, right?" Josie said. "I'm not Yvonne."

Rio's smile was edged with concern. "Yvonne just texted me to ask if you wanted her to come home and stay with you today. She says it's not that busy."

"It's not busy because you two are supposed to be on your honeymoon," Josie reminded him. "Yvonne cleared her calendar so she could have that special time with you, not me."

"We can do that later." He shrugged. "Family is more important to both of us."

"And I'm here." Isabelle came into the kitchen and immediately hugged Josie to her bosom. "I'll look after you." She put her hands on Josie's shoulders and gently shook her. "Why didn't you *tell* me about that horrible man?"

"Because I didn't want you to worry about me."

"Rio said he tried to *kill* you!"

Josie shot her brother a pointed look. He shrugged and looked guilty as hell.

"It wasn't that bad."

"But I'm your mother!" Isabelle sounded shocked. "You used to tell me everything!"

She sat down and took Josie's hand in hers. "I will not let you out of my sight. If that man thinks he can get to you again, he is *very* mistaken." She turned to Rio. "I can send for some armed guards if you wish, *meu filho?* Men who are loyal to me?"

"I think we've got things covered, *Mamãe*," Rio reassured her.

"I know—why don't you come home with me, Josie?"

Isabelle asked. "I have full-time security. I can keep you much safer on my ranch."

"I don't think the authorities would want me to leave the country right now," Josie said. "Trying to protect me in a public place like an airport would be hard."

"We could take a private plane from Morgan Ranch." Isabelle disposed of Josie's objections in one airy wave of her hand. "I'm sure Graham would be more than willing to lend us one of his fleet."

"*Mamãe* . . ." Josie met her mother's gaze. "I'm not going anywhere."

"But why? I mean—"

"I'm not prepared to run any farther."

Isabelle raised her chin and looked at her son. "Rio, tell your sister to listen to me."

Rio came to stand behind Josie and put his hand on her shoulder. "I won't do that, *Mamãe*. She's old enough to make her own decisions and I understand what she's saying."

"You want her to be killed?" Isabelle pressed her hands to her chest, her voice rising. "Your own sister? How can you do that to your mother?"

"Stop it." Josie spoke more loudly than she had perhaps intended, and everyone stared at her. "Stop it right now. This is not about you."

Isabelle gasped. "I am not—"

"Yes, you are." Josie stood up. "I love you, Mom, but I need you to listen to me. I'm staying here. If that bastard finds me, I can assure you, he'll regret it."

She held her mother's tear-filled gaze. "You taught me how to defend myself. You know I'm capable. Now allow me to deal with this myself."

Isabelle rose, too, her mouth trembling. "I can see that I am not wanted here. Please excuse me. I will retire to my room and start packing."

She left, her nose in the air, and Josie looked at her brother.

"Why did you tell her anything?"

"Because I forgot what she's like!" He shoved a hand through his hair. "I'll go and calm her down. The last thing we need is her storming out like a drama queen and complicating everything."

"Good luck," Josie muttered as he strode after their mother.

She resumed her seat and picked up her phone. Ines passed her a new plate of hot, buttered toast.

"You were right to say what you did. She'll calm down."

"Eventually," Josie replied. "And if anyone can get her to do it, it's Rio."

"Have you heard anything else from that horrible man?" Ines asked.

"Nope, but I did block his number. Nate seemed to think he'd use a burner phone to avoid being picked up anyway."

Ines frowned. "How does he have the money to do all these things when he has just got out of prison?"

"He was barely in there, Ines, and he had a good job as a software developer, so I doubt he was short of cash." Josie typed in her password and checked her messages. "Nate says they are checking all the incoming local airport flights, but they think if he really does want to come out here and get me, he'll drive."

"Would he take his own car?" Ines asked hopefully.

"Apparently not, since it's still sitting in his driveway. There are about a thousand places he could rent a car in San Francisco, so it's taking them a while to find out whether he did or not." She flipped through a whole series of messages from her co-workers and a couple of Morgan Valley residents and stopped at a newer one from Nate.

"Ah, apparently, his mom reported her car as stolen this morning, which is helpful."

Rio had reentered the kitchen. "What kind of *idiota* borrows his mom's car?"

"The smart kind who knows his mom keeps her handgun in the glove compartment." Josie continued reading Nate's message. "Great. Just great."

"Okay." Rio sat beside her. "I know you're not going to like this, but I think *Mamãe* has a point. I'm going to get you one-on-one security, twenty-four seven."

"I don't want that."

"I think we're beyond what you want, Josie, and dealing with what you need to stay safe and alive." Rio definitely wasn't playing anymore. "I would never forgive myself if I didn't do everything in my power to keep you from getting hurt."

"That's not fair." Josie glared at her brother. "You're trying to guilt me into doing something that makes me feel extremely uncomfortable."

His brow creased. "I'm trying to keep you safe."

"By making me put up with a complete stranger when you know I'm not comfortable with men right now. And for how long, Rio? Days, weeks, months? What about if they never catch Rob?"

Ines gently cleared her throat. "If you would prefer someone local to help out, Rio, you could ask Jay Williams to recommend one of his retired military buddies. Or you could ask Evan?" Ines looked inquiringly at Rio. "He's an excellent shot and I'm sure he'd be more than happy to spend every moment of his time with Josie if you squared it with Jeff."

"He's not trained, Ines," Rio insisted.

Josie leaned back and crossed her arms over her chest. "I'm not having someone foisted on me that I don't know."

"Then I'll talk to Jay." Rio rose to his feet. "Just do me one favor, Sis? Don't leave the ranch without someone with you, okay?"

"Fine," Josie said. "But I'm still not happy about any of it."

"Adam, can I ask you something?"

"What?"

His brother's tone wasn't encouraging, but it rarely was. Evan made sure Joker was walking perfectly in line with Adam's big horse, Spot, as they rode down to check the water meadows next to Morgan Creek.

"Do you think we should all be madder at Dad?"

"About what?"

"Everything." Evan made an expansive gesture. "I mean, he basically kicked Mom out, stopped her contacting us, and threatened to hide us away if she ever went to court to exercise her legal right to see any of us."

"When you put it like that it does sound bad," Adam said.

"And yet, if you listen to the local gossips, Mom's the one who's seen as the problem because she abandoned us, and apparently that's unforgiveable."

"And if you'd asked me a few years ago, I would've agreed with them." Adam leaned down to unhook the gate and waited until Evan came through before reattaching the chain. "Even though I was old enough to watch it all happen in real time, I still made a lot of wrong assumptions. I blamed Mom when maybe I should've been more even-handed with that."

"I read somewhere that when one parent leaves, suddenly the kids are so scared the other might go too, that they cling on really hard to the one that's left even if that parent is part of the problem," Evan offered.

"Makes sense." Adam nodded; his gaze fixed on the creek below. "I guess I didn't have a lot of time to think about it back then. I was too busy trying to cover Mom's chores, keep it together at school, and stop the other kids from being unkind to you all at recess."

"I don't remember much about it," Evan admitted. "By the time I got to second grade, the worst of it was over, and everyone just felt sorry for me."

"Lucky you." Adam's expression had turned inward. "The thing is, Evan, what do you want to do about it now? Calling Dad out when he's trying to be a better man, make amends, and acknowledging his faults seems kind of unnecessary."

"But doesn't that mean he just gets away with it?"

This time Adam smiled. "You obviously haven't heard

the rest of us having it out with him over the past few years. I think he knows how we feel."

He broke off and leaned forward in the saddle, his gaze intent. "Do you see that guy down by the creek?"

Evan followed the direction of Adam's pointing finger. "Yeah, cattle rustler, pot grower, or something else?"

"How about we go and find out?" Adam gathered his reins and started off down the slope as Evan checked the weapon at his hip.

They had almost reached level ground when the guy seemed to spot them and turned and ran back up the rocky slope on the other side of the creek. Adam didn't stop but carried on through the stream making a big splash with Evan following.

"Dammit."

They both heard the sound of an engine revving. When Evan reached the top of the slope, there was nothing to see except some muddy tire tracks and the rapidly retreating rear end of an SUV on the unpaved road.

"Did you get a picture?" Evan asked Adam.

"I tried." Adam held out his phone to Evan who made a face at the blurry image of the vehicle. "It's hard to manage a horse on a slope and a phone."

"I'll send it to Nate anyway." Evan took off his gloves and started typing. "Whoever the guy is, he was on private property." He frowned at his phone. "It won't send. The reception here by the creek is lousy."

Adam looked around. "Whose land is this?"

Evan tried to get his bearings and then stared at his big brother. "It's the very edge of the Ramirez Ranch."

Adam cursed under his breath. "How about you ride over there and give them a heads-up while I call Nate?"

Evan handed Adam his phone back. "You'll have to go back up the slope on the other side to get better reception."

"I'm on it." He nodded at Evan. "Now go."

Chapter Fifteen

Josie tried to text Evan, but for some reason, his cell wasn't receiving messages, so she strolled outside and went over to the bull breeding barn to see if Jaime had anything that needed doing. With Rio being home, there was always an increase in activity and a lot more tasks to perform. Jaime was awaiting a visit from the guys at the PBR who decided which new bulls to add to the available pool and was quite nervous about it.

After talking to Isabelle, Rio had disappeared into his office and Josie was quite happy to leave him there for a while. She knew he thought she was being unreasonable, but everyone telling her what she could and couldn't do when she wanted to deal with the problem herself was infuriating.

"Hey." Jaime was looking at one of the bulls that had been let out into the round pen. "And no, you're not riding this one."

Josie joined him at the fence and studied the sleek, powerful black-and-white bull as he prowled the small space and pawed at the ground.

"He still looks like a milk cow on steroids," she teased.

"Right now, he's our best hope of being picked for the PBR," Jaime said. "Rio said he wants to try him out and I'm going to video it."

"Sounds like fun. Are you sure you don't want me to ride him instead? I'm much more photogenic than my brother."

Jaime chuckled. "Josie, you know I love you, but there is nothing more beautiful on this earth than Rio Martinez on the back of a bull."

She nudged him hard in the ribs with her elbow. "Do you have his poster up on your wall as well?"

"'Course I do. Several of them in fact."

"No wonder he employed you." Josie shook her head. Jaime's devotion to Rio was well-known. "Then I'll leave you both to it. Tell Rio I'll be practicing my shooting."

"Will do."

Rio had created a shooting range just beyond the barn with proper targets set up at various points. Its steep sides formed a natural gully, meaning stray bullets weren't going anywhere. Josie collected the correct ear protectors and her 2.0 9mm M&P gun from the locked safe and headed out. Hopefully, shooting at a few harmless targets would help with her excess nervous energy. Shooting targets required both concentration and finesse, which would occupy her mind wonderfully.

She checked her phone and noticed it still hadn't charged properly. It wouldn't be the first time she'd accidentally pulled out the plug end of the charger in the wall and forgotten about it. She paused in the shade of the barn. Should she go back and recharge it first? She glanced down at the weapon in her hands and decided against it. No need to scare the bejesus out of her mom and Ines marching into the house fully armed, and she didn't want to waste time going back and securing everything again.

After twenty minutes of shooting, her restlessness still hadn't worn off and she decided to return to the house. As she walked back toward the barn her gaze was drawn to a large cloud of dust on the hill behind the ranch. She screwed up her eyes as she recognized a horse and rider coming fast like the pony express.

Even as she wondered who it was, an unknown SUV drove into the yard and came to a hurried stop. Josie stepped back into the shadows of the barn, her heart thumping so hard, she could hear it. She slowly slid her hand into her pocket to retrieve her phone and saw a screenful of messages from Nate and Adam.

Not that she needed to read them. Despite his baseball cap and dark glasses, she already knew Rob had found her. She checked her gun and took a step forward. If she could somehow get around to the other side of the car, which was currently blocking her view, she could get a good shot at him. . . .

"Josie? Is that you?" The back door of the house opened, and her mother came out and stopped dead, her gaze on Rob. "Hi!"

"Hi!" Rob was speaking way more quietly than her mom, and Josie couldn't hear the ensuing conversation.

To her horror, her mom kept smiling, linked her arm through Rob's, and led him into the house chatting away like they were already old friends.

"No . . ." Josie whispered. Dammit, she couldn't pass out right now! Her mother needed her. She took an unsteady step forward and someone wrapped an arm around her waist from behind.

Before she could scream, Evan spoke in her ear. "Don't move. It's just me."

"You scared me!" She kicked him hard on the shins and he lifted her off her feet.

"That hurt."

She tried to elbow him in the ribs. "Let me go! I need to get him before he hurts my mom!"

"Just wait a sec." Evan kept his voice low. "He's in enemy territory right now and he's got everything to lose. Let's take him down right."

"He's got my mother!" Josie hissed.

"I saw. We'll get her out of this, too." Evan set her back down on her feet and she turned to confront him. He pointed at her weapon. "Just don't shoot me, okay?"

"I'm not a fool. How did you know Rob was here?"

"Adam and I saw some guy lurking by the creek while we were out checking the water levels in the lower pastures. When we went down to have a little conversation with him, he ran off." He checked his cell. "Nate will be here in less than a minute."

Josie gazed longingly at the house. "We could go in there and sort it out in way less time than that."

"And accidentally kill someone?"

"I'm a really good shot."

"So am I, but you know as well as I do that shooting at targets and an actual firefight are two very different things, especially when your mother's in the middle of it." He checked his phone again. "Ines is already out. She's gone over to the bull breeding barn to tell Rio and the guys what's going on. She'll also be telling him to hang tight until Nate gets here."

"Good luck with that," Josie muttered. "Rio doesn't take orders well."

Evan looked past her shoulder toward the shooting range. "Nate's here. I told him to park behind the barn."

"I'm not blind, Evan. I can see him walking toward me," Josie said tartly. "Nate, he's got my mother."

"Dammit," Nate said. "I was hoping one of us would get to you before he arrived."

"Mom came out of the house and Rob was standing right there," Josie explained. "I couldn't do anything to help her."

"Did he have a visible weapon?" Nate asked.

"No, and Mom treated him like he was just a regular visitor and invited him in."

"Then she was really smart."

"I hope so." Josie only realized she was shaking when Evan put his arm around her.

Nate gestured at her gun. "If you're thinking of busting in there, I wouldn't recommend it."

"I was just practicing at the range," Josie defended herself. "That's why I hadn't checked my phone and had no idea that creep was this close to the house."

Nate held out his hand. "I'll keep it safe for you."

"Fine." Josie handed over her weapon with a sigh.

"And the magazine." Nate wasn't messing around. He double-checked the gun and made sure the chamber was clear.

"But if he hurts my mom, all bets are off," Josie muttered.

Rio came around the corner of the barn, his expression grim. "What's going on?"

Nate beckoned him to join the group. "Here's how I see it, and here's how I think we can take this guy down without a single shot being fired."

As she walked through the mudroom and into the kitchen like she didn't have a care in the world, Josie sure hoped Nate's confidence that the last thing Rob would want to do was kill her was accurate.

"Hey, *Mamãe!*" she called out, hoping Nate was picking up every word from where he was currently crouched down against the wall of the house with his backup. "Would you like me to bring you some coffee?"

"That would be lovely, darling, and don't forget to bring an extra cup because you have a visitor!"

Josie paused. Her mother didn't sound like a hostage. Maybe Nate was wrong, and Isabelle had no idea who Rob was at all. It would be just like her to invite a potential murderer into her home.

"Sure! Where are you?"

"In the family room."

"Okay, I'll just be a minute." Josie made sure to leave both the doors wide open as she hurriedly set a tray, found some cookies to put on a plate, and added a jug of cream.

Even as she exited the kitchen, she was aware of a rush of movement behind her as Nate and hopefully some of the others came to back her up. She held the tray firmly in her shaking hands, walked along the hallway, and into the sunny family room where she found her mother and Rob sitting at right angles to each other on the two couches as if it really was just a social visit.

"Hey, Rob!" Josie tried to sound surprised rather than terrified. "What brings you here?"

"Apparently Rob wants you to know that there was a terrible miscarriage of justice, darling, and that he tried to tell the police that you and he were just having a silly argument and they refused to believe him." Isabelle leaned over and patted Rob's hand. "He came all the way out here just to set the record straight! Isn't that romantic?"

Josie set the tray down and sat opposite Rob, who looked like he'd been sleeping rough for a few days. There was no sign of his gun, but his right hand was hidden under one of the cushions, which was somewhat alarming.

"You didn't need to do that, Rob." Josie looked him in the eye. "I tried to tell them the whole thing had gotten blown out of proportion, but they wouldn't listen to me."

"Maybe if you hadn't overreacted and hit your face on the glass, they would've realized that," Rob said. "You panicked over nothing and got me into a whole lot of trouble."

"Would you like some coffee, *Mamãe*, Rob?" Josie asked quickly as his expression darkened.

"Oh, yes, *please,* darling. How do you like your coffee, Rob?" Isabelle turned to face Josie's attacker, keeping his attention away from Josie and the subtle movements at the open door.

"Just black please," Rob said.

"I love mine with cream and sugar," declared Isabelle.

"I've always loved sweet things. Josie prefers hers with half-and-half. Don't you, darling?"

Josie set the two mugs down on the coffee table along with the plate of cookies. "Darn it, I forgot the sugar, *Mamãe*. I'll just go and fetch it."

"How about your mom does that so we can catch up, Josie? It's been a while," Rob said.

Josie met her mother's anxious gaze. She'd been in two minds as to whether her mom knew what was going on, but Isabelle was obviously on to Rob. "That's a great idea."

Isabelle rose with some reluctance and turned to Rob. "It was so lovely to meet you. Perhaps you'd like to stay for dinner?"

Rob stood too and awkwardly accepted her hug. "That's very sweet of you, Mrs. Martinez, but Josie and I have plans."

"We do?" Josie spoke before thinking, and Rob's gaze hardened. "I mean, if we do, you haven't mentioned them to me. Is it a surprise?"

Isabelle disappeared and Josie quickly maneuvered herself into a position where she was able to sit where Rob had been sitting. She felt the hard outline of his gun under her butt cheek and stealthily moved her hand under the cushion until she had it in her grasp.

"I don't like what you did to me, Josie." Now that her mother had gone, Rob's smile had disappeared. "I mean, I didn't want to say anything in front of your mom because she obviously doesn't know, but it's your fault I ended up in prison."

"How so?" Josie asked.

"All you had to do was agree to go out with me on one date."

"Maybe if you'd asked me that question at work, I would've given you a more positive response."

He frowned. "You think you own that place, strutting around, making all the men suck up to you just because you're the boss's sister. You would've laughed me out of town."

"But you don't know that because you never asked me," Josie said calmly, completely forgetting the script. "Instead, you chose to find out where I lived, get into my apartment building, and scream at me through my front door when I refused to let you in. And then you broke in, screamed at me some more, and shoved my face into a mirror."

He moved so fast that she was unprepared when he grabbed the front of her shirt and yanked her out of her seat onto her feet.

"See? There you go again. Thinking you're better than me, talking down to me like I'm your inferior when everyone knows you only got promoted because of your brother."

Even as he ranted and his spittle landed on her cheek, a strange sense of calm flooded through Josie.

"Let go of me, Rob."

He shook her hard. "You need to learn a few lessons, bitch."

She brought her right hand up and pressed the barrel of the gun against his skull.

"I don't think so, buddy."

He went to grab her wrist, and Nate came in through the doorway, his gun out, followed by one of the local state troopers and Conner O'Neil, a retired Navy SEAL friend of Jay's.

"Police! Drop all weapons now!"

As Rob's grip slackened, Josie stepped away and backed right into Evan's chest. She stayed where she was as Rob was tackled to the floor and handcuffed.

"You do know that wasn't part of the plan?" Evan murmured into her ear. "You were supposed to keep him sweet until Nate came in."

"As you said, things don't always go as planned in the real world," Josie reminded him. "And I have to say that this was much more satisfying."

"You sound like you wish you'd had the chance to actually shoot him." Evan exhaled. "Dammit, Josie, you scared the hell out of me."

Nate came over and held out his hand. "Can I have that gun as well, Josie? You seem to be collecting them today."

"Sure. I don't even know if it's loaded." Josie handed it over. "He hid it under one of the cushions while he was talking to Mom, and I deliberately sat on it."

"I suppose we should be grateful it didn't actually go off then," Evan muttered.

Nate was busy disabling the gun with the precision and care of a true professional. "There's definitely a bullet in the chamber, but whether it would've fired is debatable. The whole thing needs a good cleaning."

Josie nodded and then pulled away from Evan, ran down the hallway, and locked herself in the bathroom where she threw up. She splashed water on her face and tried to ignore the gentle knocking on the door as tears streamed down.

"Josephina . . ." That was her mother's voice. "Please come out. I just want to hold you and make sure you are safe."

There was a quiver in Isabelle's voice that made Josie cry even harder. The energy needed to walk over and open the door seemed beyond her. She slid down the wall, wrapped her arms around her knees, and hugged them tight.

"I'm coming in."

She looked up as Evan came through the door, which now had the lock hanging off. He shut the door, sat down beside her, and put his arm around her shoulders. As she continued to weep, he drew her onto his lap and told her how strong she'd been, how brave, how *amazing* . . .

Quite a long while later, after he'd handed her a new box of tissues, he cleared his throat.

"It's been a hell of a day, sweetness. How about we take a couple of horses and go spend some time out in Conner's hunting cabin?"

"Because Conner wouldn't like it?" Josie sniffed.

"He's not there right now. He's staying with Beth in town, and it was his idea." Evan held up a key. "He says you need to decompress, whatever that means." His voice gentled. "Humor me. I've got this stupid desire to hold you tight for at least a week and Rio would look at me funny if I started doing that around here."

Josie blew her nose. "What about your work?"

"Plenty of Millers to take up that slack," Evan reassured her. "How about it?"

Josie considered her options. She wasn't ready to deal with all the Rob fallout just yet. When she faced the authorities, she wanted to be strong enough to make sure he stayed away from her for good. And she didn't feel strong yet. She felt like a pile of rapidly melting ice cream.

"Okay."

"Great." Evan stood and offered her his hand. "You might have to speak to everyone just for a second on the way out, but other than that we're good to go."

Evan kept a careful eye on Josie on the way up to Conner's cabin, which lay in the far northernmost point of the Garcia Ranch. Her face was in shadow under her white straw Stetson, but he knew her well enough now to detect the signs of strain on her face and the way she bit down on her lip to stop herself from crying. He'd never seen himself as the kind of guy who would stick around while a woman cried all over him, but he'd do it for Josie whenever she needed him.

Listening to her take Rob to task had made him half proud of her and half terrified. He should've known she wouldn't be willing to play nice with a man who had violently invaded her personal space, and why should she be? He supposed he should be glad she hadn't gone ahead and shot the creep with his own gun. Why he cared so much and why seeing her break down after being so brave had made him want to sit and bawl alongside her was still a mystery—one he wasn't willing to investigate while Josie still needed him.

"Stable's in good shape," Evan reported as he went back to where he'd left Josie unloading their bags. Not that he had anything much to change into, but Ines had packed them two bags filled with all kinds of stuff, which hopefully contained something he could wear. "Conner definitely takes care of everything up here."

"Good to know." Josie undid the last strap of her horse's bridle and replaced it with a halter. "I'll take Madonna and come back for Joker."

"Cool. I'll take the bags in and get the fire going."

Evan unlocked the door to the wood walled cabin and went inside. There was one central room with a stone fireplace, an alcove for the bed, and a small but functional kitchen. To his relief there was a big pile of logs and kindling already in place beside the enclosed wood burner, which meant they were unlikely to run out of fuel. The cabin did have electricity, but it wasn't the best and ran off a generator.

Evan set the bags on the small couch and hunkered down in front of the fire. There was a firelighter and a couple of fake logs, which Evan intended to mention to Conner the next time they met.

"So much for being the wild man of the woods," Evan murmured.

"What's that?" Josie came in and shut the door behind her.

Evan held up the firelighter. "I thought Conner would strike a spark off his teeth or use a flint or something more barbaric."

She tried to smile, but he could see it was still an effort. He returned his attention to starting the fire as she organized the kitchen and got some coffee going on the gas stove.

"It's good to go." Evan dusted off his hands and got off his knees.

"Great. There are plenty of lamps, so I don't think we

need to use the generator," Josie said as she handed him a mug of coffee.

"Thanks." Evan took the drink and continued to look down at her. "How are you doing?"

She sighed. "I'm a complete mess."

"Understandable." He nodded. "You've been through a lot."

"I hate feeling weak and out of control."

"Yeah?" He smiled at her. "Welcome to my world."

"You're not weak." She frowned at him. "And you've never been a control freak like me, so losing control isn't such a big issue for you."

"You weren't weak." Evan decided to ignore those home truths and focus on Josie. "You faced that asshole down like a boss."

"Only because I had control of his gun." She shivered. "If Mom hadn't drawn his attention away for those vital few seconds, it could've all turned out very differently."

"Ifs and coulds never work, and there's no point going over and over them in your head," Evan reminded her. "Everything worked out the way it was supposed to be-cause you're strong and Rob's a dickhead."

He surprised a laugh out of her, and she cupped his chin. "Thanks for being here with me."

"It's my pleasure."

Okay, he'd already had twenty messages from his dad all in caps asking where the hell he was, and who he thought was paying his wages, but he didn't care. All of that faded into insignificance beside what Josie needed from him right now. He stared into her eyes, totally caught in their whiskey-brown depths.

"Dammit," Evan murmured.

He was absolutely and totally one hundred percent in love with her.

"What?"

"Nothing." He kissed her forehead. "Did Ines send any food, because I'm starving."

Chapter Sixteen

Josie had forgotten just how quiet it could get out in the wilds of Morgan Valley. With the generator off and the cabin lit with lamps and heated by a wood fire, there was very little background noise. But for once, the darkness felt like a comfortable blanket wrapped around her. She paused to look up at the sky and got lost in it, her mind more willing to fly away into the nothingness than stay pinned to the ground. Behind her, the horses whickered and stamped their feet safe in their enclosed stalls.

She'd ventured out to check on Madonna and Joker while Evan tackled the washing up. It felt like it was the first time she could breathe properly since she'd watched her mother take Rob into the ranch house that morning. She was proud of herself for not breaking down in front of Rob, but she hadn't expected the emotional backlash afterward. Thank goodness Evan had been there. She didn't care what anyone else said about him—he'd been her rock, and she would always be grateful for that.

She lowered her gaze to the two lit windows of the cabin. Smoke poured out of the chimney and the faint hint of coffee wafted toward her on the ever-chilling breeze. Even at this time of year you could taste the edge of ice on your tongue as it rolled off the snow-covered peaks. She shivered and started walking again, her hands in the pockets of her fleece as she spied Evan moving around in the kitchen.

He opened the door for her, and the scent of coffee became stronger.

"Everything okay out there?"

"Yup." She eased out of her boots and unwrapped her scarf. "The horses are settled in nicely. Do we need to call anyone before we turn in for the night?"

"It's up to you. Personally, I'm avoiding talking to anyone with the name of Miller right now, but that's nothing new." He gestured at the countertop. "If your phone won't work, Conner gave me his radio. It has a direct connection to Nate at the sheriff's office."

"Let's hope we don't have to use it." Josie accepted the coffee and went to toast her toes in front of the fire.

"I already checked in with Nate." Evan joined her. "Rob is safely on his way back to San Francisco. Nate looks forward to seeing you in his office sometime soon so he can take your statement."

"Good old Nate."

"He is a good guy," Evan agreed as he sat beside her and draped one arm along the back of the couch. "But don't let him hear you calling him old. He said he'd tell Rio and your mom that you were safe and settled up here."

"That's kind of him." Josie sighed and leaned back on the couch. "I don't know why I'm so exhausted."

"Duh." Evan rolled his eyes. "I mean it's not as if anything weird happened today or anything, is it?"

She angled her head until it rested against his shoulder. "I'm glad you're here."

"Me, too." He paused. "I wasn't kidding when I said you scared the hell out of me."

"I guess I would've felt the same if it had been the other way around," Josie acknowledged. "No one wants to see someone they care about in a difficult situation."

He nodded as his hand came to rest on her shoulder. "You okay to share that bed with me, or shall I sleep on the couch?"

She poked him in the chest. "I thought you said you didn't want to let me go."

"That's true." He covered her fingers with his own. "But I didn't want to come across as too needy."

"That's settled then," Josie said firmly. "Now, all we need to do is brave that outside bathroom and then tuck ourselves up in bed."

Evan looked interested. "Did you say 'tuck'? Or was it something else?"

"Tuck." She ruffled his hair. "I'm way too tired for anything else."

"Just checking." He grinned at her as he got off the couch. "Let me go find my flashlight."

Two hours later, she was wide-awake and staring at the ceiling while Evan snored away beside her. It was the first night she actually remembered spending together with him in a bed, and she'd already discovered that not only did he snore, but he was a sheet hogger. Outside, the grasshoppers were in full song along with the occasional frog chorus.

Every time she closed her eyes, she saw Rob staring down at her as he yanked her to her feet. She'd forgotten how fast he could move, and for a moment, she'd stared into the abyss again before anger had transcended fear and she'd reacted instinctively.

"What's up?" Evan whispered, his voice gravelly.

"Nothing important." She patted his bare shoulder. "Go back to sleep."

Instead, he rolled over onto his side and up on one elbow to study her. "Tell me."

She sighed. "I'd gone through a million scenarios of what I was going to do if I ever saw Rob again. I thought I'd covered every angle, from self-defense classes, to therapy, to even writing down my plans, and still, when it actually happened, I froze."

He frowned. "No, you didn't."

"I let him grab hold of me again."

"You didn't 'let him' do anything, Josie. Rob's the problem here. He's the responsible adult who decided he'd take what he wanted with violence and without your consent."

"I guess . . ."

"No guessing about it," Evan said. "It's one hundred percent on him. If he'd grabbed hold of your mom, would you have blamed her?"

"Of course not."

"Then why blame yourself?"

"Because I knew what he was like! He jumped me last time and I let him do it again."

"Bullshit. You had his gun. You drew him in, and when he was close enough you could've pulled that trigger."

"I'm not sure about that," Josie admitted.

"Whether you would've actually gone through with it?" Evan settled her back against the pillows with his arm firmly around her shoulders.

"Yes." She turned her face toward him and pressed a kiss on his warm skin. "But I knew Nate was right there. Once my mom was clear, I tried to believe that everything would go as planned."

"Which it did because dickhead Rob is currently on his way back to prison," Evan said firmly. "And you're here with me, which is just as it should be."

She smiled and rubbed her cheek against his chest. Sometimes she admired his ability to think in such straight lines. "Lucky old me."

"Yeah." He kissed the top of her head. "But I think I'm the lucky one."

She eased herself upright so that she could see him clearly in the moonlight. "I know it's your turn to pick something off your list, but there is something I really want to do."

"Okay, shoot."

"I need to go back to San Francisco."

He didn't say anything for so long that she began to wonder if he hadn't heard her.

Eventually he cleared his throat and smiled. "I guess that was inevitable, right?" He moved slightly away from her. "When are you leaving?"

"That depends on you."

He shrugged. "I don't have any right to stop you, Josie."

She frowned. "I *meant* that you've been away from the ranch a lot recently, and we both know your dad isn't exactly okay with that."

His eyebrows rose. "What's my dad got to do with you leaving?"

"Because I want you to come with me," Josie explained. "I've been avoiding doing this thing. If you were there, it might make it easier."

"Back up a minute." Evan held up his finger. "What 'thing' exactly?"

"My apartment in San Francisco." She looked at him expectantly. "I haven't been back to it since the night Rob broke in. I've been too scared. I thought maybe if we went there together, I'd be able to face it."

He went quiet again, his expressive face for once difficult to read.

"If it's too much to ask, I could always get Rio to come with me," Josie said quickly. "He's been on me for months to get my stuff out of there and move into the new place he found me." She reached for his hand. "It's okay if you can't get away. It's a big ask."

"I'd have to see what Adam and Danny think." Evan finally spoke. "I don't want to leave them with too much work. How long were you thinking of going for?"

"Just a weekend. Most of the furniture came with the apartment so it's really about packing my personal stuff and taking it to the new place."

He nodded and she shook off a lingering sensation that something was off.

"Did I say something wrong?" she asked.

"Not at all. I'm just thinking about how to approach my brothers." He pushed aside the covers and got out of bed. "Might as well pee now that I'm awake. I'll be back in a minute."

He took the flashlight he'd left on the table and exited

the cabin, leaving Josie with the feeling that she'd missed something important. She lay back on the pillow and tried to run the conversation through her head, looking for when it had gone off the rails. Was Evan beginning to feel like she was taking advantage of him? Was she expecting too much?

God, that was it.

Josie sat bolt upright and stared at the door. She'd come to depend on him way too quickly in the past few weeks, but that didn't mean he had to feel the same way. Everyone had told her that Evan didn't take his relationships too seriously, and she'd sure dragged him down a rabbit hole. And now she was demanding he spend every minute of his free time taking care of her needs. No wonder he'd hesitated. She took an unsteady breath, which made her heart hurt. If Evan wanted to go back to just being friends, she wouldn't blame him in the slightest.

Evan hesitated as he reached the cabin door. One thing he knew was that he wasn't good at pretending everything was fine when it wasn't. He was the family bigmouth, the guy who said the thing that everyone else was thinking and was too polite to let it out in public. He leaned back against the cabin wall and contemplated the starry sky. If he hung around out here long enough, maybe Josie would fall asleep and their awkward conversation would all be forgotten tomorrow morning.

For the first time in his life, he couldn't just walk away, and most of him didn't want to. Hearing her say she was leaving had been such a punch in the gut that he'd wanted to shout out an instant denial. It had only confirmed his suspicion that he cared about her a lot and that the thought of her going away was . . .

Evan sighed. So, he'd acted like a dumbass, and now she probably thought he was a complete idiot, which wasn't new, but somehow hurt. Now that he'd had time to think about it, Josie wasn't the kind of woman who would just casually announce she was leaving the guy she was literally in bed with at that moment. She'd be way kinder than that. The fact that even the thought of her leaving had him floundering around like a kicked calf was the problem.

She hadn't asked him to fall in love with her. She'd only agreed to help him with his bucket list while she was on vacation for a few weeks. He was the one building stupid castles in the air, not her. She was a smart, savvy businesswoman destined for big things and he was . . .

Just a stupid cowboy.

"Evan."

He jumped as the cabin door opened to reveal Josie wearing his spare fleece over her pajamas.

"What?"

"Are you coming back in, or are you planning on riding off and abandoning me in the middle of nowhere?"

"I'm coming in." She stood back and he went into the warm interior to take off his boots and coat. He could joke his way out of this. "My evil plan won't work when everyone in Morgan Valley including the sheriff knows exactly where we are."

She climbed back into bed and sat looking at him, her arms folded over her chest, her long braid of hair over one shoulder. She looked anxious again and he kicked himself for putting that expression back on her face. He went to speak, but she was quicker.

"I'm sorry." Josie met his gaze. "I've been taking advantage of our friendship. You're probably getting sick of me asking for too much from you. I *totally* understand if you have stuff to do that doesn't involve babysitting me, okay?"

Friendship. Right. He could do that as well.

"Nope." He strolled back over to the bed and slid in beside her. "You lighten up my life. I've had more fun since you came to stay in Morgan Valley than I've had the entire rest of my life."

"Fun?" She tried to smile. "I've cried all over you, almost gotten you shot, I made you get on a bull, and—"

He kissed her, cutting off her words, and she surrendered into his embrace. When he eventually raised his head, they were both breathing hard. This he could do—this part made sense. If he didn't have the right words yet to tell her what she probably didn't want to hear anyway, then he could at least show with his mouth, his hands, and his body what he really felt.

"Evan?" she whispered. "Are we okay?"

"We're absolutely okay." He groaned and kissed her again, pushing his fingers under her layers of clothing until he found her soft, warm skin.

"I want you, Josie," he murmured against her mouth. "Will you have me?"

She slid her fingers into his hair to keep him exactly where he wanted to be, and kissed him back.

"Yes, Evan. Always."

He rolled her onto her back, pulled the covers back

over both of them, which made her giggle, and grinned down at her.

"Gotta keep everything warm."

"I guess." She slid her sock-covered foot up his sweatpants-covered leg to his thigh.

"How about I make this something to check off my list?" Evan offered as he pressed one hand under her ass and gently squeezed. "How few clothes can we take off and still have sex?"

"That's certainly a challenge," Josie agreed gravely. "But I definitely think you're up for it."

He bucked his hips. "Oh, I'm up for it, all right."

It was her turn to groan as she slipped her cold fingers beneath the waistband of his sweatpants, making him shudder.

"Warm them up on my belly before you touch anything we might need later, okay?" Evan advised, which made her chuckle. "I've figured this out, Josie. I push my sweats down to my knees and you take one of your legs out of your pajamas and we'll be good to go."

By the time Evan got back home the next day, the sun was high in the sky and he'd missed his chores again. He unsaddled Joker, made sure he got some water, and then turned him out to graze with the other horses in the pasture behind the barn. It wasn't until he was just about to leave the barn that he noticed someone, probably Kaiden, had put up a new sign.

THE MILLER RANCH
UNDER NEW MANAGEMENT.

Evan was still smiling when he let himself into the house and walked through to the kitchen to find his father eating lunch at the table. He held up his hand and braced himself for impact.

"Look, before you start in on me—"

"Not my problem, Son." His dad continued eating his sandwich. "Take it up with Adam. He's the boss now."

"Are you feeling okay?" Evan asked. "I mean, it's not like you to miss the opportunity to shout at someone."

"I'm a new man." Jeff got up to refresh his coffee and poured a mug for Evan. "You know what's weird?"

Evan took the mug. "Er, the way you're behaving right now?"

"Nope." His dad's rare smile emerged. "I'm enjoying not being in charge."

"Who are you, and what have you done with my father?" Evan asked.

"Ha ha. You wait until you get to my age, Son. You'll understand." Jeff patted him on the shoulder. "Adam said you were due back about lunchtime, so I made you a sandwich. It's in the refrigerator. How's Josie doing?"

"She's okay." Evan took out the plate, noting his dad had even made his favorite sandwich, chicken salad and mayo. "Isabelle seemed to be more affected than Josie."

"She would be." Jeff returned to his seat. "She's an excitable woman."

Evan tried to be fair. "But she did totally disarm Rob with her friendliness, which gave Nate and the rest of us time to make a plan to bring him down."

"I suppose she did. Good for her."

After a slight hesitation, Evan went to sit opposite his

dad. "Josie wants me to go to San Francisco and help pack up her old apartment."

"Yeah? Why's that?"

Evan shrugged. "I guess she hasn't been there since she was attacked, and she doesn't want to do it alone."

"Good thinking." Jeff nodded. "You'll be a nice distraction."

"Thanks, I think." Evan took a bite of his sandwich. "Would you be okay with me being away for another weekend?"

"Ask Adam. He won't like it, but he's probably not going to raise hell like I would. When does she want to go?"

"Whenever suits me."

"Sounds like she really wants you to come along." Jeff chewed slowly for a while. "You like this one?"

"Josie?" Evan tried to sound nonchalant. "Yeah."

"Have you told her that?"

Evan set his sandwich back on the plate. "You might be a new man, but I am not discussing my love life with you, Dad, like ever. Period."

"Shame, because I've got a lot of experience in screwing up a perfectly good thing."

"Why would you think I'd do that?" Evan knew he should shut up, but his mouth kept on flapping.

"Because, according to your mother, Miller men aren't good at expressing their feelings and we're shit-scared of appearing vulnerable or something."

"She's got a point," Evan acknowledged. "But I think we've gotten better at it since Mom came back."

Jeff nodded. "She's a force of good, that woman." He set down his mug with a definite thump. "I told Adam

I'd take you out with me this afternoon. We need to check on the cattle in the fields bordering the creek again."

"Sure." Evan nodded, glad that his father had reverted to talking about the ranch. He could do with a nap after being up half the night with Josie, but he knew his father's newfound tolerance would never stretch that far. "Just let me finish up and I'll meet you in the barn."

Chapter Seventeen

Evan tried to ignore the surreptitious glances as he followed Josie along the busy San Francisco street to her old apartment complex. Maybe they didn't see many real cowboys complete with a Stetson and boots in the middle of the city, but that was no reason to stare. Next time he'd take Kaiden's advice and wear a baseball cap instead.

It was surprisingly dark at street level among the high-rise buildings. A strong breeze swirled around the stunted trees, reminding him of home. He was glad he'd brought his jacket because the city was notoriously chilly even in the summer.

"We're here."

Josie had come to a complete stop in front of a narrow old-fashioned building. She'd chosen to wear black pants with a soft, silky blouse under her smart ski jacket and had put her hair up in a high ponytail. Unlike Evan, she'd left her cowboy boots at home, and for the first time looked like the businesswoman she was.

He reached for her hand and she grabbed hold of it.

"You can do this," Evan reassured her.

She nodded, her grip tightening, her expression solemn,

then walked toward the glass door. There was a uniformed security guard sitting on a stool in the entranceway who waved and came to unlock the door.

"Ms. Josie! How are you?"

"I'm doing great, Izzy." She gestured at Evan. "This is my friend Evan Miller."

"Hello." Evan offered a fist bump, which was returned. "Nice to meet you."

"You, too." Izzy turned back to Josie. "Tessa had the baby three weeks ago. It's a girl. We called her Carla after my grandmother."

"What a lovely name." Josie's face lit up with a smile that made Evan want to hug her. "Give Tessa my best, won't you? And tell her to take things easy for a while."

"I sure will." Izzy gestured at the bank of elevators. "Would you like me to come up with you? Mr. Martinez told us not to allow anyone in the apartment until you came back."

"No, I'll be fine." Josie smiled. "That's why I brought Evan along. He's going to help me move my stuff."

Izzy's smile faded. "I can understand why you want to move, but I will miss chatting to you. I only wish I'd been the one on duty when that bastard came in. I would *never* have let him past the front door."

Evan reclaimed Josie's hand and drew her away from Izzy toward the elevators. "Which floor is it?"

"Third," Josie said and pressed the correct button.

The doors slid open and they stepped into the good-sized elevator, which was reassuring as Evan had never liked small spaces.

"Gee golly, gosh, shucks," Evan said. "I've never been

in one of these newfangled machines before in the big city."

For a second Josie just looked at him and then punched his arm.

"Stop it."

"Yes, ma'am."

The elevator chimed and they walked out onto the carpeted landing. There was absolutely no sound coming from any of the doors. Evan speculated that either everyone was out at work or the place was very well insulated.

"Which way now?" Evan asked.

"I just need a moment," Josie said. "I keep remembering the sight of my front door being smashed in with a fire extinguisher."

"Shame it didn't go off and shoot the jerk out the window." Evan looked down at her frozen face. "Okay. Do you want me to go ahead and unlock the door for you?"

"No, I want to see it." She took a deep breath. "It's the last door on the left. It's a corner unit."

Evan let her lead the way and kept his mouth shut as she paused again outside an inconspicuous-looking white door with the number six on it.

"They must have replaced it with a completely new one," Josie said. "The number's slightly different." She took out her key chain, which chimed in her shaking hand. "I'm going in."

Evan only realized he was holding his breath when he had to gulp in some air. He walked in behind Josie to a small area with a table containing a dried-flower arrangement. Two pairs of outdoor shoes were parked under the table and there was a bowl for keys. There was also a nail on the wall above the table, which looked odd until it dawned on him there had once been a mirror there. He turned to close the front door and noticed gouges on the frame where the previous damage had been done.

"Come on through," Josie called to him.

He walked into a large kitchen and family room that took up both sides of the corner apartment and had dual-aspect windows looking down over the rear garden attached to the building. Josie had said there was also underground parking, which was at a premium in the congested city. The kitchen area was to the right of the door with a long granite countertop and high stools. On the left were two comfortable-looking couches with blue and green pillows scattered on them.

It was pure Josie and made Evan imagine sinking into the couch with her on his lap as they watched TV together on a rainy Sunday afternoon.

"Despite what Izzy says, I guess Rio did send someone in to clean up, or else there would've been a lot of rotting food in my refrigerator by now."

Josie opened the refrigerator to display its gleaming white emptiness. She half-smiled and pointed at the countertop. "I was sitting up here eating my dinner and checking my mail when Rob rang the doorbell."

Evan just nodded and hoped she'd talk as much as she wanted.

"There's nothing left in the freezer." She checked the large pantry and turned back to Evan. "No sign that the cops were here either, to be fair."

"It looks good to me," Evan said. "Are you doing okay?"

"It's a lot." She came around the counter and walked

into his arms. He held her close. "I really don't think I could live here anymore. It feels like he . . . desecrated the place."

"I get it." Evan kissed the top of her head.

Eventually she pulled back. "Rio said he left plenty of packing boxes in my bedroom and that if I needed more to call the moving company."

"Do you want to make a start on that?" Evan asked. "Or do you need to walk away and come back later?"

She raised her chin. "I think I'd like to get it done. Are you okay with that?"

He flexed his biceps. "Honey, I've been waiting to be someone's hired muscle all my life. Lead the way."

About two hours after they'd arrived at the apartment, Josie's cell buzzed, and she checked her messages to find one from Rio.

E aí?

Bacana. We're about halfway through packing already.

Josie typed fast. Thanks for setting this all up.

Not a problem. If you want to see the new place this afternoon, and work out where you're going to put everything, it's available. You have the code and keys.

I might just do that.

Josie heard Evan cursing from the pantry where she'd left him in charge of packing all the canned food and dry goods. It sounded like he'd dropped something on his foot.

> If you don't like the new place, we can always find you something else. But you have very nice neighbors ☺

> That's you, right?

> I own the whole building, mana. Mamãe uses the apartment below yours and Yvonne and I are in the penthouse.

Before she could type a reply, he sent a new text.

> Gotta run. PBR are due in at five. I'll call you at the hotel tonight. Leave the clean-up to my guys, they're good.

Josie smiled at her phone as she typed. Obrigado x

She took a long look around her bedroom. She'd picked the wall color, drapes, and bed linen, but for some reason the serene colors now seemed jarring. Her gaze fell onto the open door of the closet, which she'd already cleared out. Rob had found her in there and dragged her back into the hall while she kicked, screamed, and begged. It hadn't made any difference. The thought of sleeping in her bed again made her feel ill.

She went back into the kitchen where Evan had set up a whole row of boxes on the countertop. He'd put in his earbuds and was humming away to some tune as he loaded them up.

"I don't want most of this stuff anymore." Josie spoke loudly so he could hear her.

He paused to take out an earbud and look at her, his hazel gaze calm. "Makes sense."

"It doesn't, but I can't help that." She indicated the packed boxes of food. "These can go to the local food bank. Everything, except my clothes and a couple of the art pieces, I'll donate to a charity. I think I want to start fresh."

He nodded. "I get that."

She found a big black marker in one of the drawers. "Let's identify what's going where, take my clothes back to the hotel, and call it a day."

"I do so love a decisive woman." Evan blew her a kiss.

She thanked the gods that he'd agreed to come with her. There was something about his ability to make her laugh, while also understanding her on an instinctual level, that was very soothing. She'd have to remember to respect his boundaries, though. He'd only signed up to be her friend and she shouldn't forget that.

"We'll have a late lunch, go and view the new place, and then take a trip to IKEA," Josie declared.

"I haven't actually been there." Evan looked thrilled. "Like for real."

"You're kidding." Josie started randomly emptying the kitchen drawers into a box. Clearing everything out and starting afresh suddenly made a lot of sense. She felt . . . liberated. She was lucky enough to have the funds to replace everything, and for once she was going to splurge and not worry about it.

"No, really. I hear they do good meatballs." Evan offered her a bottle of water. "Kaiden's been there with Julia a few times and he was raving about them."

"He's right." Josie started on the cupboard under the

sink. "They are good." She pointed at the far corner of the family room. "Let's put the trash over there so that whoever comes to clear everything out after we've left knows exactly what's going where."

"We don't have to do that?" Evan took a swig of water.

"No, Rio said he'd take care of everything."

"Man, I wish I had a brother like that."

"He's the best," Josie agreed. Every cupboard she emptied made her feel slightly like shedding her skin, which was creepy but kind of accurate. "I've packed both my suitcases and there's one box of other stuff. We can get a taxi or Uber to the hotel and take it from there."

Evan turned in a slow circle, his gaze fixated on the San Francisco skyline and the outline of the Bay Bridge right in front of him. He edged closer to one of the floor-to-ceiling windows and gulped.

"It's . . . high."

"Yes. Don't you like it?" Josie came over and linked her arm through his.

It had been interesting watching Josie move through their first day together in the city. She'd started off barely wanting to enter her original apartment and then after the decision to let everything go had visibly grown lighter and more relaxed. Her confidence in moving around the city and dealing with its inhabitants had shown Evan a different side of her. It was beginning to dawn on him that she really didn't need him there at all.

"Are you going to take this place?" he asked, although he already knew she absolutely loved the modern, sleek lines and awe-inspiring views. He was quite partial to it himself. He could probably fit his current apartment in her walk-in-closet. She'd mentioned that Rio owned the whole building and tried to imagine how much that had cost. It was a good reminder that although Josie never made a big deal of how wealthy her family was, they were loaded.

"I think I will. It's so full of light and space." She leaned forward to look down at the street far below. "I bet it will sway like heck if we have a big earthquake."

Evan tried to imagine that and swallowed convulsively.

"Don't you like heights?" Josie looked up at him.

"Not really a fan," Evan confessed. "But this place is spectacular. I can see why you'd want to live here."

"It's closer to my office as well." She danced away from him and went into the gleaming, black-and-white kitchen. "I'm glad we came here first. I have the dimensions of the place, but it always helps to see the actual layout before you commit to buying any furniture."

She took a notebook out of her backpack, counted the kitchen cabinets, and started scribbling.

"Oh, yeah, about that." Evan cleared his throat. "If you're good with everything, I can just head on home."

Her smile disappeared and she set the pad down on the countertop. "I thought you had the whole weekend off?"

"I do, but if you don't need me to wrangle anything big furniture-wise, I could go."

"Evan . . ."

He shrugged. "It's okay. You've proven you can come back here and deal with everything. I'm really proud of you."

"I couldn't have done it without you." She met his

gaze, her brown eyes steady. "I don't want you to go—unless you absolutely have to." She gave a little laugh. "I am aware that you probably have way better things to do in your life than hang around with me."

"Like what exactly?"

She shrugged. "You tell me."

He studied her in silence, torn between his longing to stay and the foolish hope that she'd admit she wanted more from him than just friendship, which was just stupid.

"I don't want you to feel like you have to keep me around just because." Evan finally spoke.

"Because what?" She strolled back toward him. "Because you're sinfully sexy, kind as they come, and most importantly, you've been my rock through all of this."

He shrugged. "I think you're mistaking me for Rio."

"No, I'm definitely not." She reached his side and cupped his chin, her thumb grazing his lower lip. "Please don't go. I want to take you to IKEA, smother you in meatballs, and then take you back to the hotel for wild sex."

"Meatballs, eh?"

He shoved down his misgivings. Surely, he deserved one more night with her? It would all end when she decided to go back to work anyway. He could already see that time approaching way too fast. If he really loved her—and he was pretty sure that he did—then he'd see it through to the end when she said thank you and goodbye and he walked away from her with a smile.

"Evan? What do you think?"

He leaned into her touch and gently nipped the tip of her thumb. "You're on."

* * *

Later that night in the luxurious suite Rio had booked for them in the center of the city it was Evan's turn to be wide-awake and staring. He didn't leave Morgan Valley very often, but there was something about the vibe of a city he loved—that sense of something always happening or evolving.

He'd even enjoyed the crowds at IKEA and had tried not to blink at the length of the bill Josie had run up once she'd swept through the store. They'd filled at least eight shopping carts and had a bag full of bigger-sticker items to collect at the checkout. The assistant manager of the store had even come out to assure Josie that everything would be delivered the very next day. Rio had already promised her that someone would take care of all the details and that when she next came back to the apartment, it would be ready to be lived in.

Evan, who had secretly looked forward to spending a few hours putting some of the furniture together, was almost disappointed to find out that Rio had already hired a team of guys to do it. Josie had suggested they pop back to the new apartment before they left for home so that they could see how things were going, but he doubted there would be any problems. Rio wasn't the kind of guy who employed anyone who wasn't good at their job.

"Here." Evan jumped as Josie handed him a bottle of water from their very own refrigerator. She'd put on the big fluffy hotel robe and had her hair up on top of her head in a messy bun. She nudged his shoulder. "Move over."

He shifted on the cushioned window seat so she could

join him and took a swig of water more out of politeness than need.

"Is everything okay?" Josie asked.

"Yeah." He risked a smile down at her. "I guess my brain's just a bit scrambled right now with everything that's going on."

"It's certainly different here." She took the bottle and also had a drink. "Do you hate it?"

"Why should I?"

She shrugged. "A lot of people who choose to live outside a city environment do so for a reason."

"I didn't get to choose," he pointed out. "I was just born there. I like this city just fine. The nice thing about where our place is that all this is just a few hours away—even closer if you choose to fly."

Josie nodded. "That's one of the reasons why Rio decided to buy the ranch in Morgan Valley."

"The other being Yvonne, right?"

She smiled. "That definitely had something to do with it." She looked out over the city lights. "Have you spoken to your dad tonight?"

"I sent Adam a text about what time to expect me home, but as Dad's decided he isn't my boss anymore, I left it at that."

"Do you think he means it?"

"I dunno. He was pretty adamant about stepping back. I think he wants to spend more time with my mom."

Evan wasn't sure why she was bringing all this up, but he was more than willing to talk in circles if it suited her. He wasn't used to feeling stuff and he was even worse at not blurting it out.

"It's a bit like my mom occasionally hanging out with

Graham—the man she threatened to kill during the custody hearing over Rio."

Evan frowned. "My mom didn't threaten anyone—my dad was the one who said if she took him to court, she'd never see us again."

"Maybe neither of them really meant it." Josie sighed. "I mean why would you ever want to reconnect with someone who treated you so badly?"

"Well, your mom can be pretty dramatic sometimes," Evan pointed out.

"She paid for it by being denied joint custody by the judge at the time. She didn't get to see Rio for years because he wasn't even allowed to leave the country."

"I guess that during a divorce people often say the worst shit they can think of just to get free," Evan said slowly. "And maybe when they get older, they start to remember the good things about the other person that attracted them in the first place."

"I still don't get how your mom has forgiven your father."

"Maybe she's just a good person?" Evan suggested. "Remember, she came back on her own terms, and she's certainly not taking any crap from my dad anymore."

"Good for her." Josie handed him back the water bottle. "I'm not sure I could ever be so forgiving."

"Me neither. I got a front row seat to watch my parents' marriage implode. I'm already skittish about the whole idea of loving someone forever, but my brothers and sister seem to have gotten over themselves, so maybe there is something in it."

"Ines said that Danny and Faith went out together when they were teenagers."

"What about it?" Evan stiffened.

"There's no need to get salty."

"I'm just wondering why you suddenly focused in on them."

She frowned at him. "I just thought it was sweet."

"Sweet?" He shook his head. "Danny nearly fell apart after she left. It took years for him to get his confidence back, and then Faith turns up, and—" He paused. "Well, we all know how that went."

"Are you still mad? I thought you'd worked things out with Danny."

"We're good."

Josie stared at him. "It doesn't sound like it to me."

"He's got way worse things to worry about right now than me. He's got to deal with Faith's parents who told them both a crock of lies about—" Evan abruptly stopped. "A lot of stuff that happened back then."

She patted his hand. "It's okay, I'm not asking you to reveal family secrets."

"Seeing as that's how I got on Danny's shit list in the first place, I'm not going to repeat the mistake. I just wish—" He let out a breath.

"What?"

"I just wish I'd told him everything."

Josie didn't say anything but watched him carefully.

Evan tried to smile. "I can't tell you that either, because it's all tied up with all the other stuff."

"The stuff you already blurted out to your family over the dinner table." Josie nodded.

"And here's the stupid thing. I can't rest easy with Danny until I tell him, but I can't tell him because he'll hate me all over again—maybe this time for good. He's got Faith now. He doesn't need me in his life."

She gripped his hand. "Didn't we just talk about our parents forgiving things that they originally thought were unforgiveable?"

Evan nodded.

"So maybe you should give Danny the benefit of the doubt and let him decide what he wants to do with what you have to tell him," Josie said gently. "He might surprise you."

Chapter Eighteen

Josie was trying to keep out of the way as Rio's crack team put together a whole series of bookshelves that would cover the whole wall that was at right angles to the floor-to-ceiling windows. Immediately on arrival, Evan had waded into the middle of the confusion, his expression thrilled, and offered his help. She'd forgotten he'd worked for Kaiden's carpentry business and that he was obviously in his element. He was soon chatting away in a mixture of Spanish, Portuguese, and English and was rapidly making friends with everyone as he banged in nails, planed down a piece that didn't fit correctly, and generally made himself useful.

At some point, if she decided to live permanently in the apartment, she would consider investing in some more expensive furniture, but until then the IKEA stuff would do just fine. Her cell buzzed and she walked through into the much-quieter bedroom to take the call.

"Mr. Howatch."

"Josie." He cleared his throat. "I understand that you are currently in the city."

"Just for the weekend. I'm moving apartments."

"So, I understand. I would appreciate it if you could come and visit me at home this evening."

Josie walked over to the window to take in the spectacular view. "I'm due back in Morgan Valley tonight. We were just about to leave."

"I assume you have no specific reason for having to return there?"

"I do have to deliver Evan Miller back home. His family are expecting him," Josie replied.

"What if you bring him with you for an early dinner and leave after that? The roads will be clearer for the drive home."

Josie frowned. "Forgive me if this sounds rude, but is there a reason we can't have this conversation over the phone, by Zoom or by e-mail?"

"Yes. The matter I wish to discuss is confidential."

"But—"

"How about this?" Graham interrupted her. "If you come, I'll send you both back on my private jet."

"What about my truck?" Josie countered.

"I'll have it returned to you by tomorrow night."

Josie considered her options. Despite everything, Graham Howatch was still her boss. "I'll have to check that Evan is okay with this."

"If he isn't, I'll pay him to drive your car home. Call my assistant if that's what he wants to do."

"And if he's okay to come, what time would you like us to arrive?"

"Let's make it five-thirty, shall we?" Graham was so used to getting his own way that he didn't even sound triumphant. "You have my address."

Josie considered checking in with Rio to ask him

whether he knew what was going on, but decided against it. Her brother was already fighting to stop himself from being totally submerged in the void left by his father's increasingly frail health. Complaining about Graham wouldn't help Rio's current struggles.

She went back into the kitchen and tried to get Evan's attention. Eventually, he looked up and came over to her.

"What's up? Do we need to leave?" He grinned at her. "It's the first time I've felt useful all weekend."

"You have other uses." She winked at him. "Graham Howatch asked us to dinner this evening."

"Rio's dad?"

"And my boss," Josie reminded him. "Well, he asked *me,* but when I said we'd come together he asked you as well. He says it's something he has to discuss with me face-to-face."

His smile dimmed. "Okay, but what about getting home?"

"Graham says he'll send us back in his private jet."

"Nice." He still looked unconvinced.

"Or—if you don't want to hang around, he said he'll pay you to drive my truck back to Morgan Valley."

"Which would you rather I did?" Evan asked.

"I'd rather you stayed, but I can see that you might prefer to get back." Mindful of her promise to herself not to monopolize Evan's time, Josie added with an airy laugh, "It's not as if Graham's going to let you hear this supposedly top-secret stuff he wants to talk to me about."

"So, basically you're saying I'd be in the way."

"That's not what I said." She met his gaze, and he didn't look away, his smile completely gone. "Don't make this into something it isn't, Evan."

He gave a sharp nod. "I'll take the truck home. Do you need a ride over to Graham's place, or should I just get going now?"

With a strong feeling of disappointment, she wrestled the car keys out of her pocket and dropped them on the countertop. "I'll get myself there, thanks."

"Great." He picked up the keys and half turned away. "I'll just go and say good-bye to the boys, and then I'll be off."

"Hold up. Graham said to call his assistant so you can be reimbursed for the gas and—"

"I don't need his money. I might not work for a multinational company, but I can afford a tank of gas."

"Evan, there's no need to get all salty here."

He reached out to pat her shoulder. "Thanks for a great weekend, I'll see you when you get back—*if* you get back."

"I'm not sure what you're trying to imply, but I'll probably be back before you," Josie said pointedly.

"Sure you will." He turned away and spent a few minutes slapping backs and laughing with the contractors before he picked up his jacket and hat and walked out into the hall. "Safe trip home, Josie."

She still hadn't decided exactly what she wanted to say to him before he'd shut the front door and gone off whistling down the hallway.

Leaving Rio's crew to finish up, she decided to walk back to the hotel to pack her stuff and take a shower before her dinner with Graham. She was glad she'd liberated a clean blouse and pantsuit from her new closet and would have something appropriate to wear.

When she reached her hotel suite, she stood for a

moment with her back against the door and listened to the silence. There was no Evan stretched out on the couch watching sports. She walked through the rooms, half hoping he'd changed his mind and stayed. He wasn't in the big bathroom taking a shower or napping in bed, either—not that she'd really been expecting him there. When Evan made up his mind, he rarely changed it. He'd obviously been back because all his stuff was gone, and he'd left her luggage on the bed.

She sank down on the couch and let out her breath. In her effort to make sure he didn't feel like she was monopolizing his time, she'd managed to convince him he wasn't necessary, and now he was pissed at her. But what else could she have said? Wouldn't he have felt even worse if they'd gone to dinner and Graham had made him feel superfluous? Her boss was very good at that.

With a groan she got up and went into the bathroom. There was no time to worry about Evan right now. She still had no idea what Graham wanted, and one thing she knew about her big boss was that she'd need all her wits about her. What would she do if he insisted she had to come back to work full-time right now? Could she do it? She'd made the first move and got over her fear of returning to her old apartment. Could she keep that motivation going forward, or was it all going to be too much?

She wished Evan had stayed.

Josie paused as she turned on the shower. There was no point denying it any longer, Evan's presence in her life had quickly become way too important. But was it because she was in such a vulnerable state that any half-decent human being who was nice to her immediately became the chosen one? Or was it simply that Evan

Miller was just what she wanted? God, she was sick of doubting every single thing that happened in her life.

Seeing as Evan was probably never going to talk to her again after today, all her feelings on the matter seemed mighty irrelevant right now. . . .

Evan's phone rang when he was about two hours into the journey. As Josie's truck was newer than his, he was able to answer the call hands-free.

"Hi, darling, just checking in with you."

"Hey, Mom. I'm on my way back. Tell Dad not to lose it just yet." Evan negotiated a steep left curve on the freeway. "Josie had to stay so I'm driving her truck."

"Oh, no, poor Josie. I wondered if she'd get sucked back into everything if she returned to the city." Leanne sighed. "Graham's probably putting a lot of pressure on her to return to work. Isabelle says he thinks she's got what it takes to run the whole company."

"I'm sure she could if she wanted to," Evan said. "In fact, she's having dinner with him tonight. That's why she couldn't come back with me. I was invited, but I thought they'd probably be talking about stuff way over my pay grade."

"It's a shame you didn't stay. I wouldn't want to face Graham Howatch by myself."

A flicker of doubt seized Evan. "Josie didn't sound as if she wanted me there."

"Then that's okay," Leanne said reassuringly. "She probably thought you'd be bored stiff."

Evan repressed a sigh. Apparently, Josie wasn't the

only one who thought he was too dumb to take out to dinner.

"Anyways, I'll stop for gas before I come over the mountain pass and I'll call you when I'm closer to home, okay?" Evan exited the freeway and headed toward the smaller roads that would take him up to the summit. "Love you, Mom."

"You too, Evan."

She ended the call and he settled into the drive, his thoughts busy. For the first time in ages, he wished he could talk things through with Danny, but until he cleared the other mess up, that wasn't possible. He tried to imagine what Danny would say to him if he was sitting there.

"He'd say you were an asshole and that just because you're supersalty about your lack of education and experience doesn't make it everyone else's fault if they point it out," Evan said out loud. "And Danny would be damn right as well."

He checked the map and tried to remember exactly where the last gas station was before things got dicey. It was going to be dark by the time he came over the summit. The last thing he needed was to be stranded up there without any gas. There might be plenty of reasons for his siblings to laugh at him, but that wasn't going to be one of them.

When she arrived at Graham's house on Steiner Street, which was popularly known as the row of painted ladies, Josie surreptitiously checked her cell before she knocked on the door. There was nothing from Evan, who must be well on his way home by now. She pulled up his name on her phone and sent him a text.

Please let me know when you get home, okay?

He didn't reply, but then she hadn't really been expecting him to. She hadn't been kidding about her arriving back about the same time as he did. If the mountain passes got busy or blocked by fresh snow, the journey back to Morgan Valley could take twice as long. In extreme weather, the cars would literally be turned around. She'd checked the weather that morning when she'd thought she and Evan would be traveling back together and everything had looked okay. But conditions could change on a dime.

"Good evening, Ms. Martinez."

She looked up to find Graham's English butler regarding her from the open front door, his expression as unruffled as ever.

"Good evening, Mr. Marr." She smiled as she went into the richly decorated interior. "How are you this fine evening?"

"Very well, Ms. Martinez. May I take your outerwear?" She surrendered her coat and he also took her wheelie case. "I have arranged for a car to pick you up after dinner and take you to Mr. Howatch's private plane for your onward journey."

"Thank you."

He lowered his voice. "Mr. Howatch becomes fatigued very easily these days, so we try not to overtax him."

"I hear you." Josie nodded. "I definitely won't overstay my welcome."

He nodded and gestured for her to follow him down the narrow hallway to the rear of the house. "Since Mrs. Howatch moved out, Mr. Howatch has taken over the ground floor for his study and bedroom."

He paused at the door and knocked. "Ms. Martinez, sir."

"Thank you, Marr."

Josie went in to find Graham sitting in an upright chair by the fire. A discreet figure wearing scrubs sat in the background and waved at Josie.

"Hey."

"Hey, Mike, how's life treating you?" She waved back before turning to her host. "Good evening, Mr. Howatch."

"Please call me Graham."

Josie was shocked at the deterioration in Graham since the wedding in Vegas. He seemed to have shrunk in his chair and could barely hold his head up. A thin tube came out of his nostril and was taped to the side of his head.

She took the seat opposite him where he indicated and forced herself to smile.

"My mother texted me earlier to say she'd got some of the wedding photos from Yvonne. Have you received any yet?"

"Not that I know of. But I am glad that I was there to witness the wedding in person. I'm pleased to see my son settling down at last."

"Aren't we all?" Josie countered. "I mean he certainly took his time."

"I suspect he had some very good reasons for that." Graham looked up as Marr brought his drink and offered Josie a glass of her favorite white wine. "Perhaps unlike his parents, his marriage will last."

"I'll drink to that." Josie raised her glass. She and Graham had always had an unorthodox working relationship because she'd never been scared of him in the slightest. He'd always allowed her a great deal more latitude to tell him the truth than he'd ever allowed his own son. She suspected she reminded him of Isabelle and that he quite enjoyed their spirited discussions.

"Rio has also been generous about taking on extra responsibilities in Howatch International."

"He's certainly been busy," Josie agreed. "One might say *too* busy."

"Which is where you come in."

Josie tensed and set her wineglass down. "Is this about me returning to my current job?"

"No, actually." Graham studied her. "I'd like you to take on the role of Chief Financial Officer for the whole of Howatch International."

Josie blinked at him. "You are kidding, right?"

She received a faint smile in return. "No, I'm not. You could do it."

"I'm neither qualified nor ready to step into that role," Josie hastened to say. "The current CFO is also fantastic at her job."

"But I want you there to support your brother when he takes over *my* job."

"Rio hasn't agreed to that, has he?" Josie said automatically.

"Not yet, but he will." Graham's quiet confidence was worrying. "And if you're by his side, I'd be much happier."

"I'm not taking Gina Mazinga's job," Josie said firmly.

"And if Rio does want my help with the company, I'm sure he'll ask me himself."

"When I die, Rio will have a controlling interest in the business. If he doesn't want to run it, he'll be risking a lot of livelihoods. I think he'll do what he was born to do, take it on, and make it even more successful than it already is."

"And I think you're nuts," Josie said frankly. "*And* I believe this is a conversation you should be having with Rio, not me."

"But it is a question that also involves you." Graham paused to take a drink. "Did your mother tell you about our recent discussions?"

"Tell me what?"

"Half of the shares in Howatch International I originally planned to leave to her will now go directly to you."

Silence fell, broken only by Graham's raspy breathing and the ticking of a clock on the mantelpiece.

"That means you will own three percent of the company. If you and your mother vote with your brother, you will be able to run the business just as you wish."

"I don't need your money," Josie said automatically.

"I am well aware of that. Your father left both you and your mother well taken care of financially. But, if you truly wish to help your brother, you can now do so—which is why my offer of the job of CFO still stands." He glanced over at Mike, his nurse. "Can you assist me into the dining room? I believe it is time to eat."

"Wait." Josie held up her hand. "I hope you don't expect me to keep this conversation just between us, because I'm fairly certain Rio needs to hear this."

Graham looked amused. "Josie, I am absolutely relying

on your loyalty to your brother to relay the entirety of this discussion to him. How else would I get him to hear me out when he refuses to discuss this with me?"

"That's not fair."

"Life's not fair and I should know because I'm not expected to live for very much longer." Graham sat forward. "I will do anything in my power to safeguard the future of the company I built with my bare hands."

"So, you want to use me as a go-between. Why not just ask my mother?"

"Because you work with Rio and he trusts you, and your mother can be somewhat excitable."

"My mother might be excitable but she's not stupid," Josie said.

"Trust me, I've never doubted her intelligence or her spirit. I believe that in this particular situation, a calmer head might help."

"And that's me?" Josie grimaced. "You do know why I've been off work for three months?"

"For entirely justifiable reasons. I understand that the man responsible has been apprehended. I can assure you that I will use my influence to ensure that he will never trouble you again."

"Must be nice to have half the government in your pocket," Josie muttered.

He smiled. "Sometimes it has its uses."

Graham beckoned to Mike who helped him transition into his wheelchair. "Now, come along. Marr assures me that chef has chosen all your favorite dishes, so you'd better not disappoint him."

"I don't intend to. I'm starving."

"Evan Miller chose not to accompany you?" Graham

asked as she moved to the side to allow him access to the door. "Sensible man."

"He's way too nice to be involved in all this mess," Josie said.

"Lucky man."

Josie waited for Mike to wheel Graham past her and took the opportunity to escape to the bathroom. When she came out, Mike was just exiting the dining room.

Josie beckoned to him to come closer. "Is Mr. Howatch telling the truth?"

"About how long he has left to live? Unfortunately, yes. His medical team have exhausted every possible treatment and have told him he has less than three months." Mike's eyes were kind. "I'm sorry, Josie."

"No, it's okay." She patted his arm. "Thanks for being honest with me."

"Don't worry. We'll make sure he doesn't suffer, and I'll stay with him until the end."

"Unlike wife number four who headed out to Florida the moment he got sick and divorced him," Josie muttered.

"He's better off without that one, I can assure you." Mike cleared his throat. "Now, go on through and enjoy your dinner."

"I will. Thanks for everything you do."

"I know you won't believe me, but Mr. Howatch has been a great employer."

Josie snorted. "Who were you looking after before him? Lucifer?"

"Get on with you." Mike gave her a gentle shove toward the dining room door.

She was still smiling as she went in and took her place

at Graham's right hand. She knew him well enough that when he immediately started talking about her mother's ranch that he was done with the earlier subject and would not be drawn on it. The question was—how much was she willing to share with Rio, and what was Graham hiding from her?

If she wanted to find out how things really stood at Howatch International, she was going to have to woman up, head into her old office tomorrow, and get ahead of the current gossip. It also meant she wouldn't be going back to Morgan Valley tonight and that things with Evan wouldn't be resolved. Even as she pictured his careful expression as he'd turned around and left, her heart hurt. He'd think she was never coming back. And what was worse, she couldn't even tell him what was going on right now, which might make him feel even more left out.

There was no easy answer. All she could hope was that he'd still be willing to hear her out when she finally got to see him face-to-face.

Chapter Nineteen

"Hey, Evan." Rio got out of Jaime's truck and came toward where Evan was just about to stable Joker after their morning ride. "I came by for Josie's truck."

"She's not back yet?"

"She got held up in the city," Rio said easily. "I gather there were some issues with the new apartment she had to deal with in person."

Even as his stomach dropped, Evan nodded. "Makes sense. It's a nice space."

"You liked it?" Rio studied Evan. "I'm just glad she agreed to take it. I'll feel much safer knowing where she is even when I'm not around."

"Understandable." Evan gestured at the house. "Do you want to come in while I get the keys?"

"Sure. I'll just tell Jaime it's okay to leave, and I'll follow you inside."

Evan went into the mercifully empty house and made sure there was fresh coffee available before getting the keys from his bedroom. With his dad back out working on the ranch, Evan was far more inclined to pop in for a well-earned break or a second breakfast. By the time he returned, Rio was standing in the kitchen running a hand over the worktops. "Kaiden does beautiful work."

"He does." Evan gave Rio the keys and poured them both a mug of coffee. "Julia's got him developing a website so he can offer his talents to all those rich folks in the Bay Area when he's there with her. You know the ones."

"I'd be more than happy to be his first customer."

"Didn't you just buy that whole building newly refurbished?" Evan asked.

"Yeah, but there's high end and then there's *custom*."

"And you're rich enough to know the difference," Evan said with a smile.

"I sure am." Rio took a sip of coffee. "I wanted to thank you for everything you've done for Josie over the past few weeks."

"She's great." Evan shrugged like he didn't have a care in the world. "I think we'll always be friends."

"Even if she decides to stay in the city?" Rio asked. "I heard she was back in the office this morning. Everyone was thrilled. You really helped her get her confidence back."

Evan took a moment to absorb that kicker. It looked like he'd been right, and Josie wouldn't be back anytime soon. "I'm sure she'll be coming out here to see you and Yvonne. We can always reconnect then."

"I damn well hope so." Rio paused. "I've never seen her take to someone quite like she has you."

"I am pretty awesome." Evan pretended to shrug, and Rio laughed.

"And so modest." Rio set his mug down on the

countertop. "I just want you to know that if you did want to continue to be 'friends' with her, I'd be fine with it."

"That's up to Josie. I'm just glad I was here for her when she needed someone like me."

"Someone like you?" Rio's brow creased.

"You know—not her usual type of boyfriend."

Rio studied him for a long moment. "I've just got one word of advice for you, Evan. Don't ever downplay who you are. You've made Josie happier than I've seen her in years, so you've obviously got something going for you."

Evan decided to keep his mouth shut as Rio continued.

"Don't blow it, okay?" He tossed the keys in the air and caught them. "Talk to you soon. Give my best to your *familia.*"

Evan remained standing in the quiet kitchen, staring at nothing for a while after Rio had left, his heart at war with his common sense. Josie hadn't returned after saying she would, and she'd gone back to work. He forced himself to remember the original promise they'd made to each other that they'd smile and wave good-bye when they reached the natural end of their relationship.

Was this it? Had she really been saying good-bye forever while she admitted he wouldn't fit in with her working life like it was all an amusing joke right in the middle of her new kitchen? Evan shook his head. No. She wasn't that cruel. If she'd wanted to dump him, she would've said it straight to his face. On the other hand, if he wanted to call it quits, he had the perfect opportunity to ghost on her now that she was permanently back in the city.

It would hurt less if he just kept up his end of the bargain and let it go. . . .

"You okay?"

He turned his head to see Danny studying him from the kitchen doorway.

"Yeah, I'm good."

"I just saw Rio leaving with Josie's truck. I thought you said she'd be picking it up herself?"

"She's staying in the city." Evan poured the rest of Rio's coffee in the sink.

"Which explains why you look like someone just kicked your favorite puppy." Danny helped himself to the coffee. "You've never had the kind of face that can hide how you feel, Ev."

"So what?" Evan shrugged. "It's okay if I'm disappointed, she's not coming back."

"Like ever?"

"How would I know?" Evan put Rio's mug in the dishwasher and shut the door with a bang. "I'm not her keeper."

"But you are going out with her, right? Seems reasonable that she'd let you know something important like that."

Evan refilled his mug and went into the pantry to find something to eat. When he came out, Danny was still leaning against the countertop.

"I'm right here if you have something you need to talk about, Evan," Danny said gently. "We've always been there for each other."

"Nothing to talk about. I knew Josie would be going back to work at some point and that things would come to an end."

"Doesn't mean you have to feel good about it though,"

Danny suggested. "If you care about her—and you obviously do."

"I'll be fine." Evan slathered mayonnaise on two pieces of bread and added chicken and tomato.

"Maybe if you talk things through, you could visit her in the city."

"Like I'd fit in there." Evan growled. "She didn't even want me to go and have dinner with her boss." He belatedly stopped talking before he revealed Graham's name. He didn't want to be accused of betraying company secrets. "She decided I'd be bored."

"You would've been bored."

"That's not the point. If I can't fit in with her life, there's no chance we can have a relationship."

"Maybe you should talk to Kaiden. He's finding a way to live with Julia while she's still working in the city. They're trying to make things work because they love each other."

"That's different."

"How?" Danny frowned.

"Because of the 'love' word. Josie and I aren't in love or anything."

"You sure about that?" Danny asked. "Because you don't half look like it."

"Bullshit." Evan slapped his sandwich together and cut it in half. "I'll take this out with me."

He grabbed his water flask and a couple of bags of chips and headed for the door. Unfortunately, he still had to get past Danny.

"Don't forget we're all going to the McDonalds' for dinner tonight."

"Do I have to?"

For the first time, Danny grimaced. "I'd appreciate the support. They still aren't happy about how everything went down with me and Faith."

"Okay, then I'll come."

"Thanks." Danny's smile was full of relief. "That means a lot to me."

"Is Dad going?" Evan asked warily.

"Everyone is."

"Cool."

Danny looked resigned. "It had to happen at some point. Faith and I decided better to have a full blowout now rather than six months down the line."

"Good thinking." Evan nodded at his brother. "I'll make sure I'm back in time to change."

Josie took the seat opposite Evangelista Smith-Orso, speaker of six languages, gatekeeper and guardian of Rio's calendar, and his executive assistant for the past three years. She was a formidable woman who had originally worked for Graham and now protected Rio like a dragon, and for that, Josie had always liked her. She was also dryly funny, loyal to a fault, and due to her exceptional networking talents, knew everything that went down in the entire organization.

They'd agreed to meet well away from the Howatch International offices for lunch after Josie had spent the morning reconnecting with everyone.

Eva picked up the menu. "Everything is good here, but I recommend the sushi platters."

Josie shuddered. "I'm not good with cold, raw, fish,

but if you can put up with the slurping, I'll happily eat a bowl of noodles."

"Slurp away." Eva beckoned to the waiter who set two glasses of iced water on the table and took their order.

She waited until the server walked away before turning her full attention on Josie. "What do you want to know?"

"First, I need to ask you if this conversation can be completely off the record—I mean you can't even mention it to Rio unless I give you the go-ahead."

"Unless it comes down to a legal case, then I'm good with that." Eva nodded. "What's up?"

"Does Rio want to run Howatch International?"

Eva pursed her lips. "Two years ago, I would've said absolutely not, but now . . . I think there are some aspects of the business that appeal to him greatly, whereas other things just frustrate him."

"So, when Mr. Howatch is gone, do you think Rio would take the job of CEO if it meant the company remained viable and operational?"

"He doesn't have to be the actual CEO to make money out of the company," Eva reminded Josie. "He's still the major shareholder. It's a private company. He could recruit a new CEO at any time."

"Only if Graham doesn't tie his hands," Josie said.

"It's possible, I suppose," Eva said thoughtfully. "Mr. Howatch could insist that Rio remain in control for a certain number of years in order to gain full access to his shares or something. Rio could fight it in court, but that would cost a fortune and might destroy market confidence in the company." Eva unwrapped her chopsticks and placed her napkin on her lap. "Are you worried?"

"I guess I just don't want Rio having his hand forced," Josie admitted.

"I don't think he'd allow that to happen. He's a very strong and independent man."

"With a deep sense of responsibility to his family and the company," Josie added. "That's the bit where Graham always gets him."

"I haven't heard anything from Mr. Howatch's company or personal lawyers for quite some time, but that might be because I refused to pass on information about Rio."

"Good for you."

Eva sighed. "Well, yes and no, because if I was still fully in the loop, I might have a better idea exactly what Mr. Howatch will do."

"What's your gut telling you?" Josie asked.

"That Mr. Howatch will do anything possible to tie Rio to the company for eternity."

"Well, that's not encouraging."

Eva sat back as the server placed her sushi platter in front of her. "It wasn't meant to be. But at least you'll be prepared for the worst."

"Graham wants me to talk to Rio for him," Josie confessed.

"Interesting." Eva picked up a piece of tuna with her chopsticks, dunked it in her soy sauce, and popped it into her mouth. She chewed slowly before eyeing Josie. "Are you going to do it?"

"Part of me thinks that if he wants me to talk to Rio then I really shouldn't, but then what if I don't, and Rio doesn't know what Graham might be planning?"

"I'd tell him. Rio's good at dissecting his father's bullshit."

"I damn well hope so, because this is a doozy," Josie said.

After lunch, Josie took a cab back to her new apartment and spent some time unpacking boxes and setting up her bedroom. She's always found it easier to think when she was busy, and she sure had a lot on her mind. Rio needed to hear what Graham was up to and she needed to talk to Evan.

He'd sent her a text to say he'd gotten home safely but nothing since.

She got out her phone and considered her options. Call or text? She decided to text.

Hey, just to let you know I'll probably be back tonight. Looking forward to seeing you.

She watched the bubbles form as he started to reply.

No need. Rio picked up your truck this morning, so we're good.

Josie frowned at the screen as she typed. You don't want to hang out?

I'm busy tonight.

Like really busy or you just don't want to see me?

Family stuff.

Okay. Are you mad at me?

No, we're good. ☺

Josie gripped her phone tight. **There's stuff I need to talk to you about.**

It's okay. I got the message loud and clear.

What message is that? Josie typed.

Look, we agreed we wouldn't get all hurt or fight when things came to an end.

Josie sharply inhaled. **We're over????**

You're back at work, so I guess so.

Fine. Josie set her phone facedown with deliberate care and spoke out loud. "Be like that." And burst into tears.

Evan was still unsettled when he walked with his parents up to the front door of the McDonalds' place. When he'd read back the texts between him and Josie, he'd realized they made him sound like an idiot—a passive-aggressive one at that. He'd never been good at texting. He was always scared he'd say the wrong thing and it would be immortalized forever and come back to bite him in the ass.

Josie had reached out to him and he'd acted like a first-class jerk. By trying to pretend that he was the better person, he'd come across as the worst. When a woman finished her conversation with the word *fine,* even he knew things hadn't gone well. But what was there to talk about? She'd gone back to work, and he was stuck on his family ranch.

"Welcome!"

Evan tried to focus as the McDonalds invited them in and led them through into the large family room and attached kitchen where everyone who was currently in town had already arrived. Daisy was currently in Silicon Valley finalizing the details of the takeover of her start-up and Ben and Silver were in Los Angeles. Faith's younger brother, Dave, was there with his partner, Dr. Tio, who ran the local medical clinic.

Danny came over with Faith to offer hugs and to take the dessert Leanne had made and Kaiden's offering of beer.

"Hey," Danny murmured to Evan. "Thanks for coming."

"I told you I would."

"I thought what with Josie coming back tonight you might change your mind."

"How did you know about that?" Evan asked.

"Mom heard from Isabelle. She's thrilled, obviously."

"I kind of broke up with her."

Danny went still. "Like, when?"

"In a text."

"Wow, smooth."

"I think I might have messed up, though," Evan confessed.

"Ya think?" Kaiden, who'd obviously been eavesdropping, joined the conversation. "Dumping someone by text is very on-brand for you though, Bro."

"I thought that was usually you," Evan hit back. "I mean weren't you the king of one-night stands at one point?"

Kaiden winked. "That definitely was me, but I'm a

different man now. Way more responsible." He hesitated. "Do you think it's fixable?"

"What? Me and Josie? Not when she's going back to work full-time."

"Oh, man. That sucks." Kaiden gave him a side hug and a noogie, which didn't really help. "Never mind, little Bro, we'll find you a new woman."

"You broke up with Josie?" Leanne asked, and Evan groaned and wished not for the first time that he was an only child.

"Can you all just stop talking about this? We're here to support Danny, not dissect my love life."

"Fine, but we'll get back to you later," Kaiden added, and raised his eyebrows. "So, you'd better have your excuses ready."

"Please come and sit down." Ron McDonald gestured at the extended table. "It's so great that you all could come over."

"There's no need to be so formal. It's not like we don't already know each other, Ron," Jeff grumbled as he found his seat. "We've been neighbors for years and we already went through all this getting together stuff when we tried to stop Danny from seeing Faith when they were teenagers."

"And that worked so well," Dave piped up, and grinned at his sister. "Welcome to the family, Danny!"

"Thanks." Danny smiled as he sat beside Faith. "It's certainly been a trip."

"Hmph." Ron's smile dipped. "You could say that. Shall we start with the appetizers? You can all just help yourself while I deal with the drinks."

Awkward would be a kind word for the gathering,

Evan decided as they moved onto roast lamb and all the trimmings. Not that the McDonalds were unfriendly or anything, but there was just this slight lack of warmth every time they looked at Danny, which Evan found annoying. Faith's dad was also drinking the wine he'd brought back from Europe like water.

"When's your wedding happening, Adam?" Mrs. McDonald asked brightly during one of the many silences.

"Next month," Adam answered. "You'll be getting an invitation anytime soon."

"Not Vegas, then?" Ron asked. "That seems to be a Miller family favorite these days."

Evan set his glass down. "I guess it's a good place to go when you want to get something done without too much hassle or attention."

"Well, obviously." Ron nodded. "I can understand why Silver and Ben made that decision. It must be impossible for poor Silver to get any privacy in this world."

"It's all right, Ron," Jeff said. "When Ben and Silver got hitched without us being there, I wasn't pleased, either, but I got over it." He nodded at Danny. "And as Faith and Danny couldn't get it done last time they tried, I'm glad they persevered."

"It would've been nice if they'd waited," Ron said pointedly. "Faith must have known we'd want to be there."

"Dad, we held a party right here in town the other week so we could celebrate with our friends, family, and neighbors. No one got left out." Faith said the words as if she'd had this argument about a hundred times, and probably had.

"She's right, Ron." Jeff chuckled. "Your problem is that you didn't like her choice of groom. It's always been the same."

"Dad—" Danny cleared his throat. "Not helping."

"Might as well bring it out into the open, Son," Jeff said. "And why Ron has a problem with his daughter marrying a hardworking, decent man who's done nothing except keep on loving Faith despite all the odds, I don't know."

Ron put his glass down so hard that the wine sloshed out onto the tablecloth. "One, I don't need a lecture from you about marriage, Jeff Miller, and two, if Danny hadn't behaved so irresponsibly when he was a teenager, my daughter wouldn't have been put in such an impossible situation in the first place."

"That's not fair." Faith spoke up, her face pale. "Danny and I were in love. We both bear responsibility for what happened."

"Except you were the one who had to suffer the consequences," Ron stated. "While Lover Boy here got off scot-free and still somehow manages to end up with you."

"We both suffered." Faith wasn't backing down. "And, if we're looking to place blame, Dad, if you hadn't chased Danny out of Vegas, he would've been with me when our son was born, and things might've ended up very different."

"We *all* decided that separating you two was necessary." Ron looked around the table. "Come on, Jeff. Back me up on this at least."

Jeff shrugged. "I certainly wanted Danny out of it. We can agree on that."

"So, maybe you could all stop getting mad at me," Ron said. "It was a joint decision and meant for the best."

"You kept things from me and Danny for years," Faith said. "You outright lied to me, and I'm not sure if I can forgive you for that." She glanced up at Danny and then back at her parents. "I'm sorry, but maybe this did need to be said."

Danny put his arm around her and faced Ron. "I get that you're mad, but it's not just about you, is it? You did some damage here. If Faith wants to keep her distance from you until you acknowledge that and somehow make it up to her, I'm good with her decision."

He rose to his feet, bringing Faith with him. "We're going to take a walk outside and get some fresh air."

Ron waited until they'd left the kitchen before taking a big slug of his wine. "I don't regret what we did back then, do you, Jeff?"

"Yeah, actually I do. I should've listened to my sister and let them bring the kid home to raise at our place."

Everyone at the table turned to stare at Jeff. Leanne took his hand.

"Like you would've been a good role model?" Ron shook his head and chuckled. "Mind you, I suppose you ran your own wife off and abandoned her, so Danny was just following the family tradition."

"That's enough." Adam, who was normally the quietest of Evan's brothers, rose to his feet. "None of us need to sit here and listen to you bad-mouth our family. You screwed up. Deal with it and apologize to your daughter, otherwise we'll be more than happy to welcome her into the Miller family for good."

He turned to Evan and Kaiden who had also stood. "Are we ready to go?" At their nods, he faced Ron. "Thanks for dinner. We'll see ourselves out."

Adam grabbed Lizzie's hand, Leanne took Jeff's, and Kaiden and Evan followed along behind as they reassembled in the driveway in front of the house where Danny and Faith already awaited them.

"What happened?" Danny asked warily as he came over, leaving Faith talking to Leanne.

"We decided to leave," Evan answered him. "Ron was being an ass. You should both come home with us."

"We'd already decided to do that." Danny lowered his voice. "I was worried I was going to be the one screwing things up, but Faith beat me to it. She obviously had a lot to get off her chest."

"Good for her," Evan said. "You missed the best part when Dad said he wished he'd listened to Rae and let you bring the baby home."

"Dad said that?" Danny's eyebrows shot up.

"And then Ron suggested our house wouldn't have been a good environment for your kid, and that's when Adam stood up and told him to shut his mouth, and that we were leaving."

"Wow." Danny shook his head. "Just wow."

Evan took a deep breath. "Did you ever wonder how Dad found out you'd gone to Vegas?"

"I assumed Ron called him. Why?"

"I told him."

Danny frowned. "I don't get it."

"I overheard you and Faith planning to get married in

Vegas. When Dad asked me where you were that night, I told him."

"Like, deliberately?"

Evan nodded, his heart thumping so hard, he thought he might pass out.

"*Why?*"

"I guess I was jealous, and I just let it out before I'd thought it through." Evan swallowed hard.

"Dad?" Danny horrified Evan by calling out to their father. "Can you come over here a minute?"

Jeff obliged. "What's up?"

"Evan said he told you Faith and I eloped to Vegas before you heard anything from Ron."

"What about it?"

"So, he did?"

"Yeah. You know Evan. He can't keep a secret to save his life."

"Except it wasn't my secret to keep," Evan said, his gaze fixed on Danny. "I wasn't supposed to know anything about it."

"What did you do when he told you?" Danny asked.

"Nothing." Jeff shrugged. "I figured you'd be married before I could stop you."

"Wait—you didn't tell Ron, or rush off to Vegas?" Evan blinked.

"Not because of anything you said, Son. I did go out there to bring Danny home after Ron called, but that was later when everything had gotten screwed up with the baby thing." Jeff looked longingly back at his truck. "Are we done now? I want to go home."

"Sure." Danny patted him on the shoulder. "We'll follow you in a minute. Can you take Faith with you?"

Soon Evan and Danny were alone with Kaiden's loud complaints about his beer still being in the McDonald refrigerator fading into the distance.

Evan was the first to speak into the silence. "I thought you'd hate me if you ever found out what I did. Ever since Faith came home, I've been waiting for her to tell you her side of the story, certain it would come out that I betrayed you."

"That explains a lot," Danny said slowly.

"I've been waiting for the blow, you know? For you to look at me in disgust. And, when I found out about the baby, I just . . ." Evan winced. "Felt even worse. How could I tell you that I was the one who betrayed you to Dad and ruined three lives?"

"Evan, you were a fifteen-year-old, big-mouthed, way-too-honest *kid*. How could I ever blame you?"

"Because you were my best friend?" Evan held his brother's gaze. "And I let you down."

"Nah, our parents let us *all* down, Ev. This really wasn't on you." Danny set his hand on Evan's shoulder and gently rocked him back and forth. "We're good, okay? We're *good*."

Evan could only nod as his throat closed up and he concentrated fiercely on not blubbing like a baby. Before he could accomplish that, Danny drew him into a bear hug and Evan hugged him back.

"Come on." Danny stepped back. "Time to go home before Ron starts shooting at us."

"He's drunk enough to try," Evan said. "And he's a terrible shot."

"So, we'd better skedaddle because I bet I'm his prime target." Danny started walking. "Faith's going to need some comforting tonight." He glanced over at Evan. "Are you going to see Josie now that dinner's off?"

"I already told her I was too busy."

"Then tell her you're not."

Evan got into the truck and put on his seat belt. "It's complicated."

"Love always is."

"I'm not—" Evan paused and then burst out. "I mean, how can I be? She's the first woman I've ever really been into. The chances of her being 'The One,' whatever the hell that means, are astronomical."

"Maybe you just got lucky," Danny suggested as he turned in a neat circle toward the exit. "Or maybe you knew what you wanted all along and waited patiently until she turned up. Look at me and Faith. I knew she was the one for me when we were sixteen."

He stopped the truck again to look over at Evan. "Don't be like me and almost screw up finding the love of your life. At least, give yourself a chance to find out whether Josie feels the same way about you."

"But she lives in the city, and—"

Danny started driving again. "And if it's meant to last, you'll find a way. Haven't the rest of us taught you that yet?"

"I guess." Evan considered the complicated love lives of his five siblings.

"Just call her and see if she's willing to talk to you."

Evan got out his phone as his brother continued to drive home and started typing.

Hey, dinner finished early. Can I come over?
You're right, we do need to talk.

He waited for a reply until his screen dimmed along with his hopes.

"She's not answering."

"Try when we get home. Reception's spotty on this stretch of the road."

"Will do."

They parked up in the crowded lot in front of the house and went in. Everyone was in the kitchen except Faith. Danny excused himself and Evan settled in to listen to his dad's dramatic recounting of the disastrous family dinner.

"Dig in." Leanne came over and handed him a bowl and spoon. "Luckily I made two peach cobblers and only took one with us."

"Good thinking."

Leanne touched his arm. "Did Josie tell you about Graham Howatch?"

"I haven't checked my phone for hours," Evan lied. "What's up?"

"He's gone into hospice care. Rio, Isabelle, and Josie are already headed back to San Francisco."

Chapter Twenty

Josie squeezed Rio's hand as they went into what had been Graham's study in his house on Steiner Street. Graham's body had just been cremated and his ashes were scheduled to be taken back to Boston and his family burial plot. After a surprisingly well-attended service, the immediate family members and staff had been invited back to the house to speak to Graham's attorney. Josie was surprised how empty the place felt without Graham at the center of it.

"You've got this, *mano*."

"Yeah." Rio visibly braced himself. "Is *Mamãe* okay?"

"She's in her element," Josie whispered as Isabelle came through the door leaning heavily on the arm of the chief attorney, her hair covered by a black lace veil, and a spectacular string of pearls around her neck. "She's channeling Jackie Kennedy."

"None of the other ex-wives were invited," Rio said. "She's definitely milking that."

"Who is?" Yvonne joined them, and Josie rolled her eyes in Isabelle's direction. "Oh."

At the last moment, before the attorney rose to speak, Rio turned to Josie. "Thanks for telling me what we might be up against today. Getting the heads-up about Dad's plans gave me the opportunity to consult my lawyer and create a defense strategy."

"You're welcome," Josie whispered. "And please remember I really do not want Gina's job."

"Noted." Rio went quiet as the attorney cleared his throat.

"Thank you all for joining me here today. We will dispense with the smaller legacies first and then the charitable donations, which are considerable. After that, Mr. Howatch asked us to restrict the rest of the will reading to the immediate family. I'm sure you will all understand."

Josie was pleased to see that all Graham's personal staff, including his butler, Marr, Evangelista, and Mike, his longtime nurse, were given sizable gifts. There were also small amounts for his other three ex-wives. She almost blinked at the millions he was giving away to his charitable foundation and local organizations in Boston and San Francisco.

Eventually, the room was cleared, leaving just Rio, Yvonne, Josie, and their mother. Rio sat on Josie's right with Yvonne on his other side, her mother was on her left. She constantly had to resist the urge to reach out and pat them.

"To my son, Aurelio, I leave my shares in Howatch International with the hope that he will continue in his role as CEO and drive the associated businesses within its folds to new heights. I also leave him my personal fortune and property in Boston and San Francisco, excluding the Steiner Street house." The attorney held up a sheet of paper. "These assets are listed here in their entirety for your later attention."

The attorney paused as Rio held up his hand.

"And?"

"And what, Mr. Martinez?"

"What conditions are attached to me taking control of his estate?"

The attorney checked the paperwork. "None that I can see, sir."

"Are you sure?" Rio frowned.

"I am more than willing to go over everything with you after I have finished reading the rest of the will, Mr. Martinez," the attorney said firmly. "There are just a few further bequests and I will be done."

"Please, go ahead." Rio motioned with his hand, his expression dazed.

"To Josephina Martinez, I leave ten million dollars, three percent of my holdings in Howatch International, and the Steiner Street house."

"Whoa," Josie blurted out. "That's nuts!"

The attorney favored her with a patient smile and carried on reading.

"To my first wife, Isabelle Maria Francesca Martinez, I leave three percent of my total shares in Howatch International, ten million dollars, and the deeds to her ranch in Brazil."

"How sweet." Isabelle dabbed at her eyes with a lace-edged handkerchief. "My ranch is in safe hands forever."

The attorney gathered up the papers and looked

inquiringly at Rio. "Would you like to speak to me now, or would you prefer to set up a meeting when you have absorbed the implications of this impressive inheritance?"

"I'll call you later," Rio said. "Thank you for everything."

Rio went to shake the man's hand and to claim a copy of the will. He escorted the attorney out and came back to where Josie, Yvonne, and Isabelle still sat in a row like they were waiting for the bus.

"Well . . ." He let out his breath. "The cunning old bastard ended up doing the right thing after all. *Mamãe* gets her ranch free and clear, Josie's set up for life, and I . . . get to do whatever the hell I want with Howatch International."

Yvonne kissed his cheek. "Don't look so shocked. I told you he might surprise you."

"You are the only person who believed that might be true," Rio said. "I can't get my head around it yet. All that worrying and planning we did, Josie."

"At least I don't have to be CFO," Josie said.

"As to that." Rio turned to her. "If I do stay on as CEO, would you work for me as my chief of staff?"

"Like your wing woman?" Josie asked.

"Kind of. You could be based wherever you want and just fly around my empire descending whenever necessary to wreak chaos and confusion."

"I like that idea." Josie nodded. "I don't think I ever want to go back to being in the same office every single day."

"You don't even need to do that." Rio watched her closely. "With an extra ten million in the bank. and a house like this, you'll never have to work another day in your life."

"But I'd get bored."

Rio patted her hand. "Think about it, okay? There's no rush. I've still got to decide whether I want to stay on as the actual CEO rather than just the acting one." He smiled at his wife. "That's something Yvonne and I need to talk about."

He got to his feet and Yvonne followed him. "Are you two okay if we head out?"

"Go ahead." Josie blew Rio a kiss. "I'll take care of *Mamãe*."

After Rio and Yvonne departed, Isabelle offered Josie a hug. "This house is a wonderful gift!"

"I'm not sure what I'm supposed to do with it," Josie confessed. "I mean, I've just moved in with Rio and Yvonne."

"You have plenty of time to decide that." Isabelle smiled. "I think that after we attend the Miller wedding, we should go back home. What do you say?"

"I'd forgotten that was coming up," Josie lied. "What with Graham being in hospice care, the last few weeks have flown by."

Josie was also aware that apart from a text expressing his condolences, she hadn't heard anything from Evan. Not that she should've expected to: he'd made it clear that their relationship was over when she'd chosen to stay in San Francisco.

"Are you still intending to go, *Mamãe*? I mean, we have just been to a funeral."

"Of course! Graham would be the first to suggest that

we attend. And to be fair, Josie, Graham isn't a blood relative of either of ours."

"Even though he just left us ten million bucks each?" Josie reminded her.

"Pshaw." Isabelle waved that away. "A mere trifle for a billionaire."

"Seems like a heck of a lot of money to me."

"It will make a nice little nest egg for you and your future family," Isabelle said. "We have to go to the wedding. I've heard such *marvelous* gossip from Leanne about a family dinner with the McDonalds that ended up with the whole Miller family and Faith walking out. How can we miss that?"

"I guess the McDonalds are still upset about Danny and Faith getting married."

"Apparently so. I wonder if the McDonalds will even attend the wedding. It might be awkward if their own daughter isn't speaking to them. I also heard that Dave is backing his sister and considering moving out to live with darling Dr. Tio and his grandmother."

"Sounds like a soap opera."

"Exactly." Isabelle sat back. "Although, I must confess that I am looking forward to being home. I wasn't anticipating spending so much time here, but what with Rio's wedding and then you and Graham, the weeks have stretched into months."

"You should definitely go home, then." Josie took her mother's hand. "The thing is—I won't be able to join you right away. I promised myself that I would stick around to help Rio."

"Ah, quite understandable." Isabelle nodded. "And

there is that little matter of Evan Miller. Leanne says he's been moping terribly since you left."

"Has he?" Josie perked up. "I mean, so what, that's his problem. We're not going out anymore."

"That's a shame."

"I thought you didn't approve of him?"

Isabelle drew herself up. "I am allowed to change my mind. He's grown on me."

"Like a weed?" Josie smiled. "He's like that."

"Then perhaps while we are at the wedding you can at least speak to him?" Isabelle looked so hopeful, Josie wanted to smile. "Leanne is very worried about him."

Josie considered her mother's pleading expression. "I'll think about it, okay?"

There was no point in telling her mother that it wouldn't make any difference because Evan had already made up his mind, but somewhere deep inside her, she still carried a ridiculously foolish drop of hope.

Evan knocked on Kaiden's bedroom door and went in to find his brother in the bathroom staring at his reflection.

"Don't crack the mirror," Evan said.

Kaiden groaned. "Ha ha, and lame. That's why I'm the jokester of the family and not you." He leaned in and kissed the mirror. "You're a beautiful man, Kaiden Miller, and don't you ever forget it."

Evan pretended to barf and Kaiden grinned at him.

"What's up?"

"I wanted to ask you something."

"Go for it." Kaiden walked back into his bedroom where he picked up his freshly ironed shirt and put it on. Adam had asked all his groomsmen to wear blue for the wedding, which was Lizzie's favorite color.

"Danny said you're setting up your carpentry business in San Francisco."

"Yup. It gives me something to do while I'm there and Julia's off being lawyer of the year. She was right about people being willing to pay top dollar for a handcrafted kitchen or piece of furniture."

"So, if I was like in that area, do you think you'd have work for me to do?"

Kaiden stopped buttoning his shirt. "Sure, but I'd expect you to take some classes like Wes is doing to improve your skill set."

"I could do that," Evan said slowly. "I mean, Wes goes to Bridgeport, right? Or I'm sure there are plenty of places I could study in the Bay Area."

"What are you up to, little brother?" Kaiden asked as he added a belt to his pants.

"I'm just trying to think outside the box."

"Good for you." Kaiden gave a firm nod. "Let me know what you decide."

Evan turned to leave and then paused at the doorway. "Do you think it's possible to make a relationship work when one of you works in the city?"

"Well, duh, of course I do. And if Julia and I can make it work, then anyone can."

Evan nodded and headed back to his own room, his mind swirling with ideas. He'd had time to think while Josie was away dealing with Graham Howatch's death,

and faced a few home truths. The first thing he needed
to do was see if she was even interested in having a relationship with him. But he had to make the effort. Not
being with her or ever having the conversation was
killing him.

He was always the guy out front shooting his mouth
off and now, when he needed to step up, he'd suddenly
gone all shy. Evan snorted as he took a shower and hurriedly got dressed. At least with the wedding being at the
ranch, he didn't have to rush too much, and if he forgot
something, he only had to run back inside and fetch it.

He ventured into the kitchen, which was currently full
of Yvonne's catering staff. As Yvonne was still away with
Rio, and Lizzie, her deputy, was the one getting married,
Sonali Patel had stepped up to take command. She took
one look at Evan and headed straight toward him.

"Can you do me a favor?"

"Sure."

"Go outside and check that all the tablecloths and
flowers in the tent are secured against this wind."

"Are you worried everything's going to fly away?"
Evan asked.

"Yes, and it's not funny, Evan. This is the first event
I've been in charge of and I want it to go off without a
hitch," Sonali said firmly.

"As Daisy did the flowers and she lives here, I bet she
made sure they were weighed down like a boss." Evan
tried to reassure her. "But I'll check."

"Thank you, Evan." Sonali was already turning away.
"I appreciate your help."

Evan went outside and round to the back of the house
where the yard he'd once played in with his siblings had

been transformed into a fancy wedding venue complete with large white tents, carpets and, where the old swing set used to be, a platform for the bride and groom to stand on.

Even Evan could appreciate the vines and flowers wrapped around the supports of the tents and the tiny white fairy lights that would look even better in the evening. One of the hotel staff was busy setting out the chairs they'd borrowed in nice, straight rows. In the distance, Tucker, who ran the historic hotel, was gesticulating at the improvised parking lot and his group of valet parkers.

"Looking good." His mom came up beside him and linked her arm through his. She'd already changed into a peach-colored pantsuit with a crisp white blouse underneath. "I must admit, I never thought I'd get to see my eldest son married here."

Evan looked down at her. "I guess this is my first Miller brother wedding, too."

"Unbelievable." Leanne shook her head. "If anyone had told me that last morning when I got on the bus sobbing my heart out and headed for New York that I'd end up seeing such happiness, I would've been a whole lot less miserable."

"Maybe the first part had to happen to get to the second part," Evan said.

"I think you're right." She leaned in and hugged him. "You're such a smart cookie, Evan."

"Right."

"Don't underestimate yourself."

Evan smiled. "That's what Rio told me, too."

"Well, if the brother of the woman you love thinks you're okay, I'd say you're on to something."

Evan sighed. "This love thing . . . it scares me. I mean, you and Dad loved each other when you got married, right? But everything went wrong."

"If you're looking for a guarantee that everyone will stay the same and that nothing will happen to affect that love, then I can't give it to you." Leanne cupped his chin, her expression serious. "But that doesn't mean you don't have to try. Look at your siblings. Every one of them has overcome their doubts and found someone to love."

"Yeah, but I'm the screwup in the family, the one who always gets everything wrong."

"You don't have to be." Leanne held his gaze. "You can change. Spread your wings and try it."

"Jeez, Mom." Evan fake-groaned. "Now you sound like someone in a movie."

"Get along with you." Leanne gave him a gentle push and headed back toward the house. "If you see young Roman around, will you grab hold of him and bring him to me? He hasn't gotten changed yet and Lizzie is starting to worry."

"Will do."

Evan walked over to the structure where they were having the sit-down wedding lunch and carefully checked that both the tablecloths and the beautiful floral arrangements were still firmly in place. As he looked over toward the barn, he thought he saw a flash of movement and headed over there.

He found Roman, Lizzie's son, in one of the stalls chatting away to the calf he was rearing with the 4-H club.

"So, I wish you could be at the wedding, but Jeff said you might crap on the carpet, and Mom said that even if that happened that Jeff shouldn't say that in front of me, and then Adam started laughing, and—"

Roman looked over at Evan who was struggling not to laugh himself. "Hey, Evan."

"Hey, Ro. What's up?"

"Just making sure Patchy isn't lonely while I'm doing the wedding thing."

"He'll be fine," Evan reassured his soon-to-be nephew. "Leanne's looking for you."

Roman wrinkled his nose. "She'll make me take another shower."

"Well, I guess we all have to scrub up when it's someone's wedding day," Evan said. "Especially when it's your mom's."

"Yeah."

Evan frowned as Roman slowly stood up and brushed the straw off his jeans. "You worried about something?"

Roman walked toward him and Evan let him out of the gate and fastened it behind him.

"What if Adam goes away, like my real dad did?" Roman blurted out.

Evan hunkered down so he was on eye level with Roman and put a hand on his shoulder. "I swear to you from the bottom of my heart that Adam would never *ever* do that to you or your mom."

"How do you know?"

"Because he's my big brother and he's the best. If he ever did anything to hurt your mom, me, and the rest of your uncles would kick his ass all the way to the state border."

"You would?" Roman looked skeptical. "He's a really big guy."

"Yeah, but if we ganged up on him, I think we could take him."

"Maybe."

"But we won't have to because Adam loves Lizzie and you so much, he'd be a fool to mess that up." Evan stood up and offered Roman his hand. "You ready to go in now? You don't want Jeff coming to look for you, do you?"

Roman took his hand and they started walking.

"I think he's funny," Roman confided. "He says all the bad words I'm not allowed to say."

"True," Evan agreed. "But when you get that old, you can get away with a lot more."

"He said I can call him Grandpa if I want to, but he didn't sound very pleased about it."

"Yeah? You should do that a lot." Evan fought a smile. "He'll love it."

Roman was skipping along so fast now that Evan had to lengthen his stride. He noticed the first couple of cars coming up the drive and checked the time. In less than an hour, Adam would finally marry Lizzie, with his family and friends all around him, which was amazing, and almost made Evan believe in the power of love.

Evan held open the door to let Roman into the house and smiled. And he'd get the chance to see Josie again and maybe find the courage to plead his own case.

* * *

Josie took her seat near the back of the groom's side and looked around her. She couldn't believe how the Millers backyard had been transformed into such a beautiful wedding venue. From what she'd overheard on the way in, the folks at the historic hotel had worked with Yvonne's catering company and Daisy's florist shop to produce the overall effect.

Isabelle was busy waving at everyone while simultaneously explaining who they were to Josie. There was no sign of the bride, but Adam Miller, accompanied by all four of his brothers had just swept past them to stand at the front by the raised platform under the big California oak tree. Seeing as they wore identical blue shirts and white straw Stetsons, she could barely make out which one was Evan.

"They must be Lizzie's family," Isabelle murmured as Adam went over to greet an older woman and her companion who certainly looked happy to be there. "I think they live in Florida. They are very fond of their grandson."

"Who wouldn't be?" Josie said. "He's a charmer."

"Oh, look! There's Ruth Morgan and she's brought Chase and January with her. I wonder if their kids are acting as Lizzie's attendants along with Roman?"

Josie didn't worry about answering any of her mother's rhetorical questions as there was always another one queued up.

Isabelle elbowed her in the side. "The McDonalds have come. Ron doesn't look very happy, does he?"

Josie was far more interested in staring at Adam's brothers who were busy working the two front rows where their immediate family were sitting. Did Evan even know she was there? She certainly hadn't contacted him directly to let him know she was coming. As though he'd heard her thoughts, he suddenly looked over and their eyes locked. He offered her a slight nod before turning away with a smile to speak to his mother and a young, redheaded woman she assumed was his half sister, Ellie.

Unless it was his new girlfriend. . . .

Before she could go down that treacherous path, music started playing and everyone was asked to stand. Roman was the first down the aisle carrying the rings on a velvet pillow. He was followed by two little girls with flower baskets. Behind them came Lizzie in a long, white dress with a veil and a crown of flowers, leaning on her father Derek's arm. Both of them were beaming.

Josie turned to look at Adam, who generally didn't have the most expressive face and was transfixed by his dazzling, slow smile as Lizzie came ever closer. When Roman ran up to him, Adam picked the boy up, settled him on his hip, and turned to greet his bride.

"I guess we're doing this all together," Adam said as Roman wiggled his way to stand between them and the local preacher cleared his throat and began the service.

"Dearly beloved . . ."

Evan was pretty sure he'd kissed, hugged, and shaken hands with about a thousand wedding guests and still not got within a mile of Josie and her mother. It was as if they were inhabiting two different universes, which he hoped wasn't a bad omen. Eventually, he managed to find himself on the edge of the fray and stepped out onto the turf. He took off his hat and wiped his brow.

"Hey."

He looked to his left and there she was.

"Hey." He set his hat back on his head and took a good, long look at her. She wore a crisp pink dress with a border of red cherries, high-heeled red sandals, and dangly gold earrings, and looked good enough to eat. "You look great."

"So do you."

"Sorry about Mr. Howatch."

She shrugged. "He was always very fair with me, but I can't say I ever got to know him well. He was very tough on Rio."

"I bet." Evan tried to think of what to say next. It wasn't like him to be either so polite or so stilted. "Do you think he'll take over the company?"

"I don't know." She sighed. "I don't even know if I want him to. It's a massive responsibility and I'd hate to lose him to his job. One of the reasons why he couldn't come to the wedding this weekend was because he and Yvonne want to talk things through."

"It's a lot." Evan nodded. "How's your mom dealing with everything?"

"She's fine." She offered him a quick smile, which made him wonder whether she was finding the conversation as difficult as he was. "She's dying to get back home, though."

"She's been here a while, right?" Even as he talked, Evan was beginning to wonder whether this was how it was going to be now between them.

"Yes, she's had to deal with Rio's wedding, me losing my shit, and Graham's death. That's quite a lot."

"I guess." He cleared his throat. "I'm glad you both could make it, though."

"Thanks."

Silence fell between them and it wasn't a comfortable one. Evan sneaked a glance at her serene profile as his confidence sank even lower.

He tipped his hat to her. "I'd better get back. I'm supposed to be keeping an eye on Roman."

"Okay." She smiled. "Maybe I'll see you later."

Evan took his cue and walked back into the throng, cursing up a blue streak under his breath.

"Smooth, Evan, smooth," he muttered as he looked for Roman. "She's really going to think you care about her now."

"You okay?" Danny touched his shoulder.

"Not really," Evan confessed. "I just spent five minutes talking to Josie."

"And?"

"We talked about everything but us."

"Hard to do that in the middle of a wedding," Danny said. "How about you try and get some time with her later in the evening when you can sneak away? I'll cover for you."

"But what am I supposed to say? She's obviously decided she's fine with us just being friends."

Danny gripped his shoulder. "Ev, stop panicking and listen to me. One of you has to take a risk and speak out, and it might as well be you. What do you have to lose?"

"Everything?"

Danny sighed. "Go for the melodrama, why don't

you? If you really want this to work, you're going to have to make yourself vulnerable. It sucks, but if anyone knows how to say the honest thing even if it isn't the right thing, it's you, Evan."

Josie sat on the edge of the newly cleared dance floor with a glass of wine in her hand and contemplated the couples twirling in front of her. Adam had danced with Lizzie to much applause. Even though she didn't know all the ins and outs of Adam's journey from grieving the death of his first wife at twenty-one to reconnecting with his best friend years later, she knew true love when she saw it.

Isabelle was off chatting to Leanne, Ruth Morgan, and some of the other local ladies, and was having a wonderful time. Josie had sent Rio a couple of pictures from the ceremony but hadn't heard back from him. Not for the first time she felt like her whole life was up in the air again. She'd totally frozen up when she'd unexpectedly ended up beside Evan and he'd obviously wished to be anywhere but with her.

"Hey."

She startled as Evan sat down next to her. "Hey."

"Can we try this again?"

"What exactly?"

"Talking to each other." He grimaced. "But if you're okay with us just being polite and friendly for the rest of our lives, I'm good with that, too."

"Weren't you the one who said we were done?" Josie asked pointedly, keeping her gaze on the dance floor.

"I was . . . upset when I heard you'd gone back to work full-time."

She finally turned to look at him properly. "Who told you that?"

"Your brother."

"Ah."

"He came to pick up your truck and said you were staying in the city."

"So, rather than talking to me about it, you decided that meant we were over."

"I'd already got the impression that you didn't need me around in San Francisco. I *thought* I would try and do what we'd promised each other and just let things go without a fight."

"That's such a cop-out, Evan. What you really mean is that you didn't think what we had together was worth saving."

He furrowed his brow. "That's not what it was at all."

"You decided you weren't good enough for me and literally walked away!" Josie only realized she'd raised her voice when the people at the table next to her looked around. "That's on *you*." She shot to her feet. "Excuse me."

Being Evan, he of course followed her out into the orchard beyond the dance floor. Moonlight filtered down through the branches of the trees and a slight breeze made the leaves rustle like they were alive.

"Go away."

"Not happening," Evan said. "If you want a conversation, you've got one."

She swung around to confront him. "What else is there to say?"

"You're right. I did run away." He shrugged. "All along I've wondered why you were hanging around with *me*—Evan Miller, the loudmouth screwup king. I guess I was just waiting for you to realize what a mistake you'd made."

"But I didn't make a mistake." Josie met his gaze. "And I'm not going to allow you to push all your crap on me."

"I get that now." He cleared his throat. "The thing is—what if I wanted to be the kind of man you could be proud of?"

"You still don't get it, do you?" Josie shook her head. "You already *are* that man, but if you don't know that, then what's the point?"

"You think I'm perfect?" Evan blinked at her.

"*Hell,* no," Josie said. "But if there is anything you want to change, you have to do it for yourself, not for anyone else."

"Okay, that's a start." He nodded. "What else?"

"About what?"

"*Us.*" He took a step toward her. "I want us to be together."

"You sure have a funny way of showing it." Josie sniffed.

He reached for her and the next moment, she found herself in his arms, which felt so right she wanted to weep.

"I'm sorry." He kissed the top of her head. "I'm so fricking sorry. I've never been in love before, and I've totally screwed everything up."

"Back up." She raised her startled gaze to meet his. "Who said anything about being in love?"

"Er, I just did?" He groaned. "Man, me and my big mouth. I meant to say it in a more meaningful way, and I just blurted it out."

"It's okay," Josie said dazedly.

"It's not okay, and you don't have to say it back." Evan frowned at her. "It's totally messing with my head."

"Really?"

"Yeah, I mean you're the first woman I've made love to, and you're going to be the last."

"Excuse me?" Josie put both hands on his chest and eased back so that she could see him more clearly in the moonlight.

"That's if we stay together, obviously, and I know there's no guarantees, but *technically* you could be my one and only."

"Evan . . ." Josie's mouth twitched at the corner as she fought an absurd desire to laugh and cry at the same time. "You're such a dork."

He gathered her close again. "I know. But I'm your dork."

She cupped his chin and drew his mouth down to hers. "Can I kiss you?"

"Always."

He opened his mouth to let her in, and for a long while there was nothing more in her world than the taste and the feel of him.

"I've missed you so much," he murmured against her lips. "I can't believe I was stupid enough to think I could walk away from this."

"Uncle Evan."

A shrill voice penetrated Josie's daze of happiness.

"Uncle Evan. Why are you kissing that lady?"

She looked down to see Roman staring at them, his hands on his hips, his tone reproachful.

"That's what you do when you like someone very much," Evan said easily as he turned toward his new nephew, one arm still wrapped around Josie's waist.

"Like Mom and Adam. They do it all the time." Roman nodded. "Although, Adam said I can call him Dad now if I want to because I call my other dad Ray."

"Adam's really looking forward to being your full-time dad," Evan said. "Now, shouldn't you be off getting some ice cream or something?"

"I came to find you." Roman looked past Evan to Josie. "Your mom was looking for you."

"Oh!" Josie patted her disordered hair and looked up at Evan. "I suppose I'd better go and see what she wants."

Evan nodded as Roman grabbed his hand and pulled him in the opposite direction. "I'll catch up with you in a while."

"Good, right, let's do that."

Josie stumbled back through the grass, her head so totally in a loop that she didn't know what to think. Evan Miller had just said that he loved her, and she'd crumbled like a wall built of sand.

"Ah, *minha filha!*" Isabelle waved at her from a table near the bar. "There you are."

"What's up?" Josie asked.

Isabelle took her hand. "I hope you don't mind, but I think I want to leave. I am very tired. Can you take me and Ines back to the ranch?"

"Like right now?" Josie might have squeaked. "Can't you drive yourselves?"

"We've both been drinking a little too much for that." Her mother laughed. "You can always come back and party without us."

"Okay, how about you go and say your good-byes, and I'll meet you at the truck in ten minutes?" Josie said.

"I'll just find Ines and we'll see you there."

Josie ran back the way she'd come, but there was no sign of Evan or Roman. She scanned the wedding guests and walked toward the dance floor. Where was he? She couldn't disappear again without telling him.

"Josie?" She spun around to find Danny watching her. "Are you okay?"

"I can't find Evan."

"What's new?" Danny's grin faded as he studied her face. "What's up?"

"I have to take my mom and Ines home, and Evan and I were right in the middle of something, and I don't want him to think I ran away or anything, because you know what he's like—"

"Okay, slow down. How about I give him a message?"

"I suppose you could do that."

"I'm completely trustworthy." He traced a cross over his heart.

"So Evan says." Josie sighed as she caught sight of her mom waving at her. "Tell him I had to go and that I'm sorry."

"Got it."

He went to turn away and she grabbed his arm. "Hang

on, don't say the 'I'm sorry' bit because he'll probably think that means I don't want to talk to him, and I do."

"He would think that because he's a lot more sensitive than most people realize." Danny nodded. "I'll tell him you had to take your mom home and that you'll be in touch as soon as possible. How does that sound?"

"Better than my effort," Josie said.

"Then you're good to go." Danny winked at her. "And may I put in a good word for him? He's totally in love with you."

"So he said."

"Yeah?" Danny's face broke into a huge grin. "He managed to get the words out?"

It was Josie's turn to nod.

"Look, I know it's none of my business, but you make him happy and I want that for him so much."

"Thanks," Josie said. "I'd better get going."

By the time she reached the temporary parking lot and the valet pulled up in her truck, she was a lot calmer and able to chat away to Ines and her mom about how wonderful the wedding had been.

Evan Miller loved her.

She drove back to the ranch in something of a dream, waved good night to her mother, and locked herself in her bedroom.

Even as she took off her wedding finery and put her high heels away, that thought dominated her mind. Did she love him back?

After a restless hour of trying to sleep, she went back out into the kitchen, made herself some hot chocolate, and sat at the kitchen table. After the attack, she'd promised

to be honest to herself about how she felt. She had a sense
that she was trying to dodge around facing the truth. But
what truth?

She wasn't a kid anymore; she couldn't immediately
assume that every relationship in her life was temporary
or that she'd never be good enough. She'd survived being
threatened in her own home and faced her attacker again.
She was a new person and somehow she needed to find
the courage to let the past go and embrace a new future.

Her cell buzzed.

You still up?

It was Evan. Of course.

Yes.

I got your message. Sorry I missed you, but Roman
took me out to the barn to check up on his calf.

Not a problem. I needed some time to think. ☺

Did I blow it?

Josie considered that. No.

Good. Just wanted to check in before I hit the
sheets.

Josie took a deep breath and punched in his phone
number. He picked up immediately.

"Hey."

"I have to go back to San Francisco tomorrow."

He took some time to answer. "I guess there's a lot
going on at Howatch International these days."

"I promised Rio I'd be there for him."

"Makes total sense. I'd want my family around me too if I was dealing with all that crap."

It was Josie's turn to pause. "Why are you being so nice?"

"Because I get it?"

"But what about you being in love with me?"

"What about it?"

It was hard to articulate the unexplainable. "I don't know what to do with that information, or what you expect me to do with it," she whispered.

"Josie, I don't expect anything. It is what it is. I can't do anything about it, and I don't expect you to, either. I'm just sharing my truth, no strings attached. Isn't that what love is supposed to be about anyway? Letting someone be themselves and trusting them to make the right choices?"

"I suppose it is," Josie said slowly. He was sharing his truth, just like she was trying to do. They might have made their choices to be honest for different reasons, but somehow they'd arrived at the same place. "I just don't want you to be mad at me."

"I'm not. Go and support your brother. He deserves it, and maybe when you get a chance or you need to like, vent, you can let me know how things are going."

"Thank you."

"You're welcome. Now, sleep tight and have a safe journey back, okay?"

"Okay."

"'Night, Josie."

"'Night, Evan."

* * *

Evan put his cell back on the charger, stretched out on his bed and groaned.

"Nice job, Bro." Danny, who was leaning up against his desk, pretended to applaud.

Evan gave him a reproachful stare. "You could've left and given me some privacy, you know."

"Why? You sounded like a concerned, reasonable human being. I especially liked that bit about trusting her to make the right choices."

Evan groaned again. "I flat-out told her I loved her, and she basically ran away."

"No, she didn't. She had to leave, and she took the time to find me and give you a message so you wouldn't get all panicky."

"She didn't say she loved me back, though."

"She didn't tell you to piss off, either," Danny countered. "You obviously took her by surprise."

"Well, yeah, like one minute we were arguing, and the next minute we're kissing, and I just started running my mouth off. Josie wasn't the only one who was surprised by what I said."

"Okay, so now's the time when you have to put in the work. Let her deal with what's happening with Rio. Be her supportive friend and don't screw it up by whining or getting all defensive because of her job."

"I know all that." Evan sat up to glare at his brother. "Don't you have something better to do than hang around here handing out useless advice?"

"Oh, I have *way* better things to be doing." Danny winked. "I just wanted to make sure my little brother stayed on the straight and narrow." He headed for the door. "But I do think you've got this. I'm proud of you, Evan."

"Oh, go to hell." Evan threw his pillow at Danny and only succeeded in hitting the closing door. He could still hear his brother laughing as he walked down the hall.

Chapter Twenty-One

"Dad? Can I talk to you about something?" Evan approached his father who was leaning on the fence, looking out over the horse pasture.

"Adam's the boss now."

"This isn't just about the ranch." Evan adopted the same pose as his father, arms folded on the top rail, chin on top, gaze straight ahead. "There's something I need to do, and I want your permission."

"Want or need? You're old enough to get married without asking me, Son."

"I'm not doing that." Evan shuddered. "I suppose I should've said I want your blessing."

Jeff snorted. "That sounds even worse."

Evan took a deep breath. "I've been taking some classes online because I want some backup skills."

"Always a good idea to be able to turn your hand to other trades," his dad said with a nod of his head. "Sometimes that can make a difference between a ranch folding or surviving."

"You kicked up a real fuss when Danny went off to

get his degree and Kaiden studied carpentry. What's changed?" Evan asked. "I thought you'd be mad."

"Nope. Although, I suppose it depends what you intend to do with those new skills." Jeff finally turned to look at him.

"Well," Evan said cautiously, "I have a plan. . . ."

Rio looked over at Josie, pen poised in his hand. "Last chance to talk me out of this."

"And I'll give you the same answer I gave you this morning," Josie said. "It's totally up to you."

Rio groaned and spread the papers out over what had once been his father's desk. The gaggle of company lawyers and attorneys had departed, leaving them alone in the office with Evangelista guarding the door.

Josie held her breath as he signed the documents that made him CEO of Howatch International.

"How do you feel?" she asked as he looked over at her.

"Terrified." Rio groaned. "There's a lot I want to change. Every time I think about that, all I can see is the huge mountain I have to scale."

"Step by step. Second by second," Josie reminded him. "That's what you've always told me."

"Nothing worse than having your own advice thrown back at you, is there?" He smiled although he looked worn-out, and who could blame him? "Will you be my chief of staff?"

"Yes, if you'll let me work from home." She rose from her seat and walked toward him. "Not that I've quite decided where home is going to be yet."

He sat back in his chair and looked up at her. "I don't have a problem with that. With the way communications are these days you'll still be accessible."

She came to perch on the edge of his desk. "I do like having a flexible boss."

"I'll be flying between here, Boston, and Morgan Valley. Maybe we can share a plane or something." He paused. "Are you still nervous about living permanently in the city?"

"A little bit," Josie acknowledged. "I hope that fear is going to lessen as time goes by, but I'm still prepared for some aftershocks."

"City living is not for everyone, even if they do own one of the famous painted ladies."

"I don't know what to do about that house." Josie sighed. "I mean, it's awesome, but it's such a huge responsibility."

"You can afford the upkeep. Just hang on to it until you come to a decision."

"It's certainly in a more open area of the city, but there are a lot of tourists." Josie smiled. "Mr. Marr told me that sometimes he'd be eating his dinner in the kitchen and find a bunch of people peering through the window taking his picture."

"I bet my father loved that." Rio chuckled. "Although he wasn't there very often. He preferred his estate in Boston."

He stacked the papers into a neat pile and put them back in the folder. "I guess we should celebrate or something?"

"Or something." Josie high-fived him. "It's been a grueling couple of months."

"Yeah, who knew sorting out the estate of a billionaire would be so complicated?"

"Everyone?" She stood and walked toward the door. "Shall I let Evangelista in on the good news?"

Even as Josie opened the door, Evangelista immediately sailed in and zeroed in on Rio's desk.

"Congratulations, Mr. Martinez. I've already drafted an announcement to send out to the whole company. Would you like to see it?"

"Thank you." Rio handed her the file. "Can you take a copy of this and send the originals back to Peterson?"

"I sure can." Evangelista smiled at both of them. "This is wonderful news."

"Glad you think so. Now can you spare some time to come and celebrate with us over lunch? Yvonne's booked a table at the hotel."

"I'd be delighted to join you." Evangelista nodded. "I'll just get this sent on its way and I'll be ready to leave when you are."

"We should call *Mamãe,*" Josie suggested.

Rio checked the time. "Yeah, let's do that."

Josie came to sit beside her brother who accessed Facetime.

"*E aí?*" Isabelle asked. "Did you do it?"

"Yup, you're looking at the new CEO of Howatch International and his chief of staff."

"That's wonderful news!" Isabelle clapped her hands together, making her gold bangles chime. "I know you will make Graham proud."

"I'm not sure he'd like what I'm going to do to his company, but I have to follow my own path and vision."

Isabelle nodded. "That's true, he was a difficult man.

But I suspect he'd appreciate you taking control and doing it your way."

"Nothing he can do about it now," Josie chipped in.

"Josephina! There is no need to speak ill of the dead!" Isabelle frowned at her.

"Why not?" Josie glanced over at her brother, who was trying not to laugh. "Not as much fun as bawling him out in front of a judge, of course, but far fewer consequences."

"I will say a prayer for Graham and for both of you when I go to church tomorrow," Isabelle said piously. "And, *meu filho,* I am very, very proud of you indeed." She blew Rio a kiss. "Now, I must go. I have calves to deliver."

Josie shook her head as the screen went black. "Dressed in a Chanel blouse, enough bling to scare the cows, and probably three-inch heeled boots."

"She's certainly her own woman," Rio agreed, stood up, and stretched. "Do you need to get anything from your office or are you good to go?"

"I'll just get my backpack and meet you by the elevators."

They decided to walk to the hotel, which was only a block from their office. For once, it was a bright, sunny day and the early-morning fog had burned off, leaving the city basking in sunlight. Josie took a deep breath. After lunch she'd call Evan and let him know what was going on.

To her surprise over the past two hectic months, he'd

become not only her cheerleader, but her closest confidant. Sometimes when she'd despaired that they'd never see an end to the complex problems and negotiations, he'd been the one to bolster her confidence by making her laugh or saying something so honest and Evan-like that she'd been able to reassess her priorities.

Now that everything was settled, she was looking forward to flying back to Morgan Valley and seeing him. He was her rock. Any doubts at how she felt about him had disappeared. It was time for her to live up to her promise and be as honest as he was.

"Come on." Rio held the door open for her. "We've got a private space so we can celebrate in style."

He kept his hand on her shoulder as he guided her past the smiling staff, through the main restaurant, and out onto one of the terraces overlooking the city and the Bay Bridge.

"Surprise," he murmured as she stopped in her tracks.

Evan stood up and grinned at her. "You did it! All hail to the chief of staff, right?"

"Oh, *Evan*." She ran toward him and he swept her up into his arms and twirled her around.

"Hey, don't cry." He kissed the top of her head as she clung to him. "It's okay."

"It's . . ." She looked up at him and swallowed hard. He wore his new blue shirt from Adam's wedding and his good pair of jeans and looked just about perfect to her. "It's more than okay."

"Yvonne brought me."

"That's so sweet of her." Josie turned to look at her

brother and his wife who were grinning like crazy. "*Obrigado*."

"I thought you might appreciate seeing him up close after two months of phone calls and texts." Rio put his arm around Yvonne. "I know how pleased I am to see this woman, and it's only been two weeks." He gestured at the table where Ines and Evangelista were chatting away. "Shall we eat?"

Josie sat next to Evan and, like teenagers, they held hands under the table. She couldn't stop staring at him, but he didn't seem to mind.

"Where are you staying?" Josie finally remembered to ask.

"Good question." He smiled at her. "I can get a room here, or I can crash at Julia and Kaiden's place."

"Or you can come home with me," Josie suggested.

"Don't you have to get back to work?"

"Not today." Josie held his hazel gaze. "Today is for celebrating."

"Then I'd love that." He brought her fingers to his lips. "It's so great to see you, Josie."

An hour later, they were walking hand in hand through the city back to Josie's apartment. Evan was trying his best to be cool and laid-back when all he wanted was to strip Josie naked and make love to her for hours. He reminded himself to take nothing for granted. There was still a lot to talk about. If the last two months had taught him anything, it was that trust and patience took time to grow, and that if he was right, he and Josie were on a much firmer foundation than they'd ever been before.

"Where's your hat?" Josie suddenly asked.

He pointed at his head. "On my head, doofus. Where else would it be?"

"That's a baseball cap from Morgantown Feed and Grain Store, not a Stetson."

He shrugged. "Maybe I'm just trying to blend in with the locals."

"I don't think you were born to blend in, Evan." She used her swipe card to access the apartment complex and they went up in the elevator.

"Doesn't hurt to try sometimes." He followed her into the apartment and stopped well short of the windows. "It looks great! I mean, I know you shared the pictures but it's good seeing it in the flesh."

"Would you like some coffee?"

"Yes, please."

He took off his jacket and boots and pulled out one of the high stools by the countertop so he could watch her in the kitchen. She looked good in her blue pantsuit with the pink blouse and her hair in a high ponytail. She'd look even better naked in his arms.

"I'm glad you came." She handed him a mug and went over to the couch. "It saved me a trip."

"You were going to come and see me?" Evan pretended to groan. "Man, I wasted all my money on a ticket?"

"Yvonne brought you on a private jet, so you'll get no sympathy from me." Josie rolled her eyes. "I wanted to thank you—for everything."

He set his mug on the coffee table out of harm's way. "I was just being your friend."

"You were way more than that. You literally kept me sane."

"It was my pleasure." He paused. "Can we talk?"

"I'd like that." She turned to face him, her arms folded over her chest, her expression so cautiously optimistic that Evan wanted to smile. "Do you want to go first?"

"Okay, you know you said you didn't want me changing myself for you, and that I had to do it for myself?" At her nod, he continued. "Kaiden offered me an opportunity to work for him if I took some professional classes and got certified or something. While you've been busy here, I've been working my ass off online and at the community college getting my skills on."

"That's great." Josie smiled. "I'm really proud of you."

"The thing is—Kaiden works in two places now, Morgan Valley, and here in the Bay Area."

"Okay."

"Which means I can choose which jobs I want to take and where they are." Evan held his breath.

"You can work here in the city?" Josie blinked at him. She'd always been the smart one. "Like while *I'm* working here?"

"That was my thought," Evan said modestly. "But there's no pressure. I mean you might not want me hanging around—umph." She launched herself into his arms and he was doubly glad he'd put his coffee down.

She framed his face with her hands and stared into his eyes. "I love you, Evan Miller."

"Yeah?" He wanted to whoop like he'd just won a

world championship, but he also didn't want to scare her off when things were going so well.

"Absolutely one hundred percent in all your adorable dorkiness." She smoothed his hair away from his face. "I was going to tell you that Rio had agreed to me working from home, and that I was planning on following his example and sharing my time between here and Morgan Valley."

"Then we *can* make it work?" Evan asked, just to make sure.

"Yes, I think so. Don't you?" She kissed him sweetly on the lips. "You're my person, Evan. You keep me honest and I love that."

"Right back at you."

They kissed for a long, long time, until she finally eased back.

"Are your family okay with you working away from home?"

"As Kaiden's already doing the same thing, they couldn't really object too much," Evan reminded her.

"Won't that leave your father shorthanded?"

Evan mock-frowned. "Whose side are you on? Kaiden and I already talked about that. We're willing to pay someone to pick up our slack if Dad, Adam, and Danny need it, or come home and help out."

"Okay, I'll let you off, then." Josie kissed him again and set her fingers on the top button of his shirt.

"Are we done talking?" Evan asked as she started to pull his shirt off.

"Yes." She kissed the patch of skin she'd exposed.

"If I don't get you naked pretty damn quick, I think I'll explode with lust."

"Well, we can't have that, can we?" Evan picked her up and tossed her over his shoulder, his heart almost exploding with gratitude and love. "Let's go to bed."

Epilogue

Unobserved by the family members streaming in and out of the kitchen with food for the upcoming outdoor luncheon, Jeff Miller leaned against the back wall of his house. It was rare to get everyone together these days, what with Daisy often in Silicon Valley, Ben in Los Angeles, and Kaiden and Evan going back and forth to the Bay Area. It was barely midday, but the heat was already rising, and the redwood trees provided some welcome shade.

Leanne had insisted they have a party, and he wasn't in the mood to deny her much these days after she'd forgiven him for being a complete ass when they were married. It was weird how he almost didn't recognize that man anymore. Sure, he still didn't suffer fools gladly, and liked to speak his mind, but since his heart attack he'd learned some important lessons.

"Trying to get out of doing any work, Jeff?"

He looked down at the diminutive red-haired woman who'd snuck up beside him.

"It's my big birthday, so I think I get the day off, right?"

Leanne elbowed him in the ribs. "I suppose so."

"Glad we're on the same page. Has Daisy arrived yet?"

"She and Jackson are popping in to say hi to their new nephew over at Cauy's place first."

Jeff snorted. "Another generation of Morgans in this valley."

"Not a Morgan this time, but a Lymond."

"No doubt they'll have one of those high falutin' double-barreled last names like everyone's doing these days."

"I like those names." Leanne slipped her arm through his and leaned against him. "Mind you if Rachel really wanted to go for it, she could have three names: Ford Morgan Lymond."

"The poor kid."

"Did Adam tell you his and Lizzie's good news yet?" Leanne asked.

"Nope, but Roman did spill the beans when we were working together out in the barn. He told me he's getting a new baby brother for Christmas."

Leanne chuckled. "That's just like him. I'm looking forward to meeting my new grandchild."

Jeff thought about that, his gaze turning to his tall oldest son who sat by the picnic table explaining something to Roman with a patience Jeff had never mastered.

"They all turned out okay despite me, didn't they?" he murmured.

"You did your part."

"I drove them too hard," Jeff admitted perhaps for the first time. "I didn't know any other way."

"They're all good kids," Leanne said firmly. "Adam's running this ranch like a pro, Ben's experimenting with his place to make it one hundred percent environmentally friendly, and Kaiden's done wonders at the Garcia's. You taught them that. You should be proud."

"I guess I did teach them good ranch management practices. Even Danny says that and he's the one with the agricultural degree."

Jeff heard the sound of a truck and turned toward the fence running along the side of the yard. "I wonder if that's Daisy?"

Leanne smiled at him. "Why don't you go and see?"

Despite insisting that he didn't have favorites Daisy had always held a special place in Jeff's heart, and everyone knew it. She climbed out of the truck and grinned at him.

"Hey, Dad! Happy birthday."

"Thanks." He accepted her hug and then looked over the top of her head at her husband, who was approaching rather more warily. "Jackson."

No man would ever be good enough for his daughter, but he supposed Jackson was just about okay.

"Jeff. Good to see you. Happy birthday." Jackson held up a gift bag. "Where should I put this?"

"There's a table out back," Jeff said. "Although I don't know why anyone's bothering. I've got everything a man needs right here."

"Glad you finally realized that, sir," Jackson murmured and then skedaddled when Jeff looked at him.

Daisy chuckled. "Trust my husband to let it out there."

"He's always had a big mouth," Jeff agreed. "But at least you know where you stand with him."

"True." Daisy walked back into the yard with him. "And he's right, you know."

"Yeah." Jeff found himself smiling as he observed the crowd milling around the table. "I'm one lucky guy."

Daisy stood on tiptoe to kiss his cheek. "I'm going to find Mom and Auntie Rae. I'll need their help setting up our new home in the summer when I'm finally free of my commitments to my old company."

"You're coming home for good?" Jeff perked up.

"Not sure about that, but we do want our own place. Now Rachel and Cauy have started a family we all agreed we need to spread out a little."

"Seems to be a trend." Jeff sighed. "Adam and Danny have their own houses on our land now, and Kaiden and Evan flit about like gadflies."

"You love it really, Dad," Daisy said. "At least they all choose to come home."

Jeff thought about that as he got a beer and went to sit in the shade. A few years ago, he'd been certain the ranch would fail because none of his children would want to work it with him. He'd been wrong about that and about a lot of other things, too. Adam and Danny worked full time, and the others weren't far away if needed.

His gaze strayed to where his ex-wife was chatting to their daughter and lingered there. If Leanne hadn't stirred everything up by coming home and insisting they all dealt with the past instead of burying their resentments deep, he wouldn't be where he was now—sitting here surrounded by his family, their partners, and their kids.

He loved it.

"What's wrong, Dad? Did you eat something weird?" He looked up to see Evan squinting down at him.

"I was just thinking how lucky I am."

Evan frowned. "Are you feeling okay? Too much sun, or is it the beer?"

"There's nothing wrong with appreciating what you have, Son."

"Took you long enough," Evan said, echoing Jackson. "But better late than never I suppose." He winked. "Ben and Kaiden are done burning the barbecue so we're ready to eat if you're up for it."

Jeff set down his beer and rose to his feet. "Lead the way. And mind you don't dish me up any of that fake meat. It's an abomination."

"Ben's put all Silver's plant protein-based stuff on a separate grill so it's not even touching your good Miller ranch beef."

"I'm glad to hear it," Jeff grumbled. "I suppose I should be pleased she didn't insist on bringing her personal chef."

"Are you dissing me, Jeff Miller?" Silver called out; her blond hair glinting in the sun as she turned around. She was flipping her fake burgers while Ben held their six-month-old baby girl in his arms and offered unnecessary advice. For a world-famous movie star, she sure mucked in with everyone and never complained.

"Not at all." Jeff grabbed a plate and a napkin. "I'm just making sure I get to eat the real stuff."

Silver sighed and came over to his side. "Won't you even try some? It's way better for your heart."

"It's my birthday. Leanne said I could eat whatever I liked."

"Oh, well then. If Leanne is okay with it, knock yourself out." Silver blew him a kiss.

He smiled at her, aware that he'd probably smiled more in the past six months than he had in the last twenty years. Something about all these daughters-in-law coddling and teasing him was softening him up and secretly he liked it. Not that he'd tell anyone that.

Finally, everyone was seated at the long tables and Adam stood and faced Jeff, Lizzie beaming at his side.

"Pipe down everyone. We're here to celebrate Dad's sixtieth birthday, so let's all sing him the song and we'll leave the cake until later so the food doesn't get cold."

Jeff rose to his feet. "I'm good if you don't sing, either." He took a moment to look around the tables and note every face. "I can't believe I made it to sixty."

"Without someone murdering you?" Kaiden asked with a grin. "It's certainly a miracle."

"I'm not going to argue with you today, Son," Jeff said. "I'm in a good mood." He cleared his throat. "Maybe I don't say this enough, but you all mean a hell of a lot to me."

"You never say that at all," Evan piped up and his fiancée Josie elbowed him in the ribs. "Ouch."

"He's right, but I'm trying to do better."

"Can't say I've noticed," Evan wasn't shutting up. "You were banging on my door this morning predawn asking why I wasn't up and out there."

"He comes over to my *house* and does that," Danny spoke up from his seat beside Faith. "Can you believe it?"

"Totally."

Jeff stared at Evan until he mimed zipping his lips.

"Anyway. I just want you all to know that I'm glad you

found the time to come out here today to celebrate with me. I appreciate it." Jeff sat down. "Now, let's eat."

"What about happy birthday, Gramps?" Roman demanded. "We have to sing it."

"Okay, fine," Jeff grumbled, loathe not to give Roman anything he wanted. "Just get on with it."

As the sun disappeared behind the Sierra Nevadas and the family started to gather up their things and leave, Jeff found himself sitting alone with Leanne at the deserted table under the twinkling fairy lights.

"It was good to see everyone," Jeff said. "I'm amazed they all found the time."

"They all wanted to be here." Leanne sipped her coffee.

"I don't deserve them," Jeff said simply. "The only reason things worked out is because of you."

She turned to look at him. "I guess I started the wheels turning, but everyone had to get onboard for us to turn things around and make a new start." She set her hand over his. "You did your part."

Jeff studied their joined hands. "We were good together once, weren't we?"

"We were."

"Do you ever think we could . . . ?"

"*Hell* no." She grinned at him. "I'm happy being your friend. Let's leave it at that, shall we?"

Jeff smiled slowly back at her, aware that he'd never really stood a chance, and that being friends with the amazing woman his ex-wife had become was way better than he'd ever hoped for. He wasn't stupid, and he wasn't going to ruin their relationship again.

"Sure thing, honey." He raised her hand to his mouth

and kissed it. "Friends with benefits as the kids like to say."

She made a face as she rose to her feet and he joined her. "They all know, don't they?"

"Yup." He kept hold of her hand as they turned toward the house. "And as it's still my birthday, I think I should take you to bed and continue this celebration in private."

Leanne squeezed his fingers. "Fine by me."

"Then let's go." Jeff winked at her, ignored the scandalized expression on his eldest son's face, walked down the hallway and shut the door behind them. Life was good, family was even better, but spending alone time with his ex?

Priceless.

RECIPE

Feijoada for Evan
(Brazilian Black Bean Stew)

Ingredients:

1 lb. dry black beans (soaked overnight)
1 Tbsp. olive oil
4 oz. slab bacon, rind removed, and diced
1 lb. pork ribs, individually cut
2 Mexican chorizo sausages, sliced
1 smoked sausage, sliced
1 large onion, chopped
4 cloves of garlic, minced
3 tomatoes, diced
1 tsp. salt
1 tsp. black pepper
3 bay leaves
Water, about 8 cups

Method:

Soak beans overnight. Rinse well and drain.

In a large heavy-bottomed pan, add oil and fry bacon until crispy. Set aside.

Brown ribs and sausages in same pot. Set aside.

Add more oil if necessary and sauté onion and garlic until soft.

Add tomatoes and cook for 3 minutes.

Add beans, bacon, ribs, and sausage back into the pan with the salt, pepper, bay leaves, and water—about 8 cups.

Cover with a lid and bring to a boil, then reduce heat to low and cook for 2-2½ hours, checking regularly until the beans are soft.

If there is too much liquid left, take off lid and cook for a further 20 minutes.

Serve with white rice.

(Recipe from CuriousCuisiniere.com)